W9-COI-773

The Way Upcountry

The Way Upcountry

Barrington King

Five Star • Waterville, Maine

Copyright © 2002 by Barrington King

This novel is a work of fiction. Names, characters, places, and incidents are either the product of the author's imagination, or, if real, used fictitiously.

Five Star First Edition Romance Series.

Published in 2002 in conjunction with Kidde, Hoyt & Picard Literary Agency.

Set in 11 pt. Plantin by Christina S. Huff.

Printed in the United States on permanent paper.

Library of Congress Cataloging-in-Publication Data

King, Barrington.
    The way upcountry / Barrington King.
        p. cm.—(Five Star first edition romance series)
    ISBN 0-7862-4407-0 (hc : alk. paper)
    1. Georgia—History—Civil War, 1861–1865—Fiction.
    2. Treasure-trove—Fiction. I. Title. II. Series.
    PS3561.I4728 W39 2002
    813′.54—dc21   2002071294

For S. from Nocoochee Valley

I

The Return

1

A man in a tattered straw planter's hat sails a curious old fishing boat toward the fine green line that divides the dark sea from towering evening thunderheads. These he watches with an anxious eye, one hand on the tiller, the other playing the sheet to an indigo sail with a large cabalistic eye painted upon it, from which fiery rays radiate out. The man is young, wears his golden-red hair braided in a pigtail, his ginger beard clipped short, clumsily, as if with seaman's shears. His fair skin is blistered, peeling, his eyes lined with lampblack against the sea glare.

The green line becomes an overgrown shore. White dunes rise from the sea, palmetto palms emerge from the green. A channel appears in the shoreline where none had been visible. He sails his strange craft into the channel with accustomed ease, gliding up to a dock as dilapidated as the boat that has improbably brought him so far. He tosses his seaman's bag onto the dock, raises an ax and smashes a plank in the hull, climbs onto the dock, watches the boat slowly sink until all he can see in the darkening water is the eye on the sail, balefully regarding him from below, like the eye of some giant squid.

Then with seaman's bag slung over his shoulder, he starts out haltingly along a sandy track beneath immense, moss-hung live oaks. It is growing dark now, and the moon slips in and out of the clouds, peopling the shadows beneath the trees with fugitive shapes, like long-ago children playing at twilight. The road is untended, unmarked, but it was always so. They had not wanted their lands accessible to strangers. They had been a world unto themselves.

At the end of a long avenue of oaks, only moonlight defined the familiar shape of the unlit house. He would have thought it abandoned but for the light coming from the kitchen, set far enough away from the big house to protect it and its treasures from fire. He paused for a minute or two, looking, listening. Fireflies winked in the dark beneath the trees, a ground fog hung over the fields of rice and Sea Island cotton, a screech owl cried. No other sound. He moved on quietly toward the lighted window.

The light came from two candelabras standing in front of an old cheval glass placed on its side atop a cupboard. In their light a man with café-au-lait skin, wearing a white blouse and cap, was sharpening a knife, the candlelight flashing from jeweled rings on his fingers. A silvery fish glittered on the wooden block at which he stood.

The young man laid down his sea bag, put a foot on the single step, and opened the kitchen door. The man in white dropped into a crouch, the knife held straight in front of him, steadied by an out-thrust thumb. His white cap had fallen off, and a headful of black, shining locks caught the light, a gold earring.

"Toussaint, it's me, Joel."

The knife was quietly laid on the cutting block, the cap retrieved.

"And so it is. When I heard the door I thought to see a deserter. They're all about now, trying to get back home. Then I saw you with your eyes all painted black, and for a second I thought you were one of the living dead, that they had finally found me, had come all the way from the islands for me." He

10

smiled. "But just for a second."

And then Toussaint stepped forward and grabbed him roughly by the arm, and he realized he had been falling, that the rising floor was about to slam into his face.

"Here, sit down." The big mulatto guided him into a kitchen chair.

"I've come a long way," he murmured.

"*Évidemment*, and it must have been the hard way." Toussaint went to the sink and brought back a wet towel. "Here, Monsieur Devereux, clean yourself up."

Toussaint went to the spice cabinet and brought out a bottle from the back of it. It had always been kept there.

"You still have some Mount Gay left?"

"It still arrives." Toussaint poured three fingers of the amber Barbados rum into two glasses. "The blockaders aren't going to waste their time chasing minnows. It's the big fish they're after."

"Cotton and guns."

"You should know, Joel. No, they don't have time for little fishing boats."

"As I found out. They could have taken me four times over."

"I figured you came by boat, not only by the black around your eyes but from the way you was swaying with a room that wasn't moving at all."

Joel Devereux took a sip of the neat rum, fiery but smooth, looked around the room. The marble mortar and pestle still stood on the dish cabinet, the copper pots hung still in their accustomed places on the wall beside the wood stove, swags of garlic and chili peppers drooped from a crossbeam, a bottle of Mount Gay rum stood on the table between them. Even the glasses were the same.

"So you thought I was a revenant. Perhaps I am. They come

11

not only from the land of the dead, but can be someone you thought gone forever who appears one day without warning."

"That's true. But wherever they come from, it is always with a purpose."

"Yes." He took another sip of rum, laid a finger beside the glass. "When I was fourteen, you poured me a finger, two when I was sixteen, three at eighteen . . ."

"And then you never came to the kitchen again."

"H.W.'s doing, that."

Toussaint laughed. That had been their code for Joel's father—His Worship.

"H.W. thought I had learned enough French, at least enough island French. He rather fancied having a son who spoke with a Creole accent. Another ornament to display . . . But you know that. Where is he?"

"Upcountry."

There had been the upcountry plantation and the low-country plantation, and each year when the fever season came, they would all move upcountry in a caravan, with Auguste Devereux in a coach and four, like some oriental potentate.

"And the others?"

"They're with him."

"Then why are you here?"

"I could say procuring necessities from the islands for His Worship, the wines and brandies, coffees and Cuban cigars that he requires, and that would be true . . . But this time I am also preparing for an unseasonal return here, am even under orders to scout out the possibilities for removing to Europe, if worse comes to worse . . ."

"Will it?"

"The smart money says so."

"And you have placed your bets accordingly."

"I have made certain arrangements." Toussaint grinned

12

and a gold tooth caught the light.

The man was a walking jewelry display. He was also a scoundrel. But for four years he had been the only friend the boy had had. Their friendship had been based on their shared view of the boy's father that emerged from their daily hour of French conversation in the kitchen of one or the other of the two houses, the boredom of which was always assuaged by a tot of rum.

In four years he had learned a great deal about the cook and winnowed the hard kernels of fact from the chaff of romance. He had been born in Port-au-Prince to a French harbor pilot and a lady of color who had named him Toussaint L'Ouverture after the Haitian hero, in hope that this would shield him from attacks on persons of light skin that erupted from time to time. It had not, and at an early age he had decamped to Martinique, where he had found work as a scullery boy in the establishment of a French sugar-cane grower, eventually replacing the Frenchman's aged cook.

From there he had moved on to New Orleans, where he had honed his skills at two well-known French restaurants, signed on as cook on a steamer plying between New Orleans and Charleston, jumped ship one night at Savannah, put a notice the next day in a local paper, describing himself as *chef de cuisine français,* just what Auguste Devereux had had his Savannah agent on the lookout for.

Toussaint offered a cheroot, which Joel refused. He lit it for himself.

"Does the father know of your return?"

"He may know by now that I have left Spain, but that I am back, no. I told no one and, of course, have been incommunicado since sailing from Havana."

"Alone?"

"Yes."

"A risky voyage that. You must have a serious purpose in coming back."

"I have unfinished business."

Toussaint regarded him thoughtfully, puffed on his cheroot. "A score to settle? There'll be plenty of that done, once things begin to *écrouler*."

Once things began to crumble, collapse, fall to pieces. The French was vivid enough, but was that what was really coming? Toussaint had always spoken in vivid terms.

"What about the war? Has it reached Georgia?"

Toussaint reached inside the dish cabinet, took out of it an Atlanta newspaper and handed it to Joel.

The lead article was headed "SHERMAN INVADES GEORGIA!" It began:

"From our Correspondent, May 12, 1864. I am not at liberty to reveal from where this dispatch has been sent, but I am in a position, I assure our readers, to confirm what I had come here to disprove. Maj. Gen. William Tecumseh Sherman has, indeed, descended from the heights around Chattanooga into the hills of Georgia at the head of an army of 100,000 men. If not the largest army in history, it is certainly the largest ever put into the field in this war. Well-equipped, uniformed and mounted, what hope do our valiant but under-armed and ill-rationed troops have to stem the forward progress of this behemoth?

"I put this question to a respected senior officer of our own army, whose name I am also not at liberty to reveal. His reply was succinct and clear: 'General Sherman has no choice, given the North Georgia terrain and our superior knowledge of it—if he means to take Atlanta—but to proceed down the single-track

Western and Atlantic railroad from Chattanooga, with all its defiles, bridges, tunnels and handy places for ambuscades. This route is surely the quickest and best to his objective, but it also could become his Valley of Death. We will certainly do our best to see that it is.' "

Joel looked up from the paper. "What's happened in the more than a month since this was written?"

"Sherman has advanced about halfway to Atlanta."

"How does the smart money say it's going to come out?"

"Atlanta will fall."

Like all those, Joel Devereux thought, who from the first had predicted disaster, what one feels, when it comes like a thief in the night, is indignation that one had not been consulted, forewarned. Atlanta about to fall? He had not counted on that, had not risked his life to storm or death staring up from an empty water bottle, to be thwarted, on his own playing field, by that William Tecumseh Sherman he had been introduced to one long-ago evening at one of his uncle's soirées: a scragglebearded, scrawny, hard-eyed army officer, come to inspect the military academy. But, he remembered his uncle enigmatically saying, not a man one would wish to face on the field of battle. So now he must change course, change course or lose all.

"You might also be interested in the item on page two," Toussaint said casually.

A brief article on the second page, headed "BANK ROBBERY IN NORTH GEORGIA," had been circled with pencil:

"Our correspondent in Catesville reports that night before last the local branch of the Devereux Bank was robbed by persons unknown. Shortly before dawn the bank vault was blown open with gunpowder, and from

15

tracks in the earth, wet from an evening rain, the cul-prits had struck out toward North Carolina with a heavily loaded wagon. A posse was formed and set in pursuit, but all that was found was an empty wagon some miles north of town. The authorities refuse to dis-cuss what may have been taken from the bank."

That was all. He looked up at Toussaint, whose face was inscrutable, as he could make it when he wished. But Joel doubted that the cook could know what had, at least in the beginning, been a secret shared by only Auguste Devereux, Joel and his three brothers, and Judge Colcock Stiles of Catesville. Within days of the firing on Fort Sumter in Charleston, Governor Joe Brown had ordered the seizure of the little U.S. mint in Dahlonega.

The mint had been established when large amounts of gold were discovered in North Georgia in the 1830s. Joel and his brothers were not made privy to how much gold was in the mint when it was seized, but whatever amount there had been was taken to the Catesville branch of the Devereux bank for safekeeping.

"Yes, interesting," he said. "Toussaint, I need to get up-country."

Toussaint cleared his throat. His eyes were sharp with possibilities.

"Is there some way I may help you, Joel?"

This was a softly spoken statement of his ability to do so, if it could be proved to be in his own interest. Toussaint had been many things—gambler, arranger, always for others, dabbler in West Indian sugar futures on his own account. What choice did he have this night, with the room still spin-ning, if more slowly, around Joel and that hard-eyed general descending onto the field of play.

"Just help me get upcountry."

"You should know that Devereux Hall is directly in the path of Sherman's army. That is why I was sent down here to prepare for retreat. And by the way, your father has seen that letter you wrote to the London *Times* calling for the emancipation of the slaves. The other plantation owners have seen it too. I would rather face Sherman's army than what's going to be waiting for you at Devereux Hall."

"I don't want to go to Devereux Hall—at least not yet."

"Where then?"

"Cherokee Rose."

Toussaint's eyebrows went up. "The summer cottage? What on earth for? But excuse me. You have a purpose, and what it is is none of my business. At least you will be out of the line of fire. There is nothing of interest to a Yankee general in the North Georgia mountains."

"But how do I get to Catesville?"

"Carefully, unless you want to go dressed in gray cloth from His Worship's mills. They are now detaining any able-bodied man of military age seen on the streets out of uniform."

"How then?"

"The railroad to Atlanta is still open, and the Savannah stationmaster, Captain Preston Marcey, owes me a rather large favor."

"Preston Marcey? Last I heard, he was in jail for defrauding the railroad company."

"Indeed. But when the war came to Georgia, they found that his skill in managing rail and telegraph together, which had allowed him to siphon off the company's funds for so long, was now essential to the cause. So they went cap in hand to the jail, offering him his freedom in return for his resuming his former position. He said that he could do that, provided he was made an officer in the CSA. There was no choice. What

17

was that old Greek thing H.W. was so fond of saying?"

"The strong do what they can, the weak do what they must."

"Exactly. It sometimes happens that a prisoner is stronger than those who imprisoned him. With proper papers provided by Marcey you might travel by rail to Atlanta unmolested. But then at Atlanta station, the military police would have you in shackles in a trice."

This was vintage Toussaint. "So then?"

"You find a way of leaving the train before Atlanta station. You have gold upon your person?"

"I do."

"I would have imagined so, after three years in Barcelona. Well, you buy the best horse you can, one that can outrun bushwhackers, Northern or Southern, who would kill you for a good pair of boots."

"Not the advice I would have expected."

"Personal qualities count for almost everything now, Joel. A fine horse and rider are worth more than all a merchant's stores. H.W. once told me you were the finest horseman the family had ever produced. No small compliment from him."

"He never told me that."

"Of course not. That was always how he wished to be known himself. Now, when do you propose to begin your journey upcountry?"

"As soon as possible. I need an element of surprise."

" 'As soon as possible' means I will have to ride into Savannah tomorrow, get the necessary papers from Captain Marcey. Two days at least—if nothing goes wrong, as it usually does these days."

"How am I to repay you?"

"If we both survive the coming débacle, you can reward me as you see fit. If we don't, we can settle our accounts in the next world."

"Fair enough. And how am I to remain invisible here until you return from Savannah?"

"You can stay in your old room on the top floor of the big house. I will leave you food and water, a bottle of Mount Gay, and a handful of cheroots. The house servants are all at Devereux Hall. The field hands dare not enter the big house. I have told them that I have placed there one of the living dead, who stalks the corridors both day and night.

"I'll give you the key to the house and a lantern to find your way up the stairs. Its light will be seen in the cabins. And while I am gone, if you were to smoke a cheroot or two at night on the back piazza, that will be seen, too. I can assure you that you will not be disturbed while I am away. Now, how would you like this sea bass prepared that I was about to fillet? À la Créole used to be one of your favorites."

"Yes, Toussaint, yes. *À la Créole.*"

He awoke to a rippling of sea light on the white surface above him and reached in vain for tiller and rope. It took him fully a minute to get his bearings. He was back in his room at Tupelo, on the top floor of the old mansion surrounded by rice fields. He did not need to turn his head to know that the ripples of light came from the big cistern out back, on the surface of which, no doubt, blue-flowered water lilies still floated. He had survived—so far.

Thus reassured, he resolved just to stay there for a while in idleness of body and mind. While he lay still, his spirit got up and explored the rooms and corridors. The four sons of Auguste Devereux had had four rooms sharing a long piazza, facing the working part of the plantation, which was screened from guests by a triple row of dark cedars. These hid a courtyard of pink earth, the cistern, stables, mule barn, slave cabins running in long rows like marching infantry,

19

pine-boarded, shake-roofed, with chimneys of pink brick made from the local earth, shadowed by old loblolly pines, and, beyond, the bright, pale green of the rice fields.

On the front side of the house there were also four rooms: in those days occupied by the head overseer, Frank Jones; the butler of uncertain race, Massey; the head gardener, the Irishman McCord; and finally the *chef de cuisine*, Toussaint L'Ouverture. No piazza there, just four small windows high up in the house's pink brick facade.

The piazza on the back of the house had been divided in two by latticework, separating the two feuding camps of brothers: the elder, Junius and Lamar, from the younger, Joel and Marion. When war had come, Auguste had declared the elder brothers essential to his support of the war economy; Joel had been sent to Barcelona to protect his cotton export business in Europe; and Marion had been sacrificed to the cause at Chickamauga.

When he next awoke it was as dark as any night at sea, the moon already down. From somewhere below came soft chanting, clapping, a fiery ripple now faint above him on the ceiling. He attempted to get up and fell to the floor. There was no strength in his legs. He must have walked from the dock to Tupelo on nerves alone.

He crawled to the piazza and looked down. Dark figures casting long shadows danced around a fire to the low beat of a drum. He dragged himself back onto the bed, drank from the water bottle. The darkness closed in again.

The third time he awoke it was late morning. The sun had already left the surface of the cistern, and there was no sound from below. Holding onto the back of a chair which he pushed in front of him, he went haltingly again onto the piazza. The pink earth of the courtyard had been swept in a circular pattern by brooms, the ashes of the fire in the center like an eye looking up at him. He would have thought he had gone a little mad, except that once-familiar things that he had forgotten were still where they had once stood: a rain barrel beneath a copper pipe running from the roof, a bucket beside it, a bar of yellow soap stuck on a spike set in the wall.

He moved back into the shadows around the doorway, soaped and rinsed himself. His skin peeled off in transparent pieces like that of a shedding snake. He ate some of the bread that Toussaint had left, cut off a couple of thin slices from a piece of sugar-cured ham, drank some more water from the bottle, slept until late afternoon when he was awakened by the sound of the workers returning from the rice fields.

He got up again, and this time his legs held. He made his way to the armoire. The mirror on the inside of the armoire door showed clearly why Toussaint had for a moment thought that a being from the land of the dead had come for him.

There were linens and clothes still in the armoire, musty but usable. In their accustomed places were his monogrammed silver hairbrushes, ivory-handled razor, shaving brush, and other appurtenances of a well-to-do young man. He pulled a chair up to the mirror and cut off his pigtail, trimmed his hair and beard, groomed his nails, selected a linen shirt and trousers and a pair of short English riding boots.

He dressed, sat on the edge of the bed, drank some Mount Gay, and lit a cheroot. He was himself again, at least in appearance. Inwardly he was a very different man from the boy who had sailed for Spain three years before. He had passed his first trial in sailing alone from Havana. There would be new trials awaiting him upcountry, but he would endure, he must endure, to atone to her for his cowardice. He had never doubted it from that awful morning in the hunting lodge in the Pyrenees, lying awake while the marquesa slept beside him, when he had finally faced the truth about himself.

21

Toussaint was right. He had a score to settle—with himself. He had always laughed at the code of honor of his class, but he had found that one does not so easily escape a heritage.

The morning of the third day there was a knock on the door. It was Toussaint, wearing what he remembered as one of Junius's English-tailored outfits. He also carried a leather portfolio and a valise that looked like Junius's. He took a piece of paper from the portfolio and handed it to Joel. It was a pass signed by Preston Marsey and countersigned by a Confederate colonel, whose scrawled name was obscured by a forcefully applied, purple-inked rubber stamp.

"I won't ask you how you got this, but I won't forget what you have done."

"I wouldn't expect you to, Joel," Toussaint said blandly. "I brought this valise along. It's not a good idea these days to travel without luggage. There's a carriage waiting out front. You'd better not waste time. The situation gets worse by the day."

Joel held out his hand and Toussaint took it. "Well, *bonne chance,* Joel. Till we meet again."

After Toussaint had left, he removed the false bottom of the armoire and took out the treasures of his youth: a fowling piece, a bamboo sectioned fly rod, a box of flies, a French brass telescope, and a compass, all given him in secret by his uncle Willy. Lastly, there was a velvet-lined leather case containing a pair of English dueling pistols from his father, meant to remind him that pride and courage were qualities expected of all Devereux men. He would take those as well. There might be a matter of honor to settle, if not in a sense that Auguste Devereux would understand.

Then Joel Devereux descended the curving grand staircase to his waiting carriage. He nodded to the driver, a Negro he had never seen, and they started off down the road to Savannah.

2

She sat in the porch swing, rocking back and forth gently to the creak of the rusty chains, an unopened copy of *The Complete Works of Samuel Taylor Coleridge* beside her on the seat. It was a fine June day, the last of the spring wildflowers in bloom, a blue sky overhead, and the cloud-capped Nantahalas just visible on the horizon. From where she sat she could look down on the valley floor, green with pasture and young corn, the river running alongside, shaded by birch and sycamore trees. It was hard to believe that not so far away, somewhere along the railroad from Chattanooga to Atlanta, it would be a day of booming cannon, bayonet charges, and death.

At the far end of the porch her uncle and guardian, the Reverend Philander Goode, slumped in his wheelchair, asleep now. She got up and went to him, took the small leather-bound book from his lap robe, moved the marker to the page where he had been reading, awakening him.

"I was reading Pascal," he said in a tremulous voice. "If only the fire-eaters of South Carolina had read him attentively. 'The sole cause of man's unhappiness,' Pascal says, 'is that he does not know how to stay quietly in his room.' If they had only been able to wait and consider, all that has befallen us might not have been."

"South Carolinians never were ones for waiting or considering, let alone staying quietly in their own room."

She pushed Philander's chair into his bedroom, drew the curtains. He was already asleep again. She went back out onto the porch and resumed her gentle swinging, picked up the book, put it down again.

From a long way off she could see Amos Boggs approaching, knowing him by his large dappled mare. He crossed the covered bridge to their side of the valley, where the summer homes of the planters were strung out along the riverbank beneath the trees. A knight-errant, she thought, a large gentle man who for thirty years had been sheriff of Cate County, by his very presence keeping law and order.

He left the road, moving up toward the mission station, as it was still known, though precious little missionary work was ever done there. He was concerned for her, she knew, saw her as the others did, as a young woman who had sacrificed her life to ministering to her missionary uncle, a recluse at twenty.

The sheriff tied his horse to the gatepost before walking to the house, hat in hand, waiting for her permission before mounting the squeaking steps to the porch.

"Good morning, Miss Susannah."

"Good morning, Sheriff."

"How's the reverend doing?"

"Not well. He hardly gets out of bed anymore."

The sheriff shifted from one foot to the other. He had something to say, but he didn't quite know how to begin.

"I guess you're going to lose him soon."

"That's what Dr. Habersham says."

"Have you made any provisions for what you'll do then?"

"I've thought about it. I might try to get a position as housekeeper."

She could tell by the look on his face what Sheriff Boggs

thought of that idea. But it was the best she could come up with. She kept the mission accounts and knew that Philander had not a single dollar to his own name. He had lived on his stipend from The Board of Foreign Missions and, when the war had cut off remittances from the North, the charity of his summer neighbors, rich planters from the low country and the Piedmont.

"That won't be easy. Don't know anyone in the county ever had a housekeeper excepting Judge Stiles, unless you count old man Devereux, who brought his with him in the summer. But of course he doesn't come anymore."

"But Junius and Lamar are at the cottage right now. Why?"

"I guess the Confederacy is pretty desperate, and they aren't giving any more deferments, even for the likes of the Devereux. You could say they are sort of staying out of the public eye. As it happens, that is just where I was headed, but I thought I should stop by and see how you and the reverend was doing."

"You have business with the Devereux boys?" Thirty-two and thirty-five, they were still known as "the Devereux boys," so much were they under the thumb of old Auguste Devereux.

"Yes. The telegraph line to Atlanta is back up at last, and there's some worrisome news on it, according to Judge Stiles. Governor Brown wants the robbers of the Devereux Bank last month brought to justice, wants the gold back, and lacking that, wants some indictments of those responsible for letting all this happen."

"Gold?"

"There are people who say that Governor Brown turned over all the gold remaining in the Dahlonega mint to Auguste Devereux for safekeeping when the war began. But I don't know that to be true."

"Sit down, Sheriff." She wanted to hear more. "How did there come to be a U.S. mint in a small North Georgia town in the first place?"

"John C. Calhoun, they say. He had a big interest in the mines and, of course, knew how to pull strings in Washington. The miners, and there were thousands of them in the mountains in those days, were all for it. They needed to have someplace official to get their gold assayed. That's when I took to being a law officer, a deputy to Sheriff Hurt. There were four deputies in those days, not just the one there is now, and Dorsey don't have a whole lot to do.

"There was plenty to do then. None of the miners got rich, but they always had money to spend. Around Catesville there sprung up any number of rooming houses and saloons and gambling houses and . . ."

"Bawdy houses."

"Miss Susannah!"

She hadn't meant to finish the sentence that the sheriff wouldn't, but she was still the woman that she was.

"Well, yes, and there were fistfights and gunfights, and public drunkenness was more the rule than the exception." He paused, looked out across the valley floor. "And then the gold began to run out just as they discovered gold in California, and all those miners went away just as fast as they had showed up. It's sort of odd to think of all that drinking and gambling and stuff turned into nothing more than gold coins, and the people who did all those things just disappearing like they had never been here, and leaving Cate County peaceful and poor again. No gold, no railroad, no cotton . . ."

"And aren't we lucky," Susannah Goode said. "That's all the Yankees are interested in."

"I guess you're right there." The sheriff stood up. "Well, I'd better be getting over to the Devereux place. You know

now, all you have to do if you need something is to get word to me, and me or Dorsey will be right over."

"Yes, I know, Sheriff. By the way, what about the other Devereux boy?"

"Joel? Still in Spain, as far as I know, and not likely to get back until this is all over. The blockade now is tight as a proper cinch."

She watched Amos Boggs ride off, and then she picked up the book, opened it at random. Lines of poetry leapt up at her.

"A savage place! As holy and enchanted/As e'er beneath a waning moon was haunted/By woman wailing for her demon lover!" She put down the book again, shaken by the image those lines evoked. Her demon lover. She saw herself once again as he must have seen her that long-ago night, aged seventeen, naked in a darkened church, her body turned rosy pink by the glow from a pot-bellied stove.

Susannah recalled that first time with Joel in all its detail. She had done this so often that it was like watching the repetition of a well-known play, and like a play there was an element of inevitability to it. Her life had not aspired to high drama, but then tragedy chooses its subjects, one does not choose tragedy. A messenger simply comes on stage and announces that fate has changed course.

In this case it began with an influenza that put the slave boy Leander to bed. He had been accustomed to driving her to choir practice on Thursday evenings and watching her from up in the slave gallery. The Cherokee boy Elias was nowhere to be found, and since she did not intend to miss choir practice, she had no choice but to hitch up the mare herself.

The temperature hovered around freezing, and the road was turning into an icy mush. She was afraid they were in for the worst kind of weather you could have in the North

Georgia mountains: rain falling on the forest and freezing on the tree limbs, until ice so weighed them down that they began breaking off near dawn with the sound of gunfire. She hoped she was wrong, but as she approached the Congregationalist church, all by itself on the country road, sleet began to fall. She had gone too far now to turn back, and there would at least be warmth and companionship.

But the church was dark. She left horse and buggy in the stable and gingerly made her way up the icy front steps. Inside she lit some candles and went to the stove in the far corner of the room, where a fire was laid. In cold weather the Eller boys laid a fire for choir practice after Sunday service. Then she pulled a bench up in front of the stove and waited for warmth and the others to arrive. After a while she realized the others weren't coming. They had looked out their windows, seen what kind of night it was, and decided to stay home. She would have done the same, had her desire to be in this place not been so strong that it had clouded her judgment. Just then she heard the hooves of a horse. Someone else had been impelled to venture out on this night.

Joel Devereux came through the door, took off his broad-brimmed hat, and the candlelight shone in his golden-red hair. He was wearing the black cloak that he had bought one summer while touring Italy, something that people of his class did but that she could not even imagine. He removed his gloves, leaned over, took her hand and kissed her lightly on the cheek, an intimacy they had allowed themselves of late, when they met at the well between the mission and Cherokee Rose, or somewhere else where they could not be seen.

She had wanted to be open and free with him, but one settled for what one could get. It had been made abundantly clear that a future together would be denied them by whatever means was required.

"You're cold, Susannah," he said, throwing his cloak over her shoulders.

"It's you who're cold," and as he sat down next to her, she brought him under the cloak.

"I came by the mission to make sure you hadn't gone out, but I was too late."

"You know why I had to come."

"Oh, yes." He smiled ironically. "The same reason I have lately taken an interest in ecclesiastical music." She laughed. "But my father will find out. He always finds out. It's time we made our decisions, and there's plenty of time for that to-night."

"What do you mean?"

"My horse nearly fell on the way here, and no horse is going to make it back now. The road is like a piece of glass."

"What are you trying to say?"

"I'm just getting you used to the idea that we're here for the night."

"But we can't . . ."

"Or we could go back, and they would find us, if not frozen, lying in the road with broken legs or whatever. Now that would be truly good for your reputation."

She laughed again. "A nice thing about the inevitable is that then you are free."

"What do you mean?"

"I mean that there is freedom in being unable to influence events, most of all the freedom to speak your mind. So let us talk, my darling."

She would later realize that it was at this precise moment that the history of Susannah Goode and Joel Devereux had its beginning.

It began with her kissing him full on the mouth, knowing for the first time the salty male taste of him. "Joel, I love you."

"And I love you, Susannah."

"Now, there is a basis for conversation."

"So what do we do to thwart Auguste Devereux, one of the most powerful men in the South, who has never had his will defied by any member of his family?"

"What can he do, Joel?"

"He has already pointed out to me that I have no income of my own and that my skills—such as they are, as he said—are confined to the business of growing, selling, or making cloth of cotton; and that he can easily assure that no one in these fields of endeavor from Charleston to New Orleans will hire me. He has also made it plain that he will not countenance marriage to you or any other sort of relationship with you. He has had the story of your mother investigated by a detective, he said, and I should be happy that he went to the trouble."

She laughed yet again, and it was not a forced laugh but that of a woman who knows that her destiny has put her on the right and only path, one that had always been there but had only needed to be pointed out to her.

"Well, at least he can say nothing against my father, since even my mother probably does not know who he is. So, what do you propose?"

"I propose that we endure, that we wait for each other wherever we may find ourselves. My father and his cronies thought, after the battle of Manassas, that the war would be a picnic, that the North would come to terms. But clearly now, they were wrong. I think the war may be our solution, Susannah."

"It may also kill us, Joel."

"Eventually something will."

"Then you are saying that we now belong to each other, no matter what?"

"I do. Will you take the same vow?"

"I will, but you may have noticed that we have not yet belonged to each other."

"Now it is my turn to be unsure . . ."

"I will show you," she said, lifting the black cloak off them and laying it in front of the now-red-bellied stove, into which she threw more logs. Then she disrobed down to her nakedness, which she knew to be beautiful and at seventeen to be at its prime. This he will know, whatever the future may hold. She stood for a moment, aglow with the glow of the flames from the stove, like some kind of witch, but hoped not that, and then she lowered herself to the warm cloak and watched as he undressed. And then they knew each other, in the way it was meant in the enormous Bible on the lectern above and beyond them in the shadows.

Afterward she lay against him and looked up at the hymn numbers posted for the Sunday before—134, 79, 233. They were like a secret code for what had passed between them, and so they would remain for a long time. She had an unseemly knowledge, all secondhand, of what the act of love was like, and she had been prepared for the usual problems that a virgin could expect. But they did not happen. She also knew what a woman could experience if a man knew what he was doing, and this did happen, the throwing of her body against his, the crying out, the final untying of the knot.

Dawn came and there was no breaking of ice-laden boughs with the sound of guns being fired. As also happened in the North Georgia mountains at this time of year, a gust of warm air blew through the valleys, and the ice fell from the trees in crystal glitter.

They lay naked in each other's arms, wrapped in his great black Italian cloak, until the stove had lost all warmth, and then he got up and began to dress, his body fairer in the early

31

morning light than she had imagined it, as she so often had. When he was dressed she stood up and let him savor her nakedness.

"Do you regret what we did?" he said gently.

"Regret? There's nothing to regret. I've always known this was the path I must take. I can't even regret taking you with me, since that too must have been ordained."

His eyes narrowed, and he observed her closely. Then he laughed and took her nakedness into his arms.

"The Reverend Philander Goode has filled that beautiful head of yours with the rubbish of predestination, has he not?"

"It was more his wife before she died. She told me I was damned. I was only twelve."

"Well, let me tell you, my seventeen-year-old emissary from the Prince of Darkness, it's all rubbish. Now we truly belong to each other and I mean to keep you, if I have to go down myself to Hell to do it. Susannah, you're not doomed to turn out like your mother. We will make our own destiny. Just keep in mind that we are up against Auguste Devereux, from whom Satan himself could learn a trick or two."

He went outside and confirmed that the road had again become passable. They left separately, she by the road in her buggy and he on his horse by some path he knew through the woods. Whether they had been observed, she did not know. But, of course, they had been, and that was the beginning of old Auguste's maneuvers to put as much distance as possible between Joel and her, which ended with Joel being sent to Barcelona.

From Spain there were passionate love letters at first, but then even letters ceased as the Northern blockade of the South tightened. After three years, she was on the brink of despair. She had, she had thought, escaped her dark destiny to enter the rational, lighted world of Joel Devereux, but now it seemed she would know only the limbo of a single woman who would never take another man, in a South going down in agony to defeat and bitterness and poverty.

The lines of poetry that had brought back that first night together were not lines one would have expected to find in a book from the library of a doctor of divinity, but even the most innocent books harbored unsettling images, she knew.

How many books had she read in the last three years? Hundreds, some even in French. Philander said she had given herself a liberal education, and perhaps she had. What else was there to do but read and hope? When Philander was gone, what would happen to the two thousand volumes, a legacy from his father and grandfather, brought South by train to Atlanta, then by wagon to Catesville, wrapped in oilcloth? What would happen to all those books when Philander Goode was buried next to the two Presbyterian missionaries who had preceded him, and their wives and his?

More to the point, what would happen to her? What course would her life have taken if they had not found themselves alone throughout the night of the great ice storm, the only two people who had ventured out for choir practice at the little isolated church? It was an idle question. What had happened had happened. The people of Catesville would never have guessed that for three years it had been her secret that she was sensuous as a cat, knew more about the act of love than most married women. Oh, she had learned a lot before she and Joel were torn apart.

The three boys were coming up the path from the river carrying fishing poles, laughing about something. Three boys, three races. There was not much time left them for laughter or even for being together. When the grandly named Mission to the Cherokee Nation closed its doors, as it soon must, they would be torn apart. There was no place in white society for Elias, the Cherokee boy. Leander would go back to Devereux Hall as a house servant; and if the South lost the war he would be free, but free to do what? Even Johnny faced a bleak future, his father killed at Chickamauga on the same day as Marion Devereux, his mother barely able to feed them on her pittance of a salary as Catesville's only schoolteacher.

And this brought her back to her own plight, that of a young woman whose reputation had been ruined, in the eyes of those few who knew, by that of her mother, before she had committed any sins of her own. A young woman who had staked everything on her grand passion for a man whose father was unalterably opposed to any form of relationship between his son and her, and who for more than two years had been as cut off from her man—if he were still that—as if he were in prison. Or perhaps it was more realistic to see herself as in prison, imprisoned by circumstance.

After Jessie Finch had finished tutoring the boys, Susannah made them tea, and they sat on the porch drinking it while the boys proudly cooked themselves lunch out of the bream they had caught, grilled over an open fire.

"I'm afraid this is the last time I will be able to offer you tea, Jessie. It's all used up, and, of course, there's no more to be had."

"These are hard times, Susannah, and getting harder. I sometimes think the hardest of all is not knowing where it will all end, except that it will end badly."

"It already has for you."

"Losing John? As much as I cared for him, my life is not over. I have responsibilities. I must see that Johnny has some kind of future, which means education, and how can I afford that? I need advice, Susannah. It is really the kind of advice I should be asking of a married woman, but I don't know anyone but you I would want to confide in."

"You flatter me, Jessie, but I'll try to help if I can."

"Amos Boggs has asked me to marry him. You look surprised."

"I am. Very surprised."

"Why?"

"I think of you two as belonging to two different worlds."

Jessie Finch put down her teacup, folded her napkin.

"We were, until recently. But one day he came over to the schoolhouse with a basket of early vegetables, said he had planted a garden out back of the jailhouse, not having much to do these days, with all the troublemakers away in the army, and was going to have more vegetables this summer than he could ever use. Lord knows I can use free vegetables, but I told him I would have to give him something in return, and it couldn't be money.

"You know what he said? He said he had always wanted to know something about geography but never got far enough in school where they taught it. Maybe I could teach him some geography while school was out for the summer. I said that was a more than fair swap, so he's been bringing vegetables a couple of times a week, and then we spend an hour studying geography.

"I guess I should have known he was interested in something more than geography. He must be awfully lonely. I have Johnny for company, but Amos and Effie had no children, and since she died, he's been living in that room above the jailhouse all alone. I do feel sorry for him, and to tell you the truth it would be nice to have some male companionship again. I miss it. That's why I said I really ought to be seeking the advice of a married woman."

"Don't just assume, Jessie, that I don't know anything

about that side of marriage. I'm not an inexperienced woman."

"Why, Susannah Goode! You of all people. I won't inquire further."

"No, please don't." She could feel herself blushing. "Well, from a practical point of view marrying Amos Boggs makes all kinds of sense, but do you love him?"

"I think I could learn to."

"Then say yes." Susannah was flustered now, wanted to leave her confession behind as quickly as possible. "You know Amos rode by while you were tutoring the boys," she said. "He was going down to Cherokee Rose to talk to the Devereux brothers about that robbery of their father's bank last month. Seems the governor wants someone held responsible."

Jessie Finch looked down at her hands folded in her lap. "Yes, and I'm real worried about that."

"Worried? Why?"

"There's a rumor around town that Amos was somehow involved in the robbery, and it seems that Givens Crenshaw started that rumor. I can't imagine why the mayor would do a thing like that."

"Maybe he had a hand in the robbery himself and is looking to blame it on somebody else. I wouldn't put anything past that snake in the grass."

"What shall I do?"

"You'd better tell Amos right away. You sure can't marry him if he's in jail, but he'll know what to do." She laughed, the tension relieved. She wanted Jessie to understand that Givens Crenshaw was no match for the sheriff.

"Bad times," Jessie said. "Sherman closing in on Atlanta, the bank robbed, and I guess you have some worries of your own."

"I have. Dr. Habersham says Philander could go any day, and then there'll be nothing to do but close the mission. I feel sorry most of all for Philander. He came down here as a young man full of enthusiasm for converting the Cherokee, but his field white to harvest was reaped by others. As soon as gold was discovered on Cherokee land, they were doomed. And he had to watch them marched off to the Oklahoma Territory, and when the best of the Cherokee leaders, Elias Budinot, was murdered by his own people for telling them they had to go, it nearly broke Philander's heart."

"And now there's the boy the Reverend named Elias to worry about," Jessie said. "He was found in the woods, wasn't he?"

"He was. Joel Devereux used to roam the mountains, and he found this Cherokee child abandoned in the forest, not old enough to know his own name. Joel brought him to the mission, and Philander was going to educate him, send him to Princeton Theological, and make him a missionary to his own people. That won't happen now, of course."

"What about you, Susannah? What will you do?"

"I'll try to find some kind of position, I guess. It looks like the war may be over soon, and something might open up for me."

A few months before, Jessie had suggested that she ought to consider marriage. With her looks she could have any young man in the county. Susannah had laughed and said that she wasn't becoming engaged to a man who would just go off to the war and be killed. But that was before Jessie's own husband had gone off to war and died at Chickamauga. And now that Jessie knew that there had already been a man in her life, she wasn't likely to raise that possibility again.

"You know what you should do, Susannah, you should talk to George Malik. He's a good friend of the Reverend's, and he has business connections all over North Georgia. He might know of something for you. Well, I'd better get to town and tell Amos the latest I've heard about what Givens Crenshaw has been up to."

"And you have to tell him that other thing."

"What other thing?"

"Yes." Now it was Jessie who was blushing.

As Susannah watched Jessie's buggy disappear down the road, with Johnny driving, she thought, Yes, of course. I should see George.

George Malik had arrived in town thirty years before with a pack on his back, selling needles and thread and other notions, and had decided to settle down, but the townspeople weren't having any Mohammedan in their midst, until Philander explained that not all Lebanese were Moslems, and that George Malik was a Christian. So he had settled down, married a local girl, and become a prosperous merchant. He had also become a kind of protector to Philander Goode's ward, knowing how unworldly Philander was and that Susannah was too pretty not to attract all kinds of male attention, including the wrong kind. Yes, she would go see George Malik.

3

An aura of death hung over the Savannah railroad station, as palpable as the dust in the air from the feet of hundreds of Confederate soldiers entering the railroad yard in ragged columns, lining up for roll call. They were emaciated, their uniforms tattered, their beards unkempt. Some wore canteens and belts and shoes scavenged from the Union dead on a field of battle. Their exhausted officers herded them onto flat-bedded railroad cars, no longer caring that the men were almost bereft of military qualities, the officers' role reduced to that of sheepdogs.

The engine built up a head of steam. They were bound for Atlanta, to reinforce the army of General Joe Johnston. Joel Devereux watched from the door of the telegraph office, smoking a cheroot and wearing a straw planter's hat he had just bought. From the dead look in the men's eyes, squatting on their blanket rolls in the open cars, he sensed they knew their cause was lost, that death, maiming, or a Yankee prison camp was likely to be their lot.

There were two closed cars for the officers at the end of the train, the last of which had a separate compartment entered from the rear platform. He picked up his brother Junius's leather bag and headed for the iron platform steps. An officer, not much more than a boy, blocked his way.

"Sorry, sir, this is a military train. No civilians."

"I have a pass, Lieutenant." He produced the document with his fictitious name, John Dabney, which he could only corroborate by the initials on his silver-backed hairbrushes.

The lieutenant looked at the document, hesitated.

"I am from President Davis's staff in Richmond, and I have business with General Johnston."

"Very good, sir."

"And I would prefer to be in the rear compartment, out of the public eye."

"As you prefer, sir."

When he entered the compartment, he was surprised to find another passenger, a scarecrow of a man with a scraggly blond beard, sergeant's stripes on his sleeve. But then he noticed that the man wore an officer's sidearm and had beside him on the seat a padlocked red metal box.

"John Dabney, from Richmond. I'm on my way to army headquarters."

"Well, I guess I am too. Sergeant Elam Scroggins, from Salt Lick Hollow, Georgia."

"Outside of Hiawassee, I believe."

"I declare. You're about the first person I've met since I've been in the army who's ever heard of it. I guess I would still be there if I hadn't gotten the idea of becoming a telegrapher. I was working in Atlanta when the war came along, and the army was onto me like a duck on a June bug."

"At least you're not in the line of battle." This telegrapher interested him. He had already figured out that if a telegrapher was on his way to General Johnston's headquarters, it was because that metal box contained military ciphers.

"That's true enough, but cannonballs don't know the difference between infantry soldiers and telegraphers. And besides, if you are a soldier, you sign up for a certain time, a year or whatever. The same's supposed to be true for telegraphers, but they's in such short supply that every time I'm due to be mustered out, there's some new order from a general saying they can't let telegraphers go yet. It's enough, sometimes, to make me think of letting myself go."

That was the reason that Sergeant Elam Scroggins had interested Joel. The furtiveness in his deep-set eyes and nervousness about his mouth. He had the look of a man who was playing with the idea of desertion. The sergeant had stopped talking and begun thinking. He reached inside his blouse and took out a crumpled letter, read it over slowly, then looked up.

"You married, sir?"

"Yes, I am."

"I was married just three weeks when the army come for me. So there wasn't no children, just me and Asa. Haven't seen her in more than two years now. She stayed on in Atlanta, and she had some schooling in bookkeeping, so with all the men gone off to war, she got a pretty good job. I've been trying to get myself back to Atlanta, but it's never worked out until now, and wouldn't you know . . ."

"What's that?"

"The mail finally caught up with my regiment in Savannah, and there was this letter from Asa. I told her that if it looked like the Yankees was going to take Atlanta, she should get herself up to Hiawassee and stay with my brother and his wife. The Yankees sure wouldn't come up that way. And that's what she done—a month ago. Now I'm on a train to Atlanta, and it ain't stopping. They going to run all night if they have to."

"They'll have to stop for water and fuel."

"Yes, and then they'll put out pickets alongside the train to make sure nobody sneaks off."

"Still, you might see a chance."

41

"You're from Richmond, you said?"

"That's right, but it doesn't matter. I wouldn't tell on you."

"I've done more than my share in this fight, and I got to get back to my woman."

"She means a lot to you."

"She's the only thing on this earth I care about." Sergeant Scroggins began to cry.

Joel opened his valise and took out a flask, filled a little silver cup with Mount Gay rum.

"Here, have a shot of this."

"I hardly ever touch a drop. My pa took to drink and used to beat me and my ma, but yes, I think I will." He downed the rum in one swallow and handed back the cup. Joel poured a shot for himself.

"You understand, then?"

"About getting back to your woman? Yes, Sergeant, I understand."

By late afternoon they had passed Augusta and were heading due west toward Atlanta, where they were expected to arrive sometime during the night. Suddenly the train ground to a halt. Gray-clad cavalrymen were conferring with the engineer of the train. Further on a pall of smoke hung over the track. Then the cavalrymen galloped off, the engineer climbed back into the cab, and they moved slowly forward. An officer stuck his head into the compartment.

"Cavalry skirmish up ahead. The Yankees were driven off. They're still around somewhere, but they aren't likely to attack a trainload of armed men."

The smoke came from two farmhouses, now burned to the ground, leaving only their chimneys standing. A dozen men in blue and gray lay dead in a trampled field of young corn.

Two horses with military saddles were grazing in the corn, horses with good conformation, officers' horses.

A little further on the train came to a stop again. Joel and the sergeant went out on the rear platform. A fireman in a leather apron got down from the cab and swung a big metal pipe out from a wooden water tank, pulled a chain that released water into the train's reservoir.

Three pickets got out of the train and looked up and down as the water was being loaded. Scroggins went to the other side of the platform.

"There's pickets on this side too—of course."

From somewhere in the pinewoods along the track, shots rang out. The pickets fell to the ground and pointed their weapons toward the sound of firing.

"Here's your chance," Joel said.

Sergeant Scroggins started to leap to the ground.

"What about your box?"

"Oh, Lordy!" Scroggins darted back into the compartment and picked up the box. Joel followed him and grabbed his valise.

"Mind if I join you?"

Scroggins flashed him a startled look, and together they went out on the platform, down the stairs and as stealthily as possible across the narrow open space between the train and tall reeds that surrounded a pond from where the water tank was supplied.

As they were entering the reeds, a voice called out, "Halt!"

Joel looked back. All of the pickets were on their feet, and one of them fired his gun in their direction. The pickets began to run toward where Joel and Elam Scroggins were half-hidden in the reeds. But not hidden enough. They could either push forward through the reeds, ankle-deep in mud, and probably be shot in the back, or they could stand with their hands raised and be shot or taken back to the train. No officer being on the scene, the pickets would probably find it easier just to shoot them and have done with it.

"What do we do now?" Elam croaked.

"Best surrender, I guess," and Joel stood up and raised his hands. There were six guns aimed at them, and the anger and fear of the pickets at having nearly let two men escape was very clear. These might be the last seconds of his life, Joel thought. Have I come so far to end like this?

An officer ran up, pistol in hand. The pickets turned, awaited orders.

"Call off those men, Lieutenant!" a voice boomed.

Joel looked back at the train. Several officers had gathered on the rear platform.

"There're two hundred and forty men to get safely to Atlanta tonight," a tall, black-bearded colonel said in a voice that carried to where they stood, hands raised, in the reeds. "I don't have any spare time for writing a report on why two men with their hands raised were shot. The general is very particular about that kind of thing. And we sure as hell ain't taking them with us. Just leave 'em."

By the time the train started off again Joel and Elam Scroggins were on the far side of the pond, where they stopped to catch their breath.

Scroggins knelt on the ground, took out a key and opened the padlock on the red metal box. There were, indeed, cipher books inside. There was also a telegraph key, which he put in his pocket.

"I'd feel naked without my key," he said, relocking the box. Then he stood up and drew back his arm as if to throw the box in the pond.

"Don't want to get caught with this, that's for sure."

"You'd better think about that."

44

"I have. Losing your ciphers is pretty much a shooting offense. Deserting with them—well, I guess that's even worse."

"What about your buddies in Atlanta? Those codes might save lives."

"Thought about that, too. When they change ciphers they send two couriers with different new ciphers. If one courier was to get shot or captured, then they just use the second cipher. Our codes ain't much good anyway. The Yankees break them right regular, though we never manage to break theirs."

With that observation, Scroggins sailed the red metal box out over the pond. It sank slowly, air bubbling up from inside it, like Joel's boat sinking to the bottom of the channel and with the same import. There was no turning back now.

"I think I know where we can find a couple of nice horses," Joel said.

"You ain't from Richmond at all, are you?"

"Never even been there on a visit."

"I thought gentlemen wasn't supposed to lie."

"That's not quite right. Gentlemen are supposed not to get caught."

Elam laughed. It was the laughter of a man who has just escaped with his life.

"Well, I like that. And we ain't dead yet, thanks to that Colonel Alexander, who kept us from getting shot for sure."

"Alexander is the commander of these troops?"

"No, that's Colonel Drake."

"Then who is Colonel Alexander?"

"Don't know, except that whatever he says goes, even when Colonel Drake don't agree."

"What else do you know about this Colonel Alexander?"

"Nothing, except that he lost a leg at First Manassas and wears a false one. Don't limp much, though. His false leg was made specially for him in Paris, they say. One fellow who claims to have seen it says it's made of ivory with brass fittings."

They set out along a path that wound through the pinewoods toward where smoke still hung in a veil around the setting sun. The horses were still grazing in the cornfield where the dead lay, one with his face half blown off, others with no sign of injury, as if asleep. Joel had the reins of the two horses in his hands before they had a chance to bolt.

"We'd better spend the night in the woods near here, wherever this may be. No point in riding off in the night toward who knows where."

"The sign at the last station we passed was for 'Social Circle,'" Scroggins said.

"I know where that is," Joel replied. "Go due north, about a hundred miles as the crow flies, and you'll be at Hiawassee. Now we'd better get these horses out of sight in the woods and be up at first light to forage for food and water before we start off."

"I've done a sight of foraging these last two years," Scroggins said. "Know just how to go about it."

Scroggins was quickly asleep. Joel took his wallet from his jacket and removed the pass he had been given by Toussaint, held it to the dying fire and read Marcey's name and the scrawled countersignature, which he was now able to decipher, that of a Col. Th. Alexander, CSA, who had let him and telegrapher Scroggins escape with secret army codes.

By the time that Joel had the two horses resaddled, the blankets turned to hide the "USA" embroidered on them, and his own gear and clean clothes packed in the saddlebags, Scroggins returned, as the sun was rising, with a small sack of cornmeal, a shank end of ham, two canteens also marked "USA," filled with well water, and a blackened skillet. They rode off northward, trying to keep to the pinewoods and red clay creek banks, avoiding settled areas as much as possible. As they rode Joel pondered why a Yankee reconnoitering party would have ventured so deep inside Confederate lines. He finally decided it must have had to do with the railroads, of which Atlanta was the hub.

By dusk of their first day together, they had covered a great deal of ground. Elam Scroggins was not much of a rider, more used to mules than horses, he said, and his stirrups he just let hang. But he was a determined man, and Joel had taken a liking to him.

They dismounted, tethered the horses where there was grass and, it being a warm evening, both of them bathed in a pool beneath a little waterfall in a stream they had been following. Then Elam Scroggins arranged some rocks in a circle, started a fire within it with small twigs, and nurtured it until there was a good blaze. Then he took the skillet he had found, fried slices of ham, poured corn meal mush into the ham grease and made a big hoecake. It was, Joel thought, just about the best food he had ever tasted.

Afterward they lay back beside the fire, using their saddles as pillows, and Joel provided some more Mount Gay while Elam explained why he was sure the South had lost the war and a man had just as well desert, if you could even call it desertion.

"I was at Missionary Ridge. We got whupped real good there. So we moved down off the mountain, and General Johnston had everyone, including telegraphers, putting up earthworks. But it didn't do no good. When ole Sherman came, it was with so many men, like I never seen before, it was like a wave, and they flanked our right and our left and we had to draw back. When we regrouped, the captain came to me and said, 'Scroggins, I got a mission for you. I want you to sneak through the enemy lines and disable the telegraph wire that runs along the Western and Atlantic track, which the Yankees have put back in service, in as many places as you can.' 'Yes sir,' I says. He didn't think to tell me what I was to do afterwards.

"So, I left that very night and got through the Yankee lines all right. Their army was all strung out. Disabling the telegraph wire weren't no problem, either. You can't just cut it. They'll have it fixed in a jiffy. They have handcars running up and down the line, finding breaks and fixing them. And that's what you have to watch for. They'll have a sharpshooter on the handcar to pick off anyone they see messing with the line. And those handcars come on you silent-like.

"No, what you have to do is cut the wire at the insulator on the pole. The only way they can find the break is to climb a ladder and look at every insulator. That can take a powerful long time. Anyway, I cut the wire at four or five places, picking a lonely stretch of rail where you could see a handcar coming from a long way off. And that's what happened. This handcar comes around the curve, and there I am atop a pole. I jumps to the ground and runs off into the woods with two of them chasing me, a couple of shot whistled right over my head. I just kept running, but they didn't give up easy. I guess finding those breaks in the wire had made them peevish.

"After a while I shook them, but I had not the slightest idea where I was. So I just kept walking, and finally I come upon a farmhouse and they told me where I was and gave me some buttermilk and cornbread and let me sleep in the barn. The next morning I thought it over. I had done my job and had no further orders, and it didn't make sense to go back through the enemy lines just in time to be in on the slaughter that was coming.

"I had seen the Yankee trains going down loaded with

fresh troops and supplies and coming back with the wounded. General Sherman had everything real well organized, and we wasn't going to be able to stand up to him. I knew then we was done for.

"So I reckoned it would be all right just to go to Asa in Atlanta. Too bad I didn't have a compass. Where I ended up was right back in our lines, and the captain telling me what a good piece of work I had done on the Yankee telegraph wire, and he promoted me to sergeant on the spot. That is the way war is. It ain't like anything else in life."

"No, I suppose not." Joel thought about the trooper with his face half blown off and wondered how Marion had died at Chickamauga. But for the choice the two brothers had made between the army and the Barcelona office, he would have been at Chickamauga and Marion in Spain. He got up.

"You smoke a pipe?"

"I do when I can get some tobacco."

"I've got a couple of pipes in my saddlebags."

Joel returned with two pipes, tamped down with tobacco, lit one pipe from a glowing piece of wood, handed it to Scroggins and then lit the other for himself. They lay back again, smoking in silence.

"So, you ain't from Richmond," Scroggins finally said. "I'll bet you ain't married either."

"No, I'm not. How did you know?"

"You don't act married. I'll tell you what I think. I think you're taking leave of the army too, though you was probably an officer. Been to school up north, too. You talk just like our colonel, who went to one of those northern schools."

"Yes, I went to Princeton University, but I've not been in the army. I've been in Europe. I had a brother though," he added, as though it somehow justified his civilian status, "who was killed at Chickamauga."

"I'm sorry to hear that. But for sure he wasn't alone. I was there, and afterwards it looked just like that cornfield where we got the horses, except a thousand times over. I telegraphed in our casualty figures—twenty thousand dead, wounded, and missing, including ten generals. I hope never to see anything like that again. Most of the dead were plain country boys like me. That's when I decided what my buddies said was about right. 'Rich man's war, poor man's fight.' But I imagine you come from a family that owns niggers."

"My father does. I wouldn't."

Another silence followed and then, "If you wasn't in the army, what are you running away from?"

"I'm not running away from anything. I did someone a great wrong, and I came back from Europe to try and make up for it."

"That someone wouldn't be a woman, would it?"

"It would."

"Well, I won't ask more. But I will ask where you're headed."

"Catesville."

"Why, that ain't all that far from Hiawassee. We can travel together."

"That's what I was thinking. Better not to travel alone these days."

"You got a side arm?"

"I have a pair of pistols."

"Well, you'd better load one and wear it. No telling what we are going to run into between here and Catesville."

4

Her plan to pay a visit on George Malik was frustrated. Philander took a turn for the worse, and she had to send Leander into Catesville to bring Dr. Habersham, who said, well, the end is near. So she waited two days, nursing Philander, until suddenly he got better again. Not the first time that had happened. He had this determination to hang onto living, as if his life's work might yet be vindicated.

The next morning Susannah had Leander hitch up the buggy to the mare and drive her into town. On the way she tried to induce him into conversation. Soon she was going to have to put it up to old Auguste Devereux what he wanted done about his young slave boy.

"What did you do down at the plantation, Leander, exactly?"

"I polishes the brass on the mules' harnesses."

"That's all?"

"That's plenty when there's more than a hundred mules. And the brass it has to shine, 'cause everything has to shine that belongs to Massa Auguste, right down to mule harnesses."

"Why do you suppose he sent you to the Mission to get some book learning?"

"He say he going to fetch me up to take ole Fraser's place as butler, when Fraser get too old for the job. My ma, April,

51

she's an upstairs maid, say there may be more to it than that, but she never say what that might be."

"You want to be a butler, Leander?"

"I wants to be free."

They drove into the town square, and Susannah realized that it had been months since she had been there. The catalpa trees were in white showy bloom around the square, around the red brick courthouse, the jailhouse in its shadow, the schoolhouse, the Masonic lodge, George Malik's Emporium and the Devereux Bank. Sure enough, a big hole had been blown in the wall of the bank, and one of the Home Guard with a shotgun on his lap was sitting in a chair in front of the exposed lockboxes. Why, after a month, hadn't they just bricked up the hole in the vault wall?

She was bound to run into a lot of people she knew, and she had almost forgotten how to act in public. But she was going to have to relearn that, and fast. She had as much determination as Philander and more reason to hang onto life. If she didn't believe that, she would give up hope. The war would end someday, someday Joel Devereux would come home, and maybe he would still love her. It was that last that worried her most. She told Leander to stop in front of the courthouse. She would walk across the square to give herself time to think about the best way to persuade people to help her.

There didn't seem to be anybody about this morning in the town square. She saw that the Confederate flag flying above George's store had the tin disk painted yellow attached to the lanyard below it. That meant the mail from Atlanta was in. Before the war it had come twice a week, but now it came when it came. That's where everybody would be, inside the Emporium picking up their mail and reading the Atlanta newspapers that Lucinda, George's wife, the postmistress, would have tacked to the walls. It was the only way that Catesville could keep up with how the war was going.

She crossed the square past the town pump, in a cast-iron gazebo with a slate roof, and went up the familiar steps to the porch along the front of the Emporium. There were two well-worn benches on the porch for the town idlers and a number of metal advertising signs nailed to the unpainted store front, but rust had made most of these almost illegible. One of them had a thermometer attached to it, but it hadn't worked in years. Since the war began, things didn't get replaced or repaired.

There was indeed a crowd inside the store, including all the town notables. Judge Stiles came over to her. He was wearing riding breeches and boots. He was the only person in Cate County who kept a pack of hounds; a heavy-set man, with a shiny bald dome, a full russet beard and crafty eyes.

"Good morning, Miss Susannah. It's good to see you out. Been a long time."

"I've had to stay close to home because of Philander."

"How's the Reverend doing?"

"Dr. Habersham says he isn't going to last much longer."

"I'm real sorry to hear that."

"When he goes, I guess I'm going to have to find a position. You wouldn't know of anything, would you, Judge?"

There was a considerable pause. "Well now, if my clerk gets called up in the militia, as well may happen, I'd need to find someone to replace him."

Susannah knew what was going around in the judge's mind from the look in his eye. He was considering the possibilities of a single woman without relatives, known as the beauty of Cate County and in bad need of money, particularly because the war gave him a plausible excuse for having a woman alone with him in his chambers.

"I think I could handle that, Judge."

A little daring, but she wasn't closing any doors just yet.

"Well, I'll most certainly keep you in mind."

They moved away from each other, and Susannah approached Amos Boggs, studying the front page of an Atlanta newspaper.

"Morning, Amos."

"Morning, Miss Susannah."

"How's the news?"

"Good, they say, very good. But of course they would, if at all possible. Anyway, it says General Johnston has given old Sherman a real trouncing at Kennesaw Mountain, the other side of Marietta. Trouble is, it's us that seems to be retreating after winning this big battle, a 'strategic regroupment,' the paper calls it, whatever that means."

Susannah waited for the sheriff to mention his proposal of marriage to Jessie Finch and her acceptance, but he said nothing. Perhaps Jessie hadn't had the nerve to speak to him yet. It was a big step for her.

The sheriff turned away from the newspapers. "Susannah, there's something you should know. There are bushwhackers operating in the area, both Yankee and our kind. If they are seen anywhere in Cate County, I'm coming to get you and bring you into town."

"But there's Philander. Where would we stay?"

"I've already spoken with Jessie. She's got room for both of you."

"I'll do whatever you say, Amos."

She didn't need any persuading. The thought of being alone in the isolated mission with only the two boys and bushwhackers roaming the hills sent a shiver through her. She had heard stories of what these irregular troops had done to women.

Across the room Lester Owens, the Devereux Bank manager, was talking with Givens Crenshaw. The mayor wore one of his usual pale tropical suits. This was meant to remind people that he came from a fine Charleston family, or so he said, but such clothes looked downright peculiar in the North Georgia mountains.

Lester Owens saw her looking at him, said something to Crenshaw, and came over to her. He wore heavy sidewhiskers, which were dyed, along with his thinning hair. He was too old for a soldier, but wanted to appear young enough to still be a person of importance in Catesville.

"Good morning, Miss Susannah."

"Morning, Lester. You know, I've been meaning to speak with you. The doctor says Philander may not live much longer, and if he goes, I'm going to have to find employment. I was wondering if the bank . . ."

"There ain't going to be no bank. The telegraph line's back up now, and I guess the robbery reminded old man Devereux that he had a branch of his bank in Catesville that hasn't made money in years. He's closing our branch. He said I could stay on until everybody had a chance to get their valuables out of their lockboxes. Then I could take a hundred dollars to help me find other employment. A hundred dollars after twelve years of faithful service. Ain't that something, and my Betsy about to have another baby. What am I going to do?"

"I'm real sorry, Lester."

"Susannah, I've got something for you," Lucinda Malik called.

She went over to the wire cage in one corner of the long room that separated Lucinda's post office from her husband's store.

"Good morning, Lucinda."

"Good morning. It's a telegram," and she slipped an envelope under the wire screen. Susannah tore it open. She couldn't imagine who would be sending her a telegram.

"From Butler and Evans, Freight Forwarders, Savannah. The merchandise you were expecting from Spain has finally arrived on a ship that ran the blockade. Will forward as soon as practicable."

This could only mean that Joel was back. For a minute she thought she would faint.

"Are you all right, Susannah? You're pale as a sheet. I hope it's not bad news."

"No, not bad news."

She would think about it later, when she was alone. For the moment, though, she still should see George Malik.

"Lucinda, I was wondering if George is in this morning."

"In the back, working on the books."

"You think it would be possible for me to see him for a minute? I wouldn't want to disturb him."

"You wouldn't disturb him. Just go on back."

She knocked on the door to the back room and went in. George Malik, sitting behind the desk, still wearing his grocer's apron, looked up from a ledger, took off his steel-rimmed glasses. His hair was graying now, blending with his olive skin, his gray-green eyes, a tall, muscular man with a big nose, his sleeves rolled back, the hairs on his arms like black wires.

"Sit down, Susannah. What can I do for you?"

"I need some advice, George."

"The best I can give, my love."

"Philander is going to die soon."

"Yes, Dr. Habersham told me he hasn't long to live."

"With no money coming from the Foreign Mission Board, the mission has been kept open, as you know, on charity from

the summer people. When he goes that will be the end of the
mission, and Philander hasn't a penny of his own to leave me
or anybody else. What's going to happen to me? I thought
maybe you might know of some place I could find work."

"What do you know how to do, Susannah?"

"Nothing much, I guess. I know how to keep house is all."

"Have you considered marriage?"

"There's someone already, but until the war is over . . ."

"I didn't know you had a fiancé in the army. You keep secrets real well, Susannah."

"It's my only one," she said and smiled. She didn't want to
lie to George.

"Well, it's a big one. Anyway, you'll soon need to find
work. You think you could be a housekeeper?"

"That's sort of what I had in mind, but I'm told that
there's no one prosperous enough in the county to have a
housekeeper but Judge Stiles, and he already has one."

"Yes, a slave woman who is more than his housekeeper.
No, I was thinking more of housekeeper at a hotel."

"A hotel?"

"The Cate Springs Hotel."

"But it's closed."

"It just might reopen soon."

"A resort hotel's going to reopen with Sherman at the
gates of Atlanta? It doesn't make any sense."

"It wouldn't make any sense except for Sherman being at
the gates of Atlanta. You see, the hotel belongs to the Georgia
Land Company, which I represent here. The shareholders
are most of the moneyed people of Atlanta, and they are
looking for some safe place to send their wives and children.
They wouldn't want anyone to know that, but I'm telling you.

"I've just had a telegram asking if I could get hold of a
hotel manager, a housekeeper, chambermaids and wait-

resses, and kitchen help, including a good cook.

"The chambermaids and waitresses and kitchen help are no problem. There are plenty of young war widows in the county, half-starved enough to take any work they can find. As for a cook, that's another matter, unless these ladies from Atlanta fancy ham hocks and field peas and collard greens. There aren't any managers about, either. The few that could claim to be are off as officers in the army. But, do I have a housekeeper?"

Susannah raised her head. "Yes, George, you do. And I may even be able to tell you where you can find a manager. Auguste Devereux is closing the Catesville branch of his bank, and Lester Owens is going to be without a job."

George nodded his head. This was obviously something he already knew.

Two nights later Susannah was awakened by the sound of gunfire, far away, but then, half an hour later, closer at hand. If these were irregulars, and it didn't matter whether they were Yankee or Confederate, a woman in an isolated house . . . Should she get up, have the two boys hitch the mare to the buggy, lead Philander out to it, and drive into town? No, it would be the death of him, and driving down a back road on a moonless night would be even more dangerous than staying put.

She went into Philander's bedroom, felt his forehead, as she did once or twice every night. It was ice-cold. She felt for his pulse. There was none. The Reverend Philander Goode, DD, had died in his sleep. She went back to her room and lay down, alone now in an isolated house with a corpse. As far as she could surmise, Joel was on his way back to her. Was the happy ending to be snatched from her at the last minute? She had never in her life felt so utterly miserable.

The gunfire was not repeated, and the next morning Susannah found she had inner strengths she hadn't known existed. She had abandoned the idea of predestination, that she was damned, and she felt suddenly a surge of optimism, that she was in charge of her own destiny, an idea that she had first been introduced to by Joel Devereux one icy dawn, as he held her naked in his arms in the little Congregationalist church. It was in the Presbyterian church on the edge of town that the funeral service for Philander was held. During the service, try as she might to feel mournful, all Susannah could think of was that Joel was on his way back to her.

After Philander was committed to the earth, Susannah rode into town in the buggy, driven by Leander and sent a telegram to Auguste Devereux, asking him what he intended to do about his slave boy. Then they drove out to the mission, and Leander and Elias lashed her already-packed trunk onto the back of the buggy. She drove herself out to the Cate Springs Hotel, after instructing the two boys to remain at the mission until they heard further from her. She intended to establish her presence at the hotel before any questions were raised by the likes of Judge Stiles and Givens Crenshaw or they put forward one of their own relatives or a friend's daughter for the position of housekeeper.

As she passed through the gate to the grounds of the Cate Springs Hotel, its name arching in wrought iron over the buggy, she pulled on the reins and brought the horse to a stop. So this was to be her home, at least until the war offered up its answer to all their destinies. The grounds were grown up in weeds, one end of the long piazza sagged, and paint was peeling from the clapboard facade. She drove the buggy on, up to the wide front steps of the hotel, got down, and tied the reins to a cast-iron hitching post in the form of a Moorish boy in a turban.

As she went up the steps she realized that she was being watched. Behind a lace curtain appeared two pale faces. These would be the Appleton sisters, Margaret and Mildred, that George Malik had told her about. Neither had married, and they had lived together in the family home in Atlanta. The year after the war began they had come up for the summer. When the hotel was forced to close from lack of business, a family member had asked the company to let them stay on. This they had done, and the colored maid they had brought with them stayed too and did their cooking.

The pale faces behind the curtain disappeared, and Susannah expected one or both of the sisters to come to the door, but from within there was only silence. Finally she took the key that George had given her from her dress pocket and inserted it in the lock. The door creaked open and she stepped inside. The entrance hall was dark and musty smelling and silent.

"Hello!"

There was no reply. She opened another door and entered a large, well-lighted room. It must have been from the nearest window of the room that the two sisters had been watching her. On a white wicker chair with cushions covered in a floral print an open book lay, on another a knitting basket. She pushed open a swinging door and entered a long pantry lit only by a skylight, with dishes and glasses and cooking pots on shelves, and a safe that must have held, if it no longer did, the hotel silver. All of these things would soon be her concern.

She heard a sound as of dishes clinking, and she walked to the far end of the pantry to another swinging door with a glass porthole in it. Through the porthole she looked into a tile-floored kitchen. At a long copper sink a colored woman with her hair tied in a bandanna stood washing dishes and putting them in a wooden drying rack. Susannah opened the door.

The woman turned, young and pretty, with rich brown skin, and was about to speak, when she saw it was not one of the Appleton sisters.

"Mercy! Who are you, ma'am?"

"I'm the new housekeeper—for the hotel. It's being re-opened."

"You mean the war's done over?"

"No, the war's not over, but the fighting is getting close to Atlanta, and there will be some ladies coming to stay here for a while."

The woman seemed unsure how to react to this news and remained silent.

"What's your name?"

"My name's Lucy and I belongs to the Appleton family." She paused. "But maybe not much longer. The Yankees, they close to Atlanta you say?"

"Yes."

It was difficult to know whether the young woman thought that being set free would be a good thing or not.

"I was looking for the Misses Appleton. I saw them as I came in, but they seem to have disappeared."

"They's probably in their room. They gets scared when somebody comes out here they don't know. They think it means the Yankees have come."

"Would you ask them if they could come down? I need to explain to them about the hotel reopening."

"Yes, ma'am." The woman dried her hands and went out the swinging door.

"I'll be in the sitting room," Susannah called after her.

It was about fifteen minutes before the sisters timidly entered the sitting room, escorted by their maid. They were pale and plump, with graying hair, and dressed identically. She could imagine they were easily scared. After she had intro-

61

duced herself and explained the reason for her presence, they sat down and Lucy was sent off to make tea.

"We were fortunate," one of the sisters said. "The hotel had a large supply of tea. You can't find it on the market now. Or coffee, or hardly anything."

"So we are going to have ladies from Atlanta joining us," the other one said. "We'll probably know most, if not all, of them. But it is worrying. Does it mean that that dreadful General Sherman . . ." She left her sentence unfinished.

"Well, of course, no one knows, but . . ." And she left her own sentence unfinished. There was an awkward silence. Whatever the Appleton sisters were thinking, Susannah was thinking that these two aging women, accustomed to being constantly cared for, would be the last of their kind.

Every counter of the hotel kitchen was covered with dishes and glasses, washed, dried, and stacked. Susannah, the sleeves of her dress rolled up to her elbows, leaned back against the stone edge of the copper sink. Lucy slumped into a cane-bottomed chair.

"Lordy, Miz Susannah, we done a heap of work today."

"Yes, we have, but help's on the way. When the ladies arrive, they're bringing three servant girls to do maid work. Then I've found three women here in Catesville, their husbands killed in the war, to wait on tables in the dining room, and Mr. Lester's scouring around for a couple of fellows who are not in the army for one reason or another, to do the heavy work, carry luggage, make repairs. There's a lot of work needed on this hotel, and the grounds."

"What about me?"

"Would you like to work in the kitchen? When we find a cook, he is going to need a helper."

"I wouldn't mind, but . . ."

"I've already talked to Miss Margaret and Miss Mildred. They've agreed to your working for the hotel now, and not just for them."

"I sure 'preciates that. They is such complainers that after a while . . ."

"Good. It'll be a change for you. This afternoon we're going to start polishing the silver."

"Well'm."

Susannah sat down in the chair that Lucy had vacated, held the ends of a dishcloth stretched over her knees. She was very tired. The silver would be a big job. After three years it was tarnished black. To her surprise the hotel silver had been left in the safe, probably safer there than down in Atlanta. She had left this chore till last, so that the silver, once polished, could be immediately replaced in the safe until the Atlanta ladies arrived.

Susannah climbed the back stairs to her dormer room and lay down on her hard, narrow bed. She had planned to nap but couldn't, her nerves were so on edge. She had to have things ready for the reopening of the hotel. She had to keep her job.

She went to the window and finally was able to loosen it enough for it to rise, the lead counterweights striking dully within the wall, was able to hold it up long enough to push in the iron pins that held the window up. Then the woods smells from outside entered the room. She leaned out and looked down on the outside fire stairs, remembering that one night she had climbed to join Joel in his room. A night when they were desperate for each other and could find no other way to be together.

It was in those months that all the torment in her mind had dissolved in the pleasures of her body, and she had begun to look on the world in a different way. The memory of those months had kept her whole in the Spanish time, as she had come to call it. Now her lover had, sphinx-like, announced his return, and she could not know whether her long exile would end or not. If not, she had traded her dreams for the routines of a housekeeper and a dry future that might be not much more than that of the Appleton sisters.

5

On the second day, as they rode on, the undulating hills of Piedmont Georgia began rising higher on the horizon. That evening they made camp again as the sun sank in the west, where the fate of the South was being determined on the field of battle. They downed another noggin of Mount Gay while the hoecake cooked.

"I cannot for the life of me understand it," Elam Scroggins said.

"What's that?"

"The moon has come up halfway, and now it's stopped and hasn't moved a dab in ten minutes."

Joel Devereux turned and looked to the horizon where a nacreous hemisphere shone palely.

"That's not the moon, Elam, which is not likely to get stuck. That's Stone Mountain."

"It is? I've heard of it but not seen it, not having been on the far side of Atlanta before. It's just like I've been told, though, a big old rock the size of a mountain sticking up out of the ground, smooth and round."

"It was a mountain once, the last mountain of the Blue Ridge, all worn down by time to its stone core."

"I don't see how time could have done that, but you've been to college, and I suppose you know. And out there behind that big rock is Atlanta, where all those boys are off the train now and been set into forts and places waiting to get blown to bits by Sherman's cannon. Except you and me. We're lucky, I guess, to be going in the opposite way. But maybe not. We don't know what lies ahead of us."

"Considering that you threw your military ciphers into a pond, I don't imagine there's anything lying ahead that could be as bad as what would be waiting for you in Atlanta."

"They'd shoot me, that's what," Elam replied tartly. "I suppose you don't have nothing to worry about?"

"Oh, I'll have some things to face."

"I reckon so. Where a woman is involved, a man can be counted on to do rash things."

Joel chuckled. "Yes, look at you."

Elam regarded him sullenly, said nothing.

"Anyway, you've got to do some more foraging in the morning, or we won't be eating ham and hoecakes tomorrow night."

"You can count on me."

There was no ham to be had, but Elam did manage to snatch a big fat hen from a chicken house and wring its neck and hang the decapitated fowl from a saddle ring. Later in the morning they came upon a moonshiner, a pot-bellied little man wearing a wool undershirt, wide canvas galluses and a black felt hat, a double-barreled shotgun slung over one shoulder. Beyond him in the woods there was a glimpse of a copper still all fired up. He sold them a sack of his stock in trade, corn meal, and they rode on.

They entered an area where there were no farms or any sign of human habitation, just an endless dense stand of loblolly pines, cutting off the sun and incensing the air with rosin. The trail that they had been following merged with a road. A hand-painted sign nailed to a tree, beside an arrow pointing north, indicated that that was the way to Gainesville, Mount Yonah, Catesville, and Hiawassee. Below, arrows pointed east and west, toward Carolina and Atlanta. The red clay earth of the road was heavily marked by horses' hooves and metal wheels.

"Maybe it's that Yankee raiding party," Elam said, "except I can't see how they would be traveling with wagons."

"Not wagons. Not coaches either. The tracks aren't widely enough spaced. Carriages."

"Like rich folks ride in?"

"Yes."

"But why would they be up here in the piney woods?"

Why indeed? He could not come up with an answer. A number of carriages, many horses. Why? They rode on.

The sound of gunfire came on them suddenly, as they reached the crest of a hill that had muffled it. Below lay another valley carpeted with pinewoods. The road cutting through it was choked with carriages, a dozen or more, not moving, while mounted men galloped back and forth, firing at each other.

Joel jumped down from his horse, took his telescope from a saddlebag, focused on the scene. The carriages were carrying a large party of women, a few of whom had got down and were fleeing into the pinewoods. A small group of Confederate troopers had dismounted and formed a circle, firing out at the larger force of men on horseback, wearing bits and pieces of blue uniform, who were closing in on them.

Joel handed the glass to Elam. "What's going on?"

"Yankee bushwhackers. Oh, those poor women! I sure am glad I told Asa to get herself up to Hiawassee when I did."

By the time that Joel took back the telescope from Elam, not a single Confederate trooper was standing. One of the bushwhackers walked among the fallen bodies, firing his pistol into the heads of those who were still alive. This was the war that he had escaped, and he felt rage at the atrocity he was looking on, at the criminal stupidity of those who had got them into this war, and most of all at himself for his inability to choose a right course.

He calmed down. He gave his own situation too much importance. He was not lying dead on the road below, not dead like his brother on the field of Chickamauga, where the winning side had taken 20,000 casualties, a figure he would not have believed, but Elam Scroggins was not the kind of man who would invent such an appalling number.

The bushwhackers had formed themselves into some kind of military order. Four of them, who seemed to be officers, were talking together, their horses, unnerved by the skirmish, so skittish that they could hardly be controlled. Some kind of decision seemed to have been reached.

Two troopers were sent up and down the line of stalled carriages, peering into them. Two young women were removed from a carriage and were taken to the carriage at the head of the line, from which several elderly women had been evicted. Meanwhile two other Yankee troopers had donned uniforms taken from the Confederate dead. The carriage into which the two girls had been put, escorted by the two false Confederates and driven by a Negro man, moved off down a side road. According to the sign further back, this would be the Carolina road. The rest of the Yankee irregulars fell into line and rode off in the opposite direction, toward Atlanta, taking several Confederate horses with them.

"What do you suppose is going on with those girls?" Elam said uneasily.

"I don't know, but you can be sure nothing good. We'd better go down and see if we can help."

When they reached the stalled carriages, most of the women were standing in small groups, talking excitedly or hysterically. Some were crying. The women were well dressed, the carriages of high quality, polished brass fittings, beveled glass. A few women stood aside, in various states of shock, staring straight ahead or at a woman who lay on her stomach in a pool of blood, clearly dead, her appearance made the more dreadful by the contrast between all that blood and her white summer frock.

Some Negro men and women had gathered in a separate group and were talking in low voices. From out of the woods came the women who had fled and four troopers who had avoided the massacre by hiding. They were all privates, very young, and scared out of their wits.

Joel approached a black-haired woman in her thirties who seemed to be in control of herself. She was dressed in a well-fitting gown that had London or Paris written all over it.

"Colonel Dabney, ma'am, CSA. The sergeant here is my aide," he added, to give plausibility to his lie. "We are on our way to Catesville. What's happened here?"

"Harriet Read, Colonel. We were on our way to Catesville too. Our husbands—or fathers—had decided to lodge us at the Cates Springs Hotel until the fate of Atlanta is determined. We had just reached this point when the Yankee bushwhackers came galloping out of the Carolina road. I suppose you saw what happened."

"We did. What about the young ladies they took away?"

"I fear the worst."

"Yes. So, I think the best course is to continue on to Catesville as quickly as possible. We will provide what escort we can, if you agree"

"I completely agree."

"Then could you see that the ladies are back in their carriages? I'll see to the drivers."

After instructing the drivers, he went over to the four troopers who had survived, Elam at his side.

"Colonel Dabney. Men, we are proceeding on to Catesville. You will take your orders from Sergeant Smith. Round up your horses, or any horses you can find, and let's get moving."

"Sir, we've got to bury our buddies first," one of the young men said in a squeaky voice.

"Sorry, son, we don't have time. We've got to escort these ladies to safety before something even worse happens."

When he got back to where Harriet Read was standing, only a pool of drying blood remained where the dead woman had lain.

"I had her wrapped in a blanket and put in my carriage," she said. "Alice was a good friend of mine. Can you see that she gets a decent burial when we get to Catesville?"

"I'll see to it, ma'am." It took a lot of grit, he thought, to continue the journey with a close friend lying dead on the seat opposite you.

In the end, the troopers could locate only three horses, and Joel gave up his horse. He could ride in the empty carriage from which the young women had been abducted.

He stood beside the carriage, holding the saddlebags containing his possessions, until he saw that all the women had remounted. As he reached for the handle of the carriage door he noticed an emblem on it. It was the Devereux family arms. He opened the door. A pale face regarded him from the far corner of the darkened carriage. It was his sister.

"Selena!"

"My God! Joel! What are you doing here?"

"What are you doing here?"

"Moving out of harm's way."

"May I join you?"

"By all means."

He put his foot on the step, and at that moment Elam rode up, this time his feet properly in the stirrups.

"Colonel, sir, I found out what happened to those girls. The bushwhackers have an understanding with some gambling men who run bawdy houses in Carolina. When they capture some pretty young things, they send them over to these men. They fetch a real good price, it is said. Ain't that the awfulest thing you ever heard? Like I said before, war ain't like anything else in life."

"You're right there. So, let's get moving, Sergeant. There's nothing we can do for those girls."

He got into the carriage. Elam had not seen Selena, and she must have heard every word he had said.

"It's a good thing I'm forty and plain, I guess."

"Who are they?"

"The Sidley girls."

"From the next plantation."

"Yes. Eighteen and nineteen."

"And virgins."

"They'd better be. Well—they won't be for long. Their father made a big mistake. Most often, when you try to run away from trouble, you just run to something even worse. I know."

"So do I."

From ahead he heard Elam bawl out, "Forward!" A few seconds later their carriage lurched ahead. Clearly, Sergeant Scroggins was enjoying his role as Colonel Dabney's aide.

"What's all this 'colonel' business, by the way?"

"It's a long story."

"I'm sure it is. I thought you were in Spain."

"And I thought you were up north."

"It's a long story." Selena buried her face in her hands. "I can't take much more of this."

"What would you say to a noggin of Mount Gay?"

Selena raised her head, smiling wanly, tears in her eyes. "You have some?"

"A small supply for casualties of the war."

"Well, I'm certainly one of those."

He took the flask out of his saddlebags and poured what remained into the silver cup, handed it to her.

"Thanks, Joel." She took a sip of rum and wiped her eyes with a lace handkerchief. "Have you ever seen me cry?"

"Never."

"I never did. It was my shield, against father, against John. I was the cool one all those years, the ugly duckling with the unfortunate pink curls, who couldn't be made to cry."

"Yes. Selena the Cool, we called you. Where is John Coffee these days?"

"As far as I know, still in our house on Lafayette Square in Washington, with one of his mistresses ensconced, still sitting in his seat in the U.S. Senate, still offering his advice to President Lincoln. I couldn't take it anymore. I came home for a visit just in time not to be able to get back, which I suppose suited both John and me well enough. But now we are coming to the end of the drama that we call Secession."

"Must be, if His Worship is sending you upcountry for your own safety."

"Not that way at all. He tried his best to keep me at Devereux Hall, figuring that even if John and I were estranged, the fact that I was married to a confidant of Lincoln might give Sherman pause before he put torch to the factories. I hope they do."

"Do what?"

"Burn everything."

"Junius and Lamar are there for the last act?"

"Hell, no. Auguste sent them up to Cherokee Rose. They were just in the way, as far as he was concerned. He sure didn't want them given guns and told to go defend the ramparts of Atlanta. He's very angry with you, you know, maybe even more so than with Sherman. You have sullied the escutcheon."

"I don't care. The old man has far worse problems now than my views on slavery, in any case."

"No reconciliation possible, I take it?"

"No."

"It's your girlfriend most of all, isn't it?"

"What?"

"You heard me correctly. Don't worry, all I know is that it's a woman in or around Catesville. Auguste wouldn't tell me any more than that she was completely unsuitable."

"Yes, he would have said that."

"Still, rather surprising, this maîtresse of the backwoods. I would have thought female companionship in the upper reaches of Spanish society more to your taste."

Selena was after information with which she could create trouble for someone, it really didn't matter whom. All her life her pastime had been fishing in troubled waters.

"All of which is none of your business, Selena."

"No, indeed, mon cher frère, none of my business."

About an hour later the caravan of carriages came to a halt, and Elam Scroggins rode up. Joel rolled down the carriage window.

"Colonel, sir, the telegraph line from Atlanta has just come alongside the road. Would you want to send a message ahead?"

"I don't understand."

"I've got my telegraph key with me. All I've got to do is attach it to the wire and I can send."

"I didn't realize that was possible. Yes, sending a message ahead would be a good idea."

Joel reached into a saddlebag on the floor of the carriage and brought out a little Spanish leather notebook with a pencil attached to it by a silk cord. He printed out a message and read it aloud.

"For Cate Springs Hotel Manager: Party of ladies from Atlanta has been delayed but should arrive late tonight. Please be ready to receive them and notify Cate County sheriff and a doctor and ask them to be on hand for arrival."

He tore the page out of the notebook and handed it out the window to Elam.

"It'll be there in minutes, sir," Elam said, taking the piece of paper.

As Elam was about to ride off Joel said, "Wait, I have another message."

He wrote out a brief message, tore out the sheet, folded it twice and handed it out to the telegrapher that chance had made his traveling companion.

6

The afternoon the Atlanta ladies were to arrive at the Cate Springs Hotel, all was as ready as possible, given the wartime lack of supplies and the inadequate help. Susannah and Lester Owens had put together a kind of kitchen staff composed of a failed restaurant owner from Dahlonega, a young war widow, and Lucy, with Susannah advising on what Atlanta ladies were likely to consider edible dishes. Now Susannah, Lester, and Lucy stood in the entrance hall, peering out at the front gate. Susannah and Lucy were dressed in their best. Lester had gone a step further. Somewhere he had found an old black frock coat with satin lapels, and this he wore with a winged collar, apparently his idea of how a hotel manager should appear.

A couple of Cate County idlers had been hired to clear the brush from what had once been the front lawn, and they were going about their task in a halfhearted way; but of the Atlanta ladies there was no sign. Susannah found this ominous. The telegram they had received from the Georgia Land Company said that the Atlanta party would be accompanied by a small contingent of Confederate troopers. The arrival of the carriages would normally be preceded by an outrider. There had been no outrider and no further telegram, and with the telegraph wire to Atlanta up again, some forewarning of delay could have been expected. But nothing. Finally, the welcoming party broke up, and Susannah, Lester, and Lucy resumed their separate tasks to pass the time.

As the sun was going down, the buggy from George Malik's store rattled through the gate, as it did almost every evening, bringing, in the trunk on the back of which was printed in yellow letters "The Emporium," additional items George had been able to find in the county for stocking the hotel kitchen. This evening, as Susannah went to the front door, it was not the delivery boy who got down from the buggy but George himself.

"Telegrams," George said, "lots of them. Since the wire to Atlanta is back up, it's like the floodgates have been opened. You mind if I sit down for a minute? I'm really wore out."

"Of course, George. Could I get you some refreshment?"

"I wouldn't mind a cup of tea."

Susannah went to the kitchen and ordered the tea, returned, and sat down across from George Malik, a glass table between them, behind it a vase filled with peacock feathers she had found in the attic.

"You know, Susannah, I've been asking myself recently what I'm doing here in Georgia, where war is about to come even to Catesville. If it weren't for the troubles in Lebanon when I was young, I wouldn't have taken ship for America. I would probably be still in Beirut, sitting cross-legged in front of my father's shop in the bazaar, smoking a narghile. You know the old folk tale 'Tonight in Samara'?"

"No."

"There was a merchant in Baghdad who sent his servant to the market, where he encounters a woman who throws up her arm in a threatening way. The servant realizes the woman is Death. He returns home, borrows a horse from his master, and rides as fast as he can for Samara. The merchant goes to the market and asks the woman why she threatened his servant. Death says that it was not a threatening gesture she made but one of surprise. She had expected to meet the merchant's servant that night in Samara."

"You can't run away from your fate, that's it?"

"That's it, I suppose. Now for the telegrams . . ."

George Malik reached into a leather portfolio and took out an envelope, handed it to Susannah.

"For Cate Springs Hotel Manager: Party of ladies from Atlanta has been delayed but should arrive late tonight. Please be ready to receive them and notify Cate County sheriff and a doctor and ask them to be on hand for arrival."

She looked up from the unsigned message. "This is a relief, George, but the sheriff, a doctor? Why?"

"I wouldn't want to speculate. I've taken the liberty of notifying Amos and Dr. Habersham."

"Thank you."

Of course, George knew what was in each and every telegram. The telegraph office was in the loft of The Emporium, the operator a telegrapher who had been crippled in a train wreck and wasn't fit for soldiering.

"And then there's this, for you."

She opened the second envelope apprehensively.

"For Miss Goode at Cherokee Mission: If church calendar has not been altered, choir practice could resume as early as tomorrow."

Again the message was unsigned. Her breath was coming fast, and she had gripped the telegram so tightly that the edges had crumpled in her hands. She looked up at George Malik, but he was fussing with the tea things on the tray that Lucy held before him. Susannah waved away Lucy's offer of tea, and George turned to her.

"There's another telegram," he said, "from Governor Joe Brown to Judge Colcock Stiles that's going to cause some lights to stay on late tonight at the courthouse."

"Oh," she said.

"Seems the Confederate government in Richmond would like the governor to look into some of the past activities of Judge Stiles. The governor has put a number of questions to the judge."

She waited for George to say more, but nothing more was forthcoming.

Shortly after nine an outrider arrived, a lad of about eighteen, his gray Confederate uniform dusted with the red soil of North Georgia. He staggered from his horse, almost falling from fatigue, made his way up the front steps and into the entrance hall, and blurted out his news to Susannah, Lester, the sheriff, George Malik, and Dr. Habersham. Their party had been attacked by Yankee bushwhackers, leaving most of his buddies dead and lying where they fell. One of the ladies had been killed, too, and her body was being brought. The rest of the Atlanta ladies, who should be arriving in an hour or so, were mostly pretty upset.

Dr. Habersham spoke first. "Amos, you'd better ride back to town and get some of the local ladies together. We're going to need help with the Atlanta party, I imagine, and you'd better let Judge Stiles and the mayor know what's happened, so they don't add to the problem. Then get the undertaker to come out for the body of the lady who's been killed."

"I'll do that," the sheriff said, "and I'll bring back three or four of the Home Guard with me, just in case, for whatever use they'll be."

Amos Boggs went out the front door, and Dr. Habersham turned to Susannah. "You have hot water?"

"We have a boiler, yes."

"Well, you'd better fire it up. In my experience there's

nothing more soothing to agitated spirits than having hot water on hand."

The sheriff returned with a dozen women from town, including Jessie Finch, armed with towels and some food and drink, and three of the Home Guard, half-criminal types judged too unreliable for military service, armed with old muskets. A few minutes later the town's part-time undertaker, who was also its only pharmacist, showed up, but of the Atlanta ladies there was still no sign. Dr. Habersham and George Malik began a game of cards. After Susannah had assured herself that sufficient beds were made up and turned down and that the kitchen was more or less prepared to serve some warm food, she sat down in an armchair in the filling entrance hall and read again the brief message she had received that afternoon.

To her alone its meaning was clear. Joel Devereux had made his way from Savannah, where his first message had been sent from the railroad station, to somewhere near Catesville, in the vicinity of which a party of ruthless Yankee bushwhackers was operating. Before she could speculate further, there was a halloo from out front, and a Confederate trooper galloped through the gate followed by a stream of carriages with blazing sidelights.

The carriages pulled up in disorder at the front entrance. Atlanta ladies spilled out in various degrees of disarray and emotional distress, came up the front steps, poured into the entrance hall. All the chairs were soon filled with women, and those who had no place sat on the floor, their backs against a wall, surely something they had never done in their lives.

"Could be a long night, depends," Dr. Habersham said to Susannah and George Malik, rubbing his unshaven chin. "Tell you what, I'll pass among them. Those that seem the least disturbed I'll point out to you, and you can get those up to their rooms for the night. Do you have some sleeping pallets?"

"Yes," Susannah said.

"Because it appears that a full half of these ladies have their maids with them, and it will calm their spirits to know that they're near at hand, either sleeping on the floor beside their beds or in the hall outside their rooms. I'll need to talk to the rest of the ladies, and talk may be all some of them need. For those that can't be calmed down, I'll give them a little dose of opium solution, which I've never known to fail in soothing ladies' nerves. By midnight, we might have them all to bed. Not as bad as I expected."

"Doctor," Susannah said, "you astonish me. You're as cool as Napoleon on the field of battle."

"Where I learned it, before I was furloughed. When you've got the dead and dying, and those out of their minds, lying all around you, you learn what works best."

Her eyes followed the doctor as he moved onto his field of battle with his black leather medical case, in his wake George Malik, Amos Boggs, the Confederate troopers, and the members of the Home Guard, to carry up baggage and ladies who couldn't make it up the stairs on their own. Lester Owens was behind the reception desk, taking down names, handing out room keys. A tall man with a ginger beard was helping him deal with the ladies, their effects, and their maids. As if she had willed it, he turned and looked straight into her eyes.

It was nearly one o'clock in the morning before the hotel was finally quiet, and even then from time to time a woman could be heard sobbing or crying out in her sleep. The corridors were dark except for small lamps in brackets on each floor to mark the location of the stairs.

Susannah slowly opened the door to her room and peered out. Nothing moved. Two colored maids slept on pallets outside the doors to their mistresses' rooms. She made her way silently down the corridor, barefoot, in her nightgown and robe, her hair down. If she encountered anyone, the housekeeper was making a final check. At the end of the corridor was a small cul-de-sac with only one room. It was the key to this room that she had slipped into Joel's hand, the first time their flesh had touched in two-and-a-half years.

One of the maids lying on the floor opened an eye, looked up at her, then closed her eye, too tired to care what was going on. Susannah reached the turning and stepped into the blackness of the cul-de-sac. After her eyes had adjusted to the dark, she could make out a chink of light beneath a door. She felt her way along the wall until her hand touched a doorknob. She turned it and the door swung open.

Joel Devereux sat on the edge of the bed, a terry cloth towel wrapped around his middle, his face and arms deeply bronzed but his body ivory in the light of a single candle. She closed the door behind her, turned the key in the lock. She had thought many times of what she would say if he returned to her, but her mind had gone blank.

"You've shaved off your beard," she finally said.

He stood up, more muscular than she remembered him.

"Beards are scratchy."

He was as nervous as she, it seemed. She relaxed the tight fists she had made of her hands. There was a lump in her throat, and the tears that had filled her eyes overflowed.

"Don't cry, Susannah."

"I've been so patient for so long."

They moved toward each other, and what had begun as romance ended as animal desire. His arms were around her and her hands felt the strong new muscles of his back. The towel had fallen off, and she let her hands slide down him until they cupped his firm buttocks.

"This much happiness in one dose will probably unhinge my mind."

He had taken her face in his hands and kissed her on the lips. She opened her mouth to him. "Or at least drive me to female hysterics."

"For which I have the antidote."

"Yes, I can feel it through my nightgown."

She stepped back from him, dropped her robe to the floor, and pulled her nightgown over her head. The hardness she had felt slid into the wet warm place between her legs.

"How can what is always the same always be new?"

"I will think on that, my philosophical mistress."

"Yes, do, later, at some much later date."

He laughed and buried his face in the thick dark hair that fell over her shoulders. She moved away and walked slowly to the bed.

"A backside that would stir the envy of Venus."

She lay down on her side and watched him approach.

"And you are my golden-haired Adonis."

He lay down on the bed facing her. Now she knew without a doubt that the Spanish time was over.

"Is there any couple like us, Joel? Are we not a law unto ourselves?"

"*Sui generis,* my love."

He touched her face, and she relaxed her body and let it happen. But what began as surrender quickly became a search by bodies to find that secret place where what happens is unspeakable, unknowable to the world, that delicious feeling that the lucky will never share with the world, even speak of. And when you arise from that dark hidden place, she thought, as her body began convulsions she could not control, even had she wished, it is with a secret smile.

The cry of an owl, returning from a night's hunting to its nest in the barn loft, announced the coming of the day, a day in which Susannah Goode was for the first time in two-and-a-half years a whole woman. Thirty months of tension had been released during the night as if the knot that had held the ropes that bound her had fallen away, leaving her lying on the bed as buoyant as though floating in a tropic sea.

It had rained during the night, leaving a thick fog over Cate County, a fog that turned the stand of tulip trees outside the window into ghostly sentinels, with dark leaves as big as hands and flowers that would glow in the sun like golden bowls. In the growing light the pale form of her own body emerged and the dark velvety place where her desire had been satisfied.

"Are you awake?" a once-familiar voice inquired, sending through her the thrill of knowing that it would become familiar again.

"Yes, my love."

"Was it all that you wanted?"

"Had it not been, would I have cried out so loudly that I may have betrayed myself to a hotel filled with women?"

"Would you care?"

"As a matter of shame, not in the least. As a matter of purdence, a bit."

"Now that we are calmer, I will ask you again if you are sure I am forgiven for everything."

"I know of only two things you wished to be forgiven for. The first was for your liaison with a Spanish marquesa, young and beautiful, you said, an affair that you need never have mentioned to me. If you had loved her, you would not have gone through what you did to return to me."

"I did not love her."

"Then, surely, I forgive you that, and you never need mention it again. The other matter was leaving me, in choosing to let your brother take your place in the army and die at Chickamauga, rather than take over the office in Barcelona. Your choice could well have led to some other outcome. Your brother was unlucky, that's all."

"It's not so easy for me to rid myself of the guilt."

"You once told me that predestination is rubbish. Now I tell you, Joel Devereux, that guilt is equally rubbish. We were not made for guilt. We were made for other things, you and I."

This thought reverberated in the space between them, and they fell silent. From below floated the sounds of a kitchen coming to life. She sighed.

"I had better get down to my duties. It seems to me that we don't want to throw off our masks quite yet. Our way forward is difficult enough without giving—who?—the world, perhaps, a chance to get its grip upon us."

"Ah, yes. You are right there. The world has a disposition to destroy those who mean to live free, and those who do tend to have few allies, but cunning and concealment are among them."

She turned on her side to look at him, equally naked on the bed.

"How is it, Joel, that we have made our way to this outrageous place where we find ourselves?"

"We took a vow three years ago, in an empty church, one icy morning, that put us on a course of collision with the world."

She said nothing in reply but got up and put on her clothes.

"We must survive this, you know," she said, her hand on the brass doorknob. "I could not live without you. For my part, I tell you that I shall never leave you, shall never fail you."

II

Devereux Hall

7

He lay in the bed, still imprinted with the form of her body, still holding her warmth, her scent, and marveled at the incredible luck that had brought him so far, through so much danger. He had fought his way back to her to find, in place of the girl he had left, a woman, as passionate as she had ever been but endowed with a maturity, a sophistication, a confidence that resonated in a most extraordinary way in her lovemaking.

From the very moment their eyes had met the evening before, he had realized that he had come back to a changed woman. She had put her finger to her lips, crossed the room, taken a room key from Lester Owens, and handed it to him, saying in a calm voice, too low to be overheard, "Everything has changed. Philander is dead, and I am housekeeper here now. I will come to you tonight when I can." Then she had turned away to attend to other business.

He got out of bed, went to the open window. The fog still hung heavy. He drew in a deep breath, savored the familiar scent of North Georgia mountain vegetation. He was home again and his woman was his again. Now began the serious business of keeping her. He took his brush and razor from the saddlebags slung over a chair back, and as he stood before the mirror shaving, he thought about how this might be accomplished. First of all, speed and cunning would be required.

He dug out the change of clothes he had reserved for his arrival. As he dressed he redefined the qualities that would be needed to those of surprise and deceit. There was nothing he wouldn't do to keep the woman who had said that she would never fail him. He must not fail her.

He sat down before the mirror and brushed out his hair with the silver-backed brushes bearing the initials "J.D." One of the first things he would have to take care of was informing Elam Scroggins and Harriet Read, among others, that John Dabney was no more. Since he was known to pretty much everyone in Catesville, that disguise had to be discarded. The second specific that came to mind was that Sheriff Amos Boggs had mentioned the robbery of the Devereux Bank and said there had been "developments."

He looked himself over in the glass. A good appearance was an asset. As he arose and turned to leave the room, the door flew open and Susannah stood there, flushed. She came into the room, closed the door, and leaned back against it.

"Joel, I need your help, now, badly."

"Speak, my love."

"The two girls who were taken off to Carolina, you must save them."

"How?"

"I don't know how. That's for you to figure out."

"Sit down and tell me more."

She sat down in a stuffed chair, and he sat on the edge of the bed. "You know, Joel, that they are to be sold to some bawdy house."

"That is what is being said, yes."

"I cannot sleep at night if something isn't done to save them."

He wasn't sure how to reply. She continued.

"How much do you know about my mother?"

"That she was leading some kind of degraded life in New Orleans, that's all. I suppose I didn't want to know more."

"Well, I'll tell you. She went south with a man who abandoned her in New Orleans. She was driven to prostitution and after a few years became a madam, eventually a very successful one, her house so successful that her name became known beyond New Orleans. It even reached her brother, who came down and took her twelve-year-old daughter away from her. That's me, Joel, as you might have guessed from what your father told you. I was raised in a brothel. Very fancy, with crystal chandeliers and red carpets and brass stair rails, champagne, and mulatto maids in starched aprons. But upstairs there was the business, nothing you would want your twelve-year-old daughter to know about. I knew all about it. Joel, you must save those girls from that."

"I'll do the best I can, but the odds are high."

"I know that. Just do the best you can."

Before he could reply she was gone.

He had told himself that he would not fail Susannah, a vow that now seemed impossible to keep, but he would make the attempt.

He went down the stairs. A few of the Atlanta women were having breakfast in the dining room, a few more sitting in the entrance hall talking. Most were probably still asleep after the adventure of the previous day and a dose of laudanum. Dr. Habersham was conversing with Harriet Read. Elam Scroggins was wandering around the room, looking lost. Joel approached him.

"Good morning, Sergeant."

"Morning, sir."

"Had your breakfast?"

"No, sir."

"Come on, then."

They were seated by Susannah. She and Joel avoided each other's eyes. Bacon and eggs were available and substitute coffee, which she advised against. She took their orders and disappeared through the swinging doors.

"Elam, I need to know some things from you."

"I'll help as best I can, Colonel."

"You can drop the colonel. My real name is Joel Devereux, as most people in Catesville know, so there's no more use pretending."

"I've heard of your family. They used to send lots of messages about cotton through the Atlanta telegraph office."

"How did you find out where those bushwhackers in Confederate uniforms were taking those young ladies?"

"One of them bushwhackers was wounded and our boys captured him. He told them."

"I'd like to talk to him. Where is he now?"

"I reckon he ain't around anymore."

"You mean our boys killed him."

"I can't say that for sure. I just know he ain't around anymore. But you couldn't blame them, after what them Yankee bushwhackers done to us."

Joel looked out the window. The fog was lifting, revealing huge old hemlocks on the hotel grounds. This was war. One atrocity led to another, until everyone's hands were covered with blood.

"Did they learn anything else about how the bushwhackers planned to get those girls to South Carolina?"

"Just that they usually takes the captured women to a big old tavern on the Tugaloo River, what's the boundary between Georgia and Carolina. They hold them there and send someone to let the gambling men know, and they come and get them and pay for them in gold."

"That would take two or three days, I suppose."

"I reckon so. The bawdy houses is in Greenville and Spartanburg."

A plan was beginning to form in Joel's mind, but he would have to think it out further.

"I suppose you'll be heading out this morning for Hiawassee."

"No sir, I won't. General Johnston's provost marshal has sent a telegram to the sheriffs in all the counties in North Georgia what's still in the Confederacy, asking them to be on the lookout for deserters who have committed hanging offenses. My name is right there at the top of the list. And that ain't all. They're sending a detachment of troopers, headed by a captain, to set up in Catesville and 'look into things'. Can't say I understand what that means."

Neither could Joel.

A maid arrived with two plates of bacon and eggs and toasted bread with butter and strawberry jam.

"I ain't et like this in a long time," Elam said with enthusiasm.

"How'd you find out about the provost marshal's telegram?"

"I was talking last night to this Levantine gentleman who runs a grocery store here, and I gave him my name. He's the one who told me. It seems the post office and the telegraph office is both in his store, so he pretty much knows everything that's going on. He said he couldn't just not tell me and see me get hanged, particular since hanging deserters wasn't going to win the war. In fact, nothing was going to win the war. He's right there, and he's a Christian gentleman."

"George Malik. Yes, he is. So what are you going to do now?"

"I was thinking I would get myself over to South Carolina. I don't reckon they'll have heard about me over there. Then

I'll try to work my way up into North Carolina and come down on Hiawassee from there."

"Oh." He wouldn't need to think out his plan any further, it seemed. "How'd you like to earn a little money on the way?"

Joel spread out a row of gold coins on the table.

"I'd say that's a lot of money."

"You'd be doing me a big favor."

"What's that?"

"Since you're going to South Carolina anyway, if you were to cross the Tugaloo where that tavern is and the girls are still there . . ."

"What?"

"And you were to offer the bushwhackers more for those young ladies than the gambling men are going to pay, I imagine they'd take your offer, particularly since you could tell the folks at the tavern that they were Yankee spies in Confederate uniforms."

"Suppose the girls done already been took to Carolina?"

"Then I'd ask you to catch up with them and bring them back, and I wouldn't care how you did it."

"Yes, I'll do it. I'd do it even without pay. I feel awful about those girls. But I sure can use the money. When I get to Hiawassee there won't be nothing, and it's too late to put in a crop. And me and Asa can't just live off my brother. He ain't got no money either."

Joel sighed with relief. "You're going to need some help in case there's trouble. I imagine if you were to give a couple of those young troopers a ten-dollar gold piece each, they'd be glad to go along with you."

"You can be sure of that."

While they were talking Elam had been eating, and his plate was now clean.

"Well, Sergeant, you'd best be going. The sooner you get on the road the more likely we are to find those girls—and the more likely you are to save your own skin."

"I wish you wouldn't joke about it, Mr. Devereux. The idea of being hanged bothers me enough as it is."

"I wouldn't joke about it, if I didn't think you were the man I know you are."

After Elam Scroggins had left, Joel sat looking out the window. The fog had lifted. It was going to be a fine day, and his run of luck was continuing.

Susannah came through the swinging doors and crossed the dining room to where he sat.

"I hope everything is satisfactory, sir."

"Very. In an hour or so there'll be three soldiers on the road, pursuing those kidnapped girls. One of these soldiers is known to me, and he's a reliable man with plenty of common sense."

"Oh, Joel, thank God you arrived when you did. I knew you wouldn't fail me." She was trying to hold back tears. "What are you going to do now?"

"I'm going into town. Is there any way that you could go with me?"

"I don't see how that would be possible. There're going to be a lot of problems I'll have to deal with once the Atlanta ladies recover and begin remembering that they're used to having their way about pretty much everything."

"Miss Susannah, Mr. Devereux."

They turned. It was Dr. Habersham. He held a handful of sheets of Cate Springs Hotel stationery, beginning to yellow with age.

"Susannah, I have a raft of messages here that the ladies would like sent to husbands and loved ones to let them know they've arrived here safely, and inquiring whether their children have reached Milledgeville, where they are being put up at a private school. They want me to send these telegrams for them. However, I don't think I should leave just yet, probably should stay here through the night, given the hysterics I'm still having to treat. You suppose there's someone who could run these messages over to the telegraph office?"

"I could do it, since you are going to be here, and I do have some other things to attend to in town."

"I'd be mighty obliged," and Dr. Habersham thrust the sheaf of messages into Susannah's hand.

Lester Owens was standing behind the reception desk in frock coat and winged collar, looking as though he had been up all night.

"Good morning, Lester."

"Morning, Mr. Devereux. You sure surprised us all by showing up last night with the party from Atlanta. Everybody thought you was still in Spain."

"Time to come home."

"I suppose you'll be going on to Devereux Hall."

"If Sherman doesn't get there first. But for right now, I have some business in town, and I suppose I should find out something about the robbery at the Devereux Bank. That's the first thing my father's going to ask me."

"I can imagine that. It's already cost me my job."

"But things haven't turned out badly for you."

"We don't know how things are going to turn out for any of us until this awful war's over."

"Tell me, Lester, what was taken when the vault was blown open?"

"Only that one big trunk your pa had put there after Secession."

"What was in it?"

"I don't know for sure, but considering that it took four men to carry it in, it must've been gold. Thinking back on it, having the trunk there must be the reason Mr. Auguste kept the bank open. The Catesville branch sure wasn't making no profit. You and your pa never did get along too well, did you?"

"No."

"Anything else you might want to know, just ask me."

"I'll keep that in mind."

As Joel started toward the front door he saw that his way was blocked by Selena.

"Going to see your *maîtresse,* Joel?"

He ignored her question. It occurred to him that Selena probably had never met Susannah. By the time Philander had brought her up from New Orleans, Selena would have been married and living in the north.

"What do you know about the bank robbery, Selena?"

He sprang the question quickly, to see if there was a reaction. There was, but she immediately regained her poise.

"Me? Nothing." She paused. "But you might ask Junius and Lamar, if you go out to Cherokee Rose."

All of her life Selena had been a troublemaker, and the remark she had let drop was no doubt meant to create some trouble. That was why he wanted to ensure that Selena didn't find out about Susannah.

"Oh, by the way, Joel, I sent a telegram to father letting him know I had arrived and that you were here."

He was about to make some caustic reply when Harriet Read stopped near them.

"Mr. Devereux, I just wanted to thank you again for all you did for us yesterday. Lord knows what would have happened if you hadn't come along when you did."

"Bad enough things happened as it was."

"Yes. Is it true that the Sidley girls were taken off as white slaves?"

"It seems so."

"And poor Alice. She's buried now, and in two or three days, when the ladies are calmer, I'll arrange a memorial service. I hope you will attend, so we can all thank you. Why did you not tell us your real name? Most of the Atlanta ladies know your family."

"I thought it best not to, in case I fell into Yankee hands. It might have been rough if they found out I was a Devereux."

"Quite right, after all the Devereux have done for the war effort. Your father will be very proud of you, adding luster to the honor of one of the great families of the South."

Selena rolled her eyes.

"Now, if you will excuse me," Joel said, "I have some urgent business in town."

No sooner was he out of the door than he ran into Judge Colcock Stiles and Givens Crenshaw climbing up the hotel steps.

"Mr. Devereux. How good to see you," the judge said with an unctuous smile. "We heard you were back from Spain. We were just coming to pay our respect to the ladies. I hope they're not too distraught after all that has happened to them."

"Doctor Habersham has things well in hand."

"Your brothers will be delighted to see you."

"I was just on my way to Cherokee Rose."

"Then I suppose you'll be joining our valiant boys defending Atlanta."

"Yes, I will."

"I'm sure Governor Brown will see that you have a colonelcy."

"Rank is not important to me. Now, if you will excuse me . . ."

As he rode away from the hotel, Joel began to reassess his situation. Maybe his luck was beginning to run out. Too many people were meddling in his affairs, and he had already lost the element of surprise. It was he who had been surprised, first by Sherman appearing at the gates of Atlanta with a huge army and by the disappearance of the gold. He had known about the gold before he had left for Spain and had figured no good would come of it. Now he would have to act immediately, and there was no latitude for subtlety.

When he reached the ruins of the Cate Gold Mine Company, he rode into the pine trees that had grown up around it, dismounted, and tethered his horse. He sat down on the pine needles, his back against a tree, lit a cheroot and waited for her, as he had often done during those few months that had been the happiest time of his life.

8

Susannah stepped up into the buggy and put on her soft leather driving gloves. Joel had given them to her in what seemed another life, and she had worn them when she drove the buggy to their assignations.

As she started off down the road, she recalled how their idyll had suddenly and brutally ended. The four Devereux brothers had been given deferments by Governor Brown at the request of their father, on the grounds that they were needed on the plantation and in the factories that produced a vast quantity of cloth for the Confederate army. However, when the war took a turn for the worse, old Auguste Devereux announced that he would have to offer up one son to the Cause and he had chosen Joel. Joel had told her that his father had undoubtedly found out that they had been meeting secretly, and this was his way of separating them. But at that point Joel's younger brother Marion had told his father that he was volunteering for the army and Joel need not go.

Not to be thwarted, Auguste had persisted in his refusal to ask for an extension of Joel's deferment unless he agreed to open an office of Devereux and Sons in Barcelona. At that early stage of the war, cotton could still be smuggled through the Northern blockade to Havana, where it was transferred to neutral Spanish ships. Or he could join the army and Marion could go to Barcelona. It was a matter of indifference to

Auguste. So Joel had chosen Spain, in the hope that he could in time return to her. Then the blockade tightened.

Yet here she was again, driving the buggy to the spot where she and Joel used to meet, only this time it was no idyll. The world they had known was falling apart, and there was no seeing what would replace it. They could only live for the day, but that she would do and not complain. Just to have him back was all that mattered. She had tried so hard to keep the fire of her passion for him damped down when she could not have him, that when she unexpectedly could, she had been apprehensive. How would it be when she once again disrobed before him?

It had been better than in her wildest fantasies. He had changed in ways that thrilled her. He was tougher, both in body and mind. His youthful bitterness toward his father had been replaced by an ironic view of their situation, and he mocked those who thought they could keep them apart. The confident and skillful way he had taken possession of her had been delicious. Most of all she recalled, with a shiver of delight, the feel of his hands, strong and calloused from sailing a boat alone from Havana, on the softness of her breasts, her stomach, her thighs.

She had been so lost in her feelings that she almost passed the ruins of the old gold-mining company. She pulled back hard on the reins. He sauntered out of the woods, leading his horse, and doffed his hat.

"You wouldn't be able to give a fellow a ride into town, would you, ma'am?"

"Better than that, I will let him drive," and she moved over on the seat.

He tied his horse to the rear of the buggy, climbed onto the driver's seat, took the reins, and soon had the mare moving at an easy trot. She had never known a man who handled horses better, even a team, with four sets of reins held in his strong hands.

"It's sure good to smell Georgia pines again," he said, as though he had nothing better to say, "and honeysuckle and wild roses. Spain's a beautiful place, but you have only one home in this life, and I guess you miss the smells more than anything. It's like the woman you love. You yearn for the scent of her."

"Do you remember the times we made love on the grass behind the old gold-mine office?" she ventured.

He smiled, said nothing.

"I knew so little of who you were then. After we had made love, you would pluck wildflowers and make a bouquet for me, all the while telling me the name of each plant and its Latin name. I had not realized until then how gentle you were, how much you loved the natural world, how much you knew of it. Do you remember?"

"I remember."

He leaned over and put his lips to her neck just below her ear, and she shivered with pleasure.

"Hey, I thought you didn't blush."

"I'm not blushing, Joel, I'm aroused, just from thinking about all the times we have made love, and especially last night, and then you touching me."

"Well, I guess we need to find some private place, don't we? I want it again just as bad as you do. How about the mission? I remember well that big hard bed of yours we tried out one afternoon when Philander went into town."

"And nearly got caught. No, the mission won't do. Elias and Leander are still there."

"Doing what?"

"Nothing, now that the mission's closed."

"Well, we need to find some spot other than the hotel,

where Selena will soon find us out. But first, I've got to stop at a couple of places. There're some things I need to explain to you. While I was on my way back here I worked out how I would get Auguste out of our affairs once and for all, which would have taken some time. But now I have to move fast. I didn't know the gold would be taken from the bank, and I didn't expect to find General Sherman on our doorstep.

"According to an Atlanta paper one of the ladies brought, Joe Johnston is going to make a stand on the far bank of the Chattahoochee. But if Johnston can't hold there, Sherman will roll right over Devereux Hall and all its works. Selena says Auguste claims he will stare Sherman down, but my guess is he'll bolt, probably to our place on the coast. I need to get to Devereux Hall before that happens and settle matters with my father. I wanted to catch him off guard, but unfortunately my dear sister has taken it upon herself to let Auguste know I'm in Catesville."

"I don't understand what the bank robbery has to do with you and me."

"Just a hunch, and I need to find out before this day is over exactly what happened. What do people here say?"

"They say there may have been a lot more gold in the U.S. mint in Dahlonega than the twenty-five thousand dollars' worth that was turned over to Jeff Davis when Georgia seceded from the Union, and that's what was stored in the bank. Also, there's a story going around—started by Givens Crenshaw—that Sheriff Boggs was behind the robbery. It's not true, but there's even talk of taking evidence against him before a grand jury. Judge Stiles is playing along with all this."

"Sounds like Crenshaw and Stiles may have something to be afraid of themselves."

"Which reminds me, Joel, that George Malik told me yesterday that the judge had received a telegram from Governor Brown that's not going to make him happy."

"There may be a lot of people who aren't going to be happy. My hunch is sounding more and more plausible. I just need some proof."

"Proof of what?"

They had come out on the Catesville town square, and Joel reined in the mare.

"I'll tell you more later. Are you still on good terms with George Malik?"

"He's been almost like a father to me."

"Would you mind if I told him about us?"

"Not at all. The only reason I didn't tell him was to protect you."

They found Malik filling a bin with nails.

"Can't even find nails anymore. I got these from a blacksmith over at Mount Yonah, made by hand from melted-down farm implements. What can I do for you?"

"George, could we see you alone for a minute?"

"Of course, Susannah. Let's go to the office."

When the door had closed behind them and they were seated, Susannah spoke.

"George, my fiancé—well, it's Joel."

George Malik smiled. "I had already guessed. Your Spanish merchandise."

"We want to be together openly," Joel said. "I'm sick of this sneaking around, and it's demeaning to Susannah. But as soon as my father finds out, he'll see that I'm forced into the army, to break us up again. We'll be right back where we started."

"You know about New Orleans, George?" Susannah said.

"Yes, Susannah, I do."

"Auguste Devereux will never accept me as a daughter-in-law, or even as his son's companion."

"So, what do you propose to do?"

"Get the upper hand with my father," Joel said. "He was responsible for the gold from the U.S. mint."

"How much was there?"

"There was talk of a million, but that's surely too high."

"Even so . . ."

"What do you know, George?"

"The gold was deliberately left in Georgia by Jeff Davis. He didn't want to be pressured into spending it. He wanted to keep it in reserve, in case things got desperate for the Confederacy. Davis made Joe Brown responsible for it, and Brown turned it over to Auguste Devereux for safekeeping. And now things are desperate, and Brown received a telegram from Davis saying he must have the gold, and now a second telegram that he is sending a cavalry detachment for the gold, except, of course, it's no longer there."

"Who took it?"

"I don't know. All I know is that the morning after the robbery Crenshaw came to see Amos and told him what had been taken and intimated that as sheriff he would probably be held responsible for not taking better precautions. Amos pointed out that nobody had told him what was in the trunk deposited in the bank, and Crenshaw said that your father had thought it prudent to inform just the judge and the mayor of Catesville.

"Seeing that he was being set up as the scapegoat, Amos made up a posse and followed the trail of the robbers up into the Nantahalas but never caught up with them. Amos can tell you more."

"One thing is pretty clear," Joel said. "No one in Cate County is capable of organizing the blowing open of a bank vault. The culprits are one or more of those who knew what was in the trunk, that is, my father, my two brothers, Crenshaw and Stiles. Whoever did it must have decided that the Confederacy was finished and the time had come to provide for the future, a very comfortable future. I think we had better go see Amos, Susannah."

At the sheriff's office, Dorsey, the deputy, told them that they could probably find Sheriff Boggs at Jessie Finch's house, where he was spending a lot of time recently.

When they got to Jessie's house they found her son Johnny and Elias and Leander churning ice cream on the porch.

"What are you boys doing here?" Susannah said.

"Mr. Dorsey come got us, said it was too dangerous to be out there alone at the mission," Elias replied. "Bad folks about."

"What kind of ice cream's that?" Joel asked.

"Strawberry."

"Save us some."

They went through the door and found Jessie and Amos sitting on a plush velvet sofa holding hands. They arose together.

"Oh, Susannah, I have the best news. Amos and I are to be married. Why, Mr. Devereux!"

"I have good news too. Mr. Devereux and I are engaged."

"Well," Jessie said. Both she and Amos were visibly adjusting their view of Susannah. "Shall we have a glass of Madeira to celebrate?"

Jessie left the room, a bit flushed and confused, and returned with a half-bottle of Madeira and four wineglasses.

"To our forthcoming marriages," Jessie said, raising a glass.

"If I don't go to jail," Amos replied glumly.

"Has it gotten that serious, Amos?" Susannah said.

"Judge Stiles is calling a grand jury. They're saying that when I took out with a posse to recover the gold, I found it and hid it away somewhere, and they got a couple of those scoundrels in the Home Guard ready to testify that's what happened."

"And if I am not arrested for evading military service," Joel said. "Judge Stiles has already taken note that I'm not in uniform. Amos, I think my family is behind the robbery, with the collusion of Colcock Stiles and his creature, Givens Crenshaw. If we could take evidence of that to Governor Brown, we'd spike their guns good."

"How you going to do that?"

"Tell me about the posse."

"I saw that Stiles and Crenshaw were trying a noose on me for size, and I decided the best thing to do was catch the robbers and get the gold back, and that would put an end to their game. So I got together some of the Home Guard and a few of those Cherokee half-breeds that hang around town and Judge Stiles' pack of hounds, which he could hardly refuse me, and I took off after wagon tracks leading from the bank. They headed north toward the Nantahalas, and where the road becomes a path there was the wagon with the empty trunk sitting in it and the two mules that were pulling the wagon gone.

"The Cherokees picked up the tracks of the mules and four horsemen that had joined the party, and these led off down to a shallow little river that flows out of one of those clefts in the cliffs.

"The Cherokees were having no part of going up there, it being a sacred tribal burying ground. So we turned around and come home."

"So, you think the gold is hidden somewhere up that canyon?"

"Could be, or it could be that those four horses and two

mules, saddlebags full of gold, went up the other branch of the river and came out just about anywhere, like a fox would do to lose hounds. By now the gold could be in North Carolina."

"Junius and Lamar are still at Cherokee Rose?"

"Yes, they are. I told them to leave, but having lost their deferments, I guess they're more afraid of the recruiting officers than of the Black Band that's terrorizing the countryside. That's why I brought your boys down from the mission, Miss Susannah."

"They can stay with me and Johnny for a night or two, Susannah," Jessie said, "until you figure out what you want to do about them."

"Thank you, Jessie. I'll have someone pick them up tomorrow. They can help out around the hotel."

"This Black Band," Joel said to Amos, "they're bushwhackers?"

"Worse than that. Deserters and common criminals who've got hold of enough horses and guns to make up a gang. They're going around the mountains breaking into houses where they think there's silver or other valuables, killing men that get in their way, raping women. They've made themselves a black flag with skull and crossbones, like pirates, to scare people. With nearly every able-bodied man down fighting around Atlanta, there's no one to stand in their way. It's sure that me and Dorsey and that miserable Home Guard can't."

"So Junius and Lamar have lost their deferments."

"Well, they sure couldn't claim they was down at Devereux Hall helping your pa."

"I think I ought to pay a call on my brothers. They may be able to tell us the rest of the story."

"I thought you and they wasn't much on speaking terms."

"That doesn't matter now. They'll talk to me."

The cottage was in sad shape. The sign with "Cherokee Rose" carved on it hung by one hook. The yard was covered with last winter's fallen magnolia leaves, paint peeled from the shutters. Joel rang the bell.

The door was answered by a stooped, gray-haired Negro man in worn livery. It was Robert, Lamar's body servant.

"Why, Massa Joel, we sure weren't expecting to see you." He looked at Susannah, whom he certainly knew, but must have decided that there was nothing he could safely say to her.

"Are my brothers in?"

"Yessir, they are in the study. Shall I announce you?"

"Don't bother, Robert. I'll surprise them."

They passed through the darkened salon, its furniture and chandelier hung with muslin dust covers. He opened the library doors. Junius and Lamar sat at a round mahogany table, a bottle of brandy on the table between them. It was nearly noon, but both were still in their dressing gowns. They rose, looking surprised but not all that surprised.

"Joel," Lamar said, "Selena sent us a message that you and she were at the Cate Springs Hotel. We can almost have a family reunion. And Miss Goode . . . Do sit down. I'll have Robert bring two more glasses."

"No thanks," Joel said. "I'm here on business."

Lamar looked at Susannah again. "Does Father know you're back?"

"Yes, he does."

Junius's brow was furrowed. He could tell something not normal was happening, but he was unable to grasp what it was. Junius was the oldest of the brothers, tall, big-boned, and slow-witted.

"Business?" Lamar said. "What business?"

"Where's the gold, Lamar?"

"Gold?"

"Gold?" Junius echoed, the first word he had spoken.

"The gold from the U.S. mint in Dahlonega that is now missing from the Catesville branch of the Devereux Bank."

"Oh, that gold. Yes, Father is very upset."

"I'm sure he is."

"And I'm sure I've no idea where the gold is."

Lamar was not going to panic. He had a long and successful history of avoiding issues, such as what did he propose to do with his life, which Auguste was constantly demanding. At thirty-two he was beginning to go to fat, and there were dark rings under his eyes from a life of dissipation that had begun when he and Joel were at Princeton together.

Joel broke a long silence. "Perhaps I can refresh your memory by telling you that I have enough evidence of a conspiracy to steal the Confederacy's gold, or the U.S. government's gold, depending on your point of view, to put all of you in jail for a long time."

"All of us?"

"You, Junius, Auguste, Judge Stiles, and Givens Crenshaw."

"You don't have any such evidence."

"What evidence I have I will present to Governor Brown. Anyone who's ready to talk now can probably avoid jail."

Junius guffawed. "You can't put anyone in jail for stealing rocks."

Lamar leapt to his feet, red in the face. "Goddamn you, Junius, keep your mouth shut."

It was a few seconds before it dawned on Joel what was being said. "So that's it. That trunk was full of rocks. There never was any gold in it. The gold was taken from the mint maybe some time ago. Years pass, and then the gold has to be produced and you can't. So you stage a bank robbery. What did you do, hire professional bank robbers from Atlanta?"

"How much do you want, Joel?"

"Nothing. I just want to know where the gold is."

"I don't know."

"Lamar, don't waste my time. I swear to you I'm going straight to Governor Brown."

"I don't know because Father never told us. He had it taken somewhere. You'd better ask him."

"That's just what I'm going to do." Joel stood up. "Come on, Susannah, let's go."

As they drove away from Cherokee Rose, Susannah said, "That was masterful, Joel. For a long time I didn't under-stand what you were up to. Now I see. You finally have your father where you want him."

"As they say, the shoe is now on the other foot."

"That must be sweet."

"To overcome is always sweet. Too bad it comes so swiftly. Like making love, the slower the better. Which re-minds me we have an appointment to keep at the mission."

"I don't need reminding. That wide, hard bed again, with the windows open, and I can cry out all I want without anyone hearing. Love in the afternoon. Could there be any-thing better in life?"

"Continuing on into the night."

"What about my Atlanta ladies?"

"Let them start learning how to take care of themselves. It'll be good practice for when they no longer have slaves."

"But should we be out at the mission, all alone at night, with those bandits on the loose?"

"It's just for one night, and it wouldn't be smart to be seen in town. Lamar is quite capable of having Judge Stiles arrest me on some trumped-up charge. Do you have riding clothes?"

"Boots and breeches."

"I propose we leave at first light tomorrow, before anyone has a chance to cause us trouble, and ride down to Devereux Hall and pay a social call."

"Much as I hate to say it, wouldn't it be better if I stay here?"

"No, not the way things are. From now on I'm not letting you out of my sight."

9

They saddled their horses by lamplight, in the hour before dawn. By the end of the first day he wanted them out of the hill country, which was infested with raiding parties, bushwhackers, and now outlaws. With luck they should be able to reach the little town of Devereux by the evening of the second day, spend the night there, and make a proper entrance at Devereux Hall the next morning, provided Sherman hadn't already crossed the Chattahoochee and turned one of his three armies north to begin the encirclement of Atlanta.

"There. Do I look like a man?"

Susannah had finished saddling her mare and had put a wide-brimmed hat atop her pinned-up hair.

"My dear Susannah, there is nothing that you could possibly do that would make you appear as other than a woman. The best we can hope for is that at a distance you might be mistaken for a boy. Are you frightened?"

"Of course I'm frightened. But if we run into real trouble, I won't lose my head. You can count on that. I've too much to live for now."

They exchanged a warm glance. There would be much to say when this was all over.

"Can you use a pistol?"

"Yes. George Malik insisted I learn, living out here in isolation with a war on."

"I'll give you one of mine. It's loaded. If you have to use it, shoot to kill. You're not likely to get a second chance. What else are you taking?"

"My prettiest dress, as you asked me to. The cupboard was bare, but I did make some cornbread. We can live off that for a day or two if we have to. Then your letters from Spain, the few that got through. Oh, and there's a letter that came for you at Cherokee Rose, a long time ago, when no one was living there, and the postman left it with us. From Princeton University."

"Really? They must have wanted money. What about your personal things? We may not be coming back."

"I really have no personal things that I care about, and I leave with no regrets. All I want now is to be with you."

"As I said yesterday, from now on I'm not letting you out of my sight. It's beginning to get light. We'd better be on our way."

As they rode past the house, Susannah said, "So ends The Mission to the Cherokee Nation. I didn't even bother to lock the door."

They rode all morning, through pine woods and past small farms, but the country was so rough that they probably hadn't made more than ten miles of the twenty-five they needed to cover. About noon they came upon a wide, well-made road.

"The Unicoi Turnpike," Joel said. "The only decent road in these parts, all the way from Tennessee to the Tugaloo River and South Carolina."

"And that tavern where the Sidley sisters are being held before being sold into a life of prostitution. When will we hear, Joel?"

"No way of knowing. We'll just have to hope Elam Scroggins and his boys do their work well. Now, we can make good time if we take the turnpike, but the risks will be greater. What do you say?"

"Take the turnpike."

"All right then."

They rode off down the road, breaking into a trot, which their horses were eager for. After half an hour they slowed their mounts to a walk. Ahead a plume of smoke rose.

"A tavern, probably," Joel said. "Maybe we can get a meal, pick up some gossip even."

Around the bend in the road stood a wood-frame building with a dozen horses tethered in the trees to one side. They would undoubtedly have gossip with lunch. But as they came up to the building, which seemed more a house than a tavern, a breeze stirred. From a pole stuck into the porch railings a black flag unfurled, exposing white skull and crossbones. At the instant that they saw it, a man sitting on the porch steps, drinking from a whiskey jug, saw them.

"Hey, boys," he yelled, "we got company."

There was no need for a word to pass between them. They spurred their horses into a gallop, and within seconds the house occupied by the outlaws was out of sight. But Susannah's hat had blown off, and her dark hair streamed behind her.

"What do we do?" Susannah called to him as they galloped abreast down the road.

"They'll come after us on fresh horses. We can't outrun them." Ahead loomed a covered bridge. "Down the bank and under the bridge."

Both of their horses nearly fell as they hurtled down the bank. They stayed in their saddles in the darkness beneath the bridge, their panting, lathered horses fetlock-deep in water.

Bars of light fell across their faces from cracks in the flooring of the bridge, giving the impression that they were in a dank prison. Joel had drawn his revolver and cocked it, and Susannah followed his example, but it was a full five minutes before they heard the hooves of horses approaching.

"They were probably all drunk," Joel said.

That was some encouragement, but he knew well that in the next five minutes they might both be dead. The hooves of four or five horses thundered across the bridge.

"What now?"

"Back into the woods."

"I guess taking the turnpike wasn't the best idea I've ever had," Susannah said and laughed.

Joel was reminded of Harriet Read traveling across North Georgia with her murdered friend on the seat opposite her. There weren't many, man or woman, with real courage, but Harriet Read and Susannah Goode were among them.

They did not dine at all badly that evening. Joel shot two pigeons with his fowling piece and, mostly to impress Susannah, went down at sunset to the stream by which they had camped, put together his fly rod, and caught a big brown trout.

Afterward they sat beside the dying fire, she huddled against his shoulder.

"We are like two asteroids," he said, "hurled into space from the explosion of a planet, headed God knows where."

"What planet?"

"The South of our fathers and grandfathers, the last of those worlds of honor and pride and arrogance that will be no more, soon to be crisscrossed by railroads and telegraph wires and studded with mills belching dark smoke."

"You are something of a poet, Joel Devereux."

"Were I not, would I ever have got the Reverend Goode's young ward in my sights?"

"How the rest of the population lives," Joel said, "and there's nothing in between this and the mansions."

"What about the slaves?"

"They're not part of the population, they're property, like horses and cows."

"Do you believe that?"

"Of course not. But if you own slaves and don't at least pretend to believe that, you wouldn't be able to live with yourself. Susannah, nobody believes they're bad. Everybody believes they're good, and they have to justify what they do to that end."

They rode on, mostly silent now, beginning to give in to fatigue. The shadows lengthened, lines of colored field hands trudged home along the road, powdered with the red dust that had settled on Joel and Susannah and their mounts. Another plantation seat appeared on the horizon.

"The Sidley place," Joel said. "I'll have to go there and tell them. I can only hope that Elam and his boys were able to rescue the girls."

"And if not?"

"I'll have to go anyway. It would be the most unpleasant duty I've ever done. Can you imagine having to tell parents that their young daughters have been sold into prostitution, and particularly parents who could have seen nothing but prosperity and good marriages for them."

"In that case, may I go with you?"

"But why?"

"Having seen the reality at close hand, I just might, without revealing my past, know some words to say that would help—although God knows what they would be."

As the sun was setting they rode into the little town of Devereux and up to a barn-like building, with a sign above the open doors, "Jenkins Livery Stable". A stooped old man with a goatee hobbled out into the street.

"Mr. Jenkins."

"Why, Mr. Devereux. I thought you was somewhere across the ocean."

"I was, but I've come home. Do you still have a room or two upstairs for travelers?"

"I certainly do, but they are mostly empty these days."

"We're going out to Devereux Hall, but I can't go like this at this hour. I was wondering if you could let us have a room for the night, with a bath if possible."

Jenkins stole a glance at Susannah, a very quick one. It was not his place to question the behavior of his betters. "There's a tub, yes, and I can have my boy heat some water and bring it up."

"That's good news. By any chance would the carriage that we used to keep here for visitors on their way to our place still be around?"

"Oh, it's here but all covered with dust. This has not been a year for visitors."

"I can imagine, but maybe your boy could wash it down in the morning and polish the brass."

"Well, of course, he could do that, but I've got no carriage horses. The army came through and took any horse that could make a trot."

"If your boy could scrub down our horses and curry them and give them some oats and stalls, I imagine I could drive them out."

"Normally, I would say that trying to hitch two strange saddle horses to the same carriage would lead to a real ruckus. But knowing who you are, if you think you can do it, I imagine you can."

"Thank you, Mr. Jenkins. We would like to start off about midday."

"You'll find everything ready. Give my regards to your father. Haven't seen him in quite a spell."

"I'll be sure to do that."

10

At first their two horses, harnessed to an elegant carriage, kicked and butted and bucked some, but within minutes Joel had them moving along at a good, steady pace. They passed the Devereux mills with their waterwheels turning in the stream that, as it flowed toward the Chattahoochee, powered the looms that produced the cotton and woolen cloth. From there the road ran as straight as an arrow to a white house, its columned massiveness obvious even from a great distance.

"Devereux Hall?" Susannah said.

"Yes."

"At last. What feelings do you have at this moment, Joel?"

"Relief that this will soon be over."

"You are confident of winning, then?"

"Not totally confident, but the odds are such that I will play to."

"What shall I do?"

"Just keep your beautiful head held high."

"Yes, my love."

They had entered a long avenue of oaks leading to the great house, and she felt her mouth dry. She had never faced anything quite like this before.

"Exactly one mile long. My grandfather was a very precise man, a stickler for detail. A Huguenot from La Rochelle, the main slave-trading port of France, so he took easily to the rice and Sea Island cotton economy of coastal Georgia. He bought this tract of land while they were still arguing in Washington about whether or not it belonged to the Cherokees."

Several carriages trailing plumes of dust passed them, headed away from Devereux Hall.

"What's that about?"

"A council of war just ended, I imagine, the big planters confronting the unthinkable. The Yankees have come to take their money and slaves from them."

At the end of the avenue of oaks a large formal garden, mainly of boxwood, surrounded the mansion.

"How beautiful," Susannah said. "Worthy of a castle in England."

"Done by an Irish landscape architect, actually. He went on to do the grounds at our Sea Island place, Tupelo. I remember him from when I was a child."

Two carriages were drawn up beneath the trees, their Negro drivers sitting on the edge of a marble watering trough, conversing quietly.

"Well, this is it," he said as they went up the wide steps together and through the open glass doors.

The dark mahogany-floored hall was empty and silent. To one side, as they advanced, a chandelier still blazed in a room where a long dining table held the remains of a dozen or more desserts, coffees and liqueurs, large linen napkins tossed on the table, not neatly folded as they would have been at the Mission when visiting clergymen came for dinner.

Across from the dining room, double doors opened slowly. A tall, white-haired Negro butler stepped aside to let pass two florid-faced men, as white-haired as he, in well-tailored plantation garb.

"Good afternoon, Mr. Beauchamp," Joel said. The man

looked at him, said nothing, and moved toward the front doors.

"Mr. Singleton."

"Joel, you have deeply wounded your father. You have chosen to return, and I can only hope it is to make amends to him," and he too strode toward the entry. Neither man had deigned even to glance at Susannah.

Joel turned his head and her gaze followed his. A figure stood in the doorway from which the two planters had just emerged. He appeared to be about sixty-five, ramrod straight, with white hair down to his shoulders. He was dressed entirely in black, a black ribbon tie held to his snow-white ruffled shirt by a gold pin. He rested one hand on a gold-headed black cane.

"Sir."

"Come, my dear boy, give your old father a kiss."

Joel crossed the room and kissed Auguste Devereux on the cheek.

"The kiss of a traitor. Thus did Judas Iscariot make himself known."

"Father, there are some things we need to discuss."

"I have nothing to discuss with you, but I do have one or two things to tell you after my siesta."

"I think I have something to tell you that you will find it in your interest to discuss."

"We'll see about that."

"You haven't greeted Miss Goode."

"Nor do I intend to."

"You will before this day is over."

"We'll see about that as well. In the meantime you will find company in the Gun Room with whom to while away the time."

Then the older Devereux turned and started up the stairs

without another word, accompanied by the butler who had been staring all the while at Joel as though he were seeing a ghost. Joel led Susannah through the open doors.

"The Gun Room," he said, "the center of power for all of the counties hereabouts."

There were indeed many guns, shotguns, pistols, muskets, rifles in glass cases around the walls. In the center of the room a large round table was as covered with debris as the dining table—empty and half-empty bottles and glasses of various brandies, open boxes of cigars. Seated beside the table, his polished riding boots on another chair, lounged a slender man with long gray hair, smoking a cigar, a glass of brandy held to the light. He wore a black string tie, paisley vest, and canary yellow breeches.

"Uncle Willy!"

"Yes, dear boy, and about as welcome here as you are. You really should try some of this exquisite forty-year-old Armagnac. Whatever else you may say of Auguste, you cannot criticize his cellar, reputedly the finest between Philadelphia and New Orleans."

The man arose and approached Susannah, took her hand in his, and kissed it.

"You would be the Miss Goode I've heard about, and certainly more beautiful than my nephew has any right to expect."

"I'd like to talk to you," Joel said, "if you have the time."

"At your disposal."

"You have a carriage?"

"No, rode my horse over from Marietta."

"But how? Isn't that behind Union lines?"

"Have a pass from my old friend, Cump Sherman. I believe you met him at my house some years ago."

"Yes, the year before I went off to Princeton."

"He was paying a visit to the military academy there, back when we were one happy united nation and the cadets wore blue, not gray. A little Armagnac, Miss Goode?"

"Yes, please."

Joel's uncle poured a splash of amber liquid from a dust-covered bottle into two glasses.

"Make yourselves comfortable," and he motioned toward two vacated chairs. "You've spoken with your father?"

"Yes. He has one or two things to tell me, he says, after his siesta."

"Ah, yes, nothing interferes with Auguste's siesta, neither General Sherman nor God. There goes April now with his camomile tea."

Through the open door a light–coffee-colored, very pretty maid was carrying a tray up the stairs.

"Don't tell me that's still going on."

"Oh, yes."

"What do you think my father has to tell me?"

"For one thing, that you are disinherited. He's let everybody know. Whether he's actually done so, I don't know. What I do know is that his amour propre has been badly damaged. It's not just what you said about slavery in your letter to the London *Times*, it's that he had to hear about it from another planter. What else he has to tell you, I have no idea, although nothing pleasant, to be sure."

"What's been going on here?"

"The plantation elite has gathered here to hear a little proposition of mine, which was not well received—to say the very least. My idea is that the time has come for Georgia to take itself out of the war. Since I am one of the few who know both General Sherman and Governor Brown, I have been going back and forth between them. I also travel with light baggage. No slaves, no fields of cotton. I've made my way on cotton futures, on knowing cotton like every Devereux. At least I did as long as I could work the telegraph line between New Orleans and New York.

"Anyway, Joe Brown hates Yankees but he hates Jeff Davis as much, if not more. He'd like to sue for peace, but if Georgia leaves the war, the Confederacy may just collapse, and Joe Brown will go down in history as the man responsible.

"On the other hand, if Sherman has to storm Atlanta with great losses, he may just devastate the whole state. So, Brown's wavering. I thought maybe if I could convince Auguste and the other big planters to support my plan it would tip the balance. But, of course, they've too much pride to do it—honor and all that, the curse of the South."

"What now?"

"I suppose the war will just have to take its course. What about you?"

"I have to settle a couple of things with my father, and then I intend to take myself and Susannah out of the war."

"Good luck, but let me warn you that when I report back to Sherman on my lack of success, he will most probably come across the Chattahoochee with pretty much everything he's got. Then there'll be hell to pay. I've already warned Auguste. After all, he is my brother, though he would rather see a lot of boys die than admit that he and his class were wrong."

"Yes," Joel said, "that's the way it is. Rich man's war, poor man's fight. And afterwards, Uncle Willy?"

William Devereux poured himself a bit more Armagnac, studied Joel as though he wondered if his nephew was up to hearing the raw truth.

"Afterward? Afterward another world will be born, like a strange new plant growing out of the rotting corpse of our old world."

Susannah winced at this too-vivid expression. She did not need, did not want, to hear more. The sun had moved now, covering her in the luminescent shadow of a swagged linen shade. She felt herself a shadow, a silent, unseen witness to the playing out of a grim family drama she barely understood. At least Uncle William was sympathetic.

"But 'plant' is perhaps the wrong simile," Joel's uncle continued. "Not a plant, a machine. Machines, that's what the new world will be about. Do you understand, dear boy, why the South lost the war?"

"I . . ."

"And don't prattle to me about cavaliers and roundheads, slavery, and Puritanism, all that. The South has lost the war because of four inventions that doomed it: the railroad, the telegraph, the repeating rifle . . . and banks. These are trumps in the little game that is now coming to an end, trumping . . . how shall I sum it up? . . . the horse, the handwritten note, the dueling pistol . . . and gold. You know something about that last, I believe."

"The Dahlonega gold?"

"Exactly. Stay away from it. There's already someone from Richmond nosing about, asking questions about the gold and . . ."

"And?"

"Nothing. Gold is nothing now. Remember the story of King Midas, and besides, now the world operates on tele-graphed messages, wisps in the air, that transfer wealth from one institution, one person to another."

"Your world?"

"No, yours. You, Joel, and your young lady," and he nodded his head toward Susannah, "will have to deal with all that. I'm taking my winnings off the board, sailing back to France with Nicole, to live in the old way that the French know so well. At least Auguste and I had that in common. We understood what living well was.

"So I had better get going, before some Confederate sentry wakes up from his nap and shoots me off my horse. Good luck, my boy."

"And to you, Uncle Willy. I won't forget."

William Devereux stood up, took the silver-handled riding crop from the chair arm where it hung, bent it until Susannah thought it would break.

"In the end that's all there is, Joel, experience and memory."

After William Devereux had left, Joel directed a servant to show them to a guest room, at Susannah's request. She needed some rest herself. It had been a day that had drained her emotions, and the worst was perhaps yet to come. As she lay on the bed, after having removed only her shoes and dress, something occurred to Susannah.

"The maid April, what were you and your uncle talking about?"

"April has been—among others—Auguste's mistress, for years now."

"Oh. Leander, the boy that your father sent up to the Mission, told me that April was his mother. I sent a telegram to your father asking what I should do about Leander but didn't receive a reply. I was going to ask you to raise it with your father."

"I'm glad you told me this. I won't raise it. I would rather see to Leander's future myself."

"Why?"

"After all, he's my half-brother."

"Jesus," Susannah said. "What feeling does that knowledge give you?"

"Certainly not surprise. No doubt there are other children on this plantation to whom I am related."

"I was raised in a brothel, but what would you call this?"

"The way things were on the great plantations."

When she awoke from a sleep that had taken her by surprise, the sun was lower in the sky and Joel was not there. She rose, groggy, uneasy in her mind, and put on her dress and shoes, went out and down the curving, red-carpeted staircase. The hall was silent again, but then she heard voices behind a half-open door next to the Gun Room. She was drawn to the sound, stood near the door and listened.

"You have no proof."

"I have Junius's and Lamar's confessions."

"I don't believe that."

"Believe it or not, I'm prepared to go to Governor Brown with what I know."

"What do you really want?"

"I want to be left alone. In particular I want you to quit interfering in my relations with Susannah Goode."

There was a harsh laugh. "When you were my son, I tried as best I could to keep you from a foolish liaison. But after that disgraceful letter you wrote to the London *Times*, which dishonored the family name, you ceased to be my son. Now it is of no consequence to me what you do to your reputation. You will excuse me, but I have other business to attend to. As a practical matter, I suppose you will have to spend the night here, but after that I would hope never to set eyes on you again."

"That would be perfectly agreeable with me."

There was a scraping of chairs, and Joel emerged from the room followed by his father. Susannah stood frozen.

"My fiancée, Father."

Auguste Devereux slightly lowered his head toward her.

"You have my best wishes, Miss Goode, that happiness will come of this union, in a world that I will never enter."

She nodded to him. Ironic even in defeat, she thought.

She was awakened by the flickering of lights on the ceiling, noises from the courtyard below. She got up and peered out the open window. A coach and four and two carriages were lined up in the light of lanterns. Servants moved back and forth, loading boxes and valises into them. Several Negroes climbed into the carriages, including April. Then Auguste Devereux and another white man emerged from the house and stood talking.

"Joel, come."

Already half-awake, he got up and approached the window.

"Who is that other man?"

"His doctor. He travels with him whenever there is a move between the upcountry house and the low-country one. We are leaving the field to the Yankees, it seems."

There was the crack of a whip, and the little caravan moved out of the lantern light into the half-light preceding dawn.

Dawn came, and Joel Devereux and Susannah Goode found themselves master and mistress of Devereux Hall.

11

The sight of the coach and attendant carriages of Auguste Devereux proceeding into the dawn drew Joel back to Spain and the passage of the coaches and carriages of the rich and powerful through the streets of Barcelona, rattling empty at dawn, being taken to the places where a grandee would emerge from his immense residence, smoking a cheroot, expecting confidently to have a carriage door opened for him by liveried lackeys, tossing an end of cheroot into the gutter, the carriage, now with footmen behind, rolling more heavily over the cobblestones.

It was a seductive life he had led there, one that drew him into intrigue and romantic adventure. He was treated like a grandee himself, heir to vast plantations and slaves, in the view of the Catalans, particularly of Luis Molinas, who would himself always be an outsider. It was also, from the first, the conception—a misconception—of Luis's high-born wife Manuela.

He had not loved Manuela. He was as sure of that as that she had not loved him. What had passed between them the evening they first met was what he had heard called animal magnetism, nothing more, but it was irresistible. He was starved for female affection, she was a young, intelligent, beautiful, and very unhappy woman. Her family was among the very oldest and noblest of Spain, so old and noble that no thought was given to money, which had existed in immeasurable amounts as long as anyone could remember. But then one day the silver of America was spent, and the family was poor. Nothing even to pawn, just a great name and a lovely daughter.

So Manuela had been sold to Luis Molinas, an Indiano, as those Spaniards who had made fortunes in Cuba were called, his from slave-grown sugar cane. She was ripe for an affair, and there would be others. He did not see a happy old age for her, but he would always have a fondness for her. She was wise in the ways of the world, and she had told him some home truths. One was that nothing ever turns out the way you expect it will, because what you expect has nothing much to do with the way that the universe works, heedlessly crushing or sparing lives as it turns.

Joel thought this as he stood with Susannah, watching his father's caravan drive off into the dawn. Who would have imagined that he would find himself, alone of his family, in Devereux Hall this morning, with the woman for whom he had thrown away everything?

"What happens now?" she said.

"I haven't the slightest idea. I suppose we could start by going downstairs and searching out some breakfast."

To his surprise the table in the breakfast room was set for two with the Boston silver and the Wedgwood china. The door to the pantry swung open and Fraser, the Devereux Hall butler for forty years, emerged. He was wearing a tail coat, winged collar, and striped vest.

"Massa Joel, will you be having the usual?"

Joel had forgotten what the usual was.

"That would be?"

"Coffee, biscuits, scrambled eggs, and hominy grits."

"There's coffee?"

"Oh, yes indeed."

"Then that would be fine."

"Would missus like the same?"

"Yes, please," Susannah said, clearly startled.

Fraser disappeared into the pantry.

"Uncanny," she said.

"Even I am a bit astonished, used as I once was to having every desire anticipated. It's sad really. Fraser cannot imagine that his comfortable and privileged position, even though as a slave, is about to be swept away. He will be free, but who in the world that is coming is going to need an aged butler?"

As in answer to his rhetorical question, Fraser emerged again and filled their glasses with water.

"Massa Auguste wouldn't let me go with him down south. Said I was too old. Now don't that beat all, him being sixty-six and me only sixty-three?"

"What will you do, Fraser, if it's all over at Devereux Hall?"

"I've got some money put aside. The kind of guests your father had all these years always left a little something for me, sometimes more than a little. They would have been embarrassed not to. Now, if you will let me stay on at my cabin . . ."

"I'm afraid I don't have anything to do with Devereux Hall anymore. My father has taken me out of his will."

"I heard that, but I didn't really believe it. I just couldn't imagine Massa Auguste would do something so mean."

"You probably know him better than I ever knew him, but that's what they say he did."

"Massa Robert is out back. He wants to talk to you after breakfast about some problem he's got."

"I'll be glad to talk to Mr. Henderson, Fraser, but I've got no authority to make any decisions about anything concerning Devereux Hall."

"Yes, sir, I'll tell him that. Your breakfast will be ready shortly."

"Who's Mr. Henderson?" Susannah said after the butler had disappeared again.

"The head overseer."

"My, you look cross." Susannah giggled. "Massa Joel, the reluctant squire."

"Well, I don't have any authority. What is very unlike my father is to leave nobody in charge of his valuable property. There's some reason, though. He never does anything without a reason."

"I overheard the last of your talk with your father yesterday. Do you think we are really free of him now?"

"Oh, yes. Although he admits to nothing, he is well aware I can go to the governor with what I know. That business about my ceasing to be his son was just to save face."

"Where do you think the gold is?"

"God knows. By now it could be in a bank vault in Europe. He must have believed from early on that the South was going to lose the war, and that with it he might lose all his lands and slaves and factories."

Fraser entered again, bearing breakfast in covered silver dishes.

"Where's the good silver, Fraser?"

"Massa Auguste put it away some time ago, I don't know where."

Again they were alone. "This isn't the good silver?"

"No, this is the everyday silver. The good silver is antique, British and French, and literally worth a fortune. I would have expected my father to put it in a safe place, so why has he left Devereux Hall with no one in charge? No doubt the answer will soon rise to the surface."

Fraser served their plates from the covered dishes and poured out coffee, disappeared again.

"The smell of coffee," she said. "How long has it been?"

135

"Oh, there's everything to delight the senses here, no matter what others may do without. But we can't stay here long, if Uncle Willy is right and Sherman is about to attempt a crossing of the river with his entire army. I've got what I came for, but where can we go? We might ride out of here and straight into a Union artillery barrage. Gentlemen don't hide, or at least that's the way I was brought up. Then maybe we should just sit tight and hope that if the Union army does arrive on our doorstep, there will be sufficient discipline imposed from on high that we won't be molested."

"That seems to make the most sense. After all, Joel, everybody hereabouts thinks you are nothing short of an abolitionist. General Sherman will probably embrace you."

"No doubt Uncle Willy has told him that I don't support the Southern cause, but we aren't going to see Sherman. If the Yankees come this way, it will be some lesser commander, and when he finds out who owns the mills producing cloth for the Confederate army, he may just burn Devereux Hall. Worse still, we are more likely to be visited by foragers looking for loot . . ."

He left this thought in mid-sentence. To describe the physical danger they might then face, particularly Susannah, would be to thoroughly alarm her. She must already be frightened enough.

"But that's just speculation. The most prudent course is to stay here for the time being. I'm sure there are plenty of provisions and, as Uncle Willy said, the best wine cellar between Philadelphia and New Orleans."

"There's only one problem."

"What's that?"

"I have nothing to wear."

He laughed. "The eternal feminine complaint."

"I'm serious. I have this one dress I'm wearing, and it's already dirty."

"Selena is about your size. I'm sure she has closets and closets full of the most expensive gowns. Help yourself."

"I can't do that."

"Of course you can. My dear Susannah, in times like these there are no longer any rules."

When Fraser returned to clear the breakfast table, Joel decided the moment had come to clear up things a bit.

"Fraser, this is Miss Goode. We are engaged to be married, and we will be staying on a few days."

"Oh, I remember Missus Goode real well from the summers we used to spend at Cherokee Rose, and I do congratulate you, Massa Joel."

"Why don't you tell Mr. Henderson to come on in now."

This time when the door closed behind Fraser, Susannah said, "Am I missing something? He never gave the slightest hint that he knew who I was until just then."

"You aren't butler at Devereux Hall for forty years unless you are absolutely discreet, and then some."

Robert Henderson was dressed in his accustomed way, in boots and breeches, a wide leather belt, and a loose-fitting linen shirt. He held a straw hat and a riding crop. He looked tired and anxious.

"Robert, this is my fiancée, Miss Goode."

"Pleased to meet you, ma'am."

"Sit down."

"Oh, I wouldn't be comfortable doing that. After twenty-three years standing in your father's presence, I'm not sure I could get my legs to bend."

"As you wish. Now, what's this problem you're having?"

"The field hands refuse to work, and some have already run away. They say the Yankees are coming in a day or two

137

and they're as good as free, and they won't work anymore unless they're paid. Even if I was told to pay them, I don't have any money for that. The only way I could make them work is by flogging a few of them. But the time's past for that. If and when the Yankees do arrive, I don't much fancy sleeping with a pistol under my pillow every night. What am I supposed to do?"

"Robert, I can't give you any advice. I'm no longer an heir to the Devereux estate."

"So I have heard, and that's a real shame."

"However, if I were you I guess I'd just let the field hands be. I don't imagine any cotton's going to get picked this year anyway. I'm not giving you an order, just an opinion."

When the overseer had left, Joel said, "So what would you like to do for the rest of the day? I can give you a tour of the carriage house and its twelve carriages, of the wine cellar, of the ballroom with its ceiling painted by an Italian artist, of the library with its family portraits."

"I'd like to see the mule barn."

"The mule barn?"

"I'd like to see if there really are a hundred sets of mule harnesses with brass fittings that Leander says it was his job to polish."

The morning passed in ominous quiet. The field hands were nowhere to be seen. Perhaps they had gone into the woods to await the arrival of the Union army. There were no travelers on the road until about noon, when a single horseman galloped up the long drive. A Confederate lieutenant, covered in road dust, got down from his horse.

"Am I speaking to Mr. Auguste Devereux?"

"No, he is traveling. But I'm Joel Devereux, his son."

"Sir, I was ordered by General Johnston to alert your father that the Yankees have crossed the Chattahoochee River in force."

"Has there been a battle?"

"No, sir. There was too many of them for us. We had the strongest fortifications imaginable for miles along the river facing the enemy. But Sherman sent one of his three armies way upriver and crossed over a pontoon bridge they put down at Roswell. They would have come at us from our rear, so there was nothing to do but give up our fortifications and cross the Chattahoochee. We'll reform somewhere between here and Atlanta, and there we will stand and fight."

"Good luck to you, Lieutenant."

"Thank you, sir. We're going to need it. What shall I tell General Johnston?"

"Tell him that my father by now is on the way from Atlanta to Savannah, and that we will stay put here. It's less dangerous than traveling on the road with what's going on."

"You're right there, sir. Nobody can say what's going to happen next." The lieutenant looked at Susannah. "Excuse me, Mrs. Devereux, for not introducing myself. Lieutenant Colson."

"I'm pleased to meet you, and thank you for bringing us the warning."

As the Confederate officer rode away Joel studied Susannah's face. She seemed calm, almost tranquil.

"Are you afraid?"

"A little, but as long as you are with me, it's all right." She looked at him. "I love you with all my heart, Joel, but I also admire you. You always do what is right and honorable, and you are brave. When I'm with you I feel safe."

"I'll do my best," he said and smiled, though he had no idea what he might be called on to do. He would try to put the best face on things, and not let her become aware of his fears.

He knew from Spain the kinds of things that were done to civilians caught between opposing armies.

They ate a cold lunch in the shade of an ancient oak tree, where Fraser had brought out a wicker table and chairs. Just as they were finishing lunch, Confederate outriders came thundering across the cotton fields, and half an hour later the first column of gray-coated soldiers appeared on the road.

They got little sleep that night as an army in retreat passed Devereux Hall, with the sound of hooves, the shouted commands and the lanterns, like a string of fireflies, lighting the way for the marching men.

By dawn it was over, and the landscape was empty again. Joel began searching with his telescope for the first Union scouts on the horizon, but none appeared. The house servants, all of whom were in their places, went about their chores silently. It was impossible to know what they were thinking.

Finally a small group of horsemen appeared on the road, headed not away from but toward the Union lines. He trained his glass on them.

"Four Confederate troopers and a civilian. I can't imagine what this is all about."

"Perhaps they're going to ask for a truce," Susannah said.

"That's possible."

But the horsemen turned into the drive to Devereux Hall. As they came closer Joel realized that the civilian was not a man at all. It was his sister, Selena.

"Selena!" Susannah cried out. "I told you I shouldn't have put on one of her dresses."

"You let me handle Selena. But what can she have in mind, riding right into the path of Sherman's army? It's crazy, and that's one thing Selena is not."

The riders came right up to the front steps. He noticed how well Selena sat her horse. She brought it to a stop at the bottom of the stairs, dismounted, and walked up as though she was not even tired.

"Well, Joel, I wondered where you had gone. And our missing housekeeper, as well."

"Susannah Goode, my sister, Selena."

"Philander Goode's ward?"

"Yes."

"So, that's it. I'll say this for you, Joel, she's pretty enough. Pretty dress, too. I think I'll have a bath and change into something nice myself. Then you can tell me what you're doing here, and I'll tell you why I'm here."

At the front door, Selena turned. "Oh, would you mind asking Fraser to send up my maid?"

"No, of course not."

He turned to the troopers standing beside their horses, hats in hand, waiting to be told what to do next. They were the same young troopers who had escaped being killed by the party of bushwhackers, including the two who had gone to Carolina with Elam Scroggins to rescue the Sidley girls.

"Come on in, boys, and refresh yourselves."

They looked up at the imposing facade of Devereux Hall.

"We couldn't, sir. We're all covered in road dust."

"Well, sit here on the steps, and I'll have some refreshments brought. What would you say to some whiskey and spring water?"

"Yes, sir," one of them said enthusiastically.

Joel rang the gong that hung beside the door, and Fraser appeared almost instantly.

"Fraser, Mrs. Coffee has just arrived. Would you send her maid up to her, and then if you would bring these gentlemen who accompanied her some whiskey and water."

When Fraser had gone back inside, one of the troopers said, "Who was that?"

"The butler."

"Don't reckon I've ever seen a butler before."

"Which of you went to Carolina with Sergeant Scroggins?"

Two of the troopers held up their hands.

"Did you rescue those young ladies?"

"Yes sir, we did."

"Where are they now?"

"Maybe we'd better tell you the whole story."

"Fine," and Joel sat down on the steps with them.

Susannah moved to a chair some distance away but close enough, Joel noted, to be able to hear.

"Well, sir, we rode down to that tavern on the Tugaloo, and they had been there, just like Sergeant Scroggins said, but the gambling men had already come for them and took them into Carolina. So we followed them and caught up pretty easy, since the young ladies were in a carriage. The two gambling men were riding on horses behind them . . ."

"And then?"

"We rode up to the two gambling men and shot them dead. We figured if we didn't, that's what they would do to us."

Joel stole a glance at Susannah. There was a look of horror on her face.

"Then we rode into the town of Easley for the night and put up at a boarding house. But the next morning the young ladies said they had talked it over and they wasn't going back with us. They had been," and the trooper lowered his voice, "violated, even before they reached the tavern on the Tugaloo, and they had lost their honor. And besides, their brother had told them if the South lost the war, they was all going to be poor. So they had decided to stay in Carolina and make their way and have some fun, too. There was no changing their minds. When we left they was in the boarding house parlor with two men, laughing and talking."

Fraser had arrived with the whiskey and water for the troopers and mint juleps for Joel and Susannah.

"So, I suppose Sergeant Scroggins is on his way home."

"No, sir. That's the rest of the story. Before we could leave Easley we ran into some boys from the sergeant's regiment, and one of them hollered out, 'That's Scroggins, and there's a reward on his head.' And two or three of them jumped him, and the last we seen of him was with hands tied, being ridden back to the provost marshal's people who are set up in Catesville to catch deserters. He's in jail there, and Judge Stiles is going to try him, and they say he may hang."

"Try him when?"

"Next week sometime."

The troopers had already gulped down their whiskey and now stood up.

"We'd better be getting on the road before we're listed as deserters, seeing as they're hanging deserters. If you could let us have a little food and some feed for our horses, we'll rest up under those trees out there and then be getting on back to Catesville."

"Of course. Mrs. Coffee has given you something?"

"Oh, yes, sir, she paid us real well for coming down with her."

The troopers led their horses away, and Joel sat down next to Susannah.

"I'm numb," she said. "Look what I have done in my self-righteousness. I made you send those soldiers off to save two girls from being forced into prostitution, and as a result two men have been killed, Sergeant Scroggins will probably hang, and the Sidley sisters seem not to care that much about their virtue."

"As you told me, Susannah, guilt is rubbish. It could have turned out quite differently. I don't mourn the gambling men. Elam Scroggins, like my brother at Chickamauga, was unlucky, and since the trial is not until next week, there may be a chance to do something about that, General Sherman permitting. As for the Sidley sisters, who can say what their future will be? But I just can't imagine how I'm going to explain to their parents what happened."

Selena walked out on the porch, in a summer frock, a mint julep in her hand. Now she looked tired. She sat down with them.

"So, tell me, Joel, what are you doing at Devereux Hall?"

"I had business to settle with Auguste. I want him out of my life, and he wants me out of the family. So we were able to agree. In the night he left for Tupelo without a word to anybody."

"Yes, he sent me a telegram. He has deeded the plantation and the factories to me. I figured if I weren't on the spot as Senator John Coffee's wife, Devereux Hall might have been burned down before Sherman's boys found out who the new owner was."

"You always did have nerve."

"I've had to. You, of course, understand what the old man's game is. If this stratagem works, and his property is saved, he will expect me, after the war is over, to hand everything back to him. That's where he's in for a big surprise."

12

Late that afternoon Susannah got another little lesson in what the Devereux were all about, relentless in the pursuit of their ambitions, impervious to the thoughts and desires of others, confidant that what they wanted they would have. Except for Joel, she thought as she dressed, who was not like that at all, a man she had told she loved with all her passion, and certainly that was true. He was still something of a mystery to her, but was that not the stuff of which grand passions are made?

As evening approached, and they had all had their siestas and, yes, she and Joel had made love again, there was a knock. A young maid was at the door, carrying an elegant lavender evening gown on a hanger and an envelope of fine ecru paper. It held a note from Selena. She wondered if the three rebels against the Devereux order might not dine together and savor their victories. Susannah was astonished. She had seen Selena, as much as any, as one of the enemy, but of course this might simply be a tactical move of some kind on Selena's part. In any case, there was no question but that she must accept the invitation. She decided not to wake Joel, who slept still wrapped in a sheet, only his bare feet and golden-red hair showing.

The maid directed her down the corridor to a tiled room where a copper tub had been filled with hot water and a table furnished with all kinds of perfumes, creams, rouges, kohl for the eyes, and silk undergarments. The maid proceeded to strip away Susannah's clothes until she was, in front of a full-length mirror, quite naked, which she had never been in the presence of another woman. She was washed, her hair shampooed, and her body dried with a large, rough towel, and she was then left alone to dress and apply cosmetics. The maid had treated the whole operation as though she were grooming a horse or a dog.

There was a table set for three in the "supper room" at the opposite end of the house from the breakfast room, and identical to it. The cloth on the round table was of fine lace, the candelabrum had been polished till it shone, as had the silver bowl that held an arrangement of pink roses. Selena was standing at the bookcase looking at a small leather-bound volume that had the Devereux family arms embossed on the cover.

"It's nice to be back among familiar things," she said, putting the book back on the shelf. "I couldn't bear to lose Devereux Hall, and I'm probably the only one who could save it, if it's discovered by Sherman's commanders that the cotton and woolen mills across the way are making cloth for rebel uniforms."

Joel seated the two women and then sat down between them. He too was back among his own things, and he looked particularly handsome by candlelight in a white ruffled shirt and black silk jacket. Selena was wearing a gown whose color Susannah had seen described in a magazine as "champagne".

"Your . . . fiancée . . . looks particularly beautiful tonight, Joel," Selena said.

It was a word that kept being used, but in fact she and Joel had never discussed marriage.

"You do indeed, my darling. This is the first time I've ever seen you in other than the Mission clothes."

Susannah looked at herself in the mirror, and it was true. In addition to the low-cut lavender gown that exposed her bosom, she had tied a lavender ribbon at her neck. From the cosmetics in the dressing room she had put a touch of lavender on her eyelids, a touch of scarlet on her lips, and had sprinkled her dark hair with a bit of silver powder, which glittered now in the candlelight.

"Thank you," she said. "There was never an occasion to dress at the Mission."

The doors opened and Fraser entered the room accompanied by two maids. They carried silver serving dishes, which they placed on the sideboard, a candle under each. Fraser took three plates from a warmer and served the first course, fish dumplings with crayfish under a pink sauce.

"Ah, *quenelles de brochet aux queues d'écrevisses, sauce Nantua*," Selena said, "my favorite dish."

"Your French pronunciation is impeccable," Joel said.

"It should be after four years at a convent school in Paris, where the nuns rapped your knuckles every time you made a mistake."

She tasted one of the quenelles. "A little on the heavy side."

"But delicious," Susannah said.

"I asked Fraser if the cook could make this dish, and he said he could but it wouldn't be as good as Toussaint's. Now we know why father sent Toussaint to Tupelo. After the South lost the battle of Missionary Ridge and Georgia lay open to Sherman, I could see he was making preparations to decamp. That's probably when he had papers drawn up deeding Devereux Hall to me. In his telegram he told me where to find them. But if the Union forces had failed to reach here, he would have just torn them up."

"Sounds about right."

Fraser had taken a bottle of champagne from an ice bucket, uncorked it, and filled their glasses.

"So you don't intend to return Devereux Hall to Auguste when the war is over?"

"Of course not. I'm as much a Devereux as he. He made his choice and he'll have to live with it. He would have done exactly the same to me. It's not as if he will be destitute. I'm sure he has money put away somewhere."

Susannah and Joel exchanged glances. "You need have no doubts on that score. Tell me, do you intend to live here—if the house survives?"

"Probably for a season each year, but certainly not all the time. That would be a deadly bore. No, I'll go back to Washington."

"And Senator John Coffee?"

"Oh, yes."

"I thought you and he . . ."

"Had fallen out of love? Oh, come now, Joel. There was never any of that. I'm not exactly a romantic. He married me for money, and I married him for position and protection from father's constant meddling in my life. However, when I return to Washington I'll bring Devereux Hall and three thousand acres, and I mean to set some rules of public behavior for John as the price of a reconciliation."

Susannah was astonished by this exchange. She was unused to such frankness, even between brother and sister. Apparently the Devereux were a law unto themselves, doing and saying what they pleased. The conversation on family matters continued through supper, but Susannah noted that Joel managed to evade questions about his plans for the future.

"About time for bed, Selena. You'd better get your sleep if

you're going to outfox the Yankees tomorrow."

When they left the supper room Joel said, "I think I'll go out and smoke a cheroot. I'll be up shortly."

Susannah and Selena went up the stairs together. At the top of the stairs Selena paused and studied Susannah.

"You are delectable, you know. I rather envy Joel," and she kissed Susannah fully on the mouth.

Susannah was so taken aback that she gasped, unsure of the significance of what had just taken place. The ambiguous look on Selena's face did nothing to clarify matters.

"Good night," Selena said and continued toward her room.

While the three of them were eating breakfast the next morning, the long silence was finally broken. There was a rumbling in the distance that could only be the hooves of many horses. They got up from the table and went out on the piazza. The rumble grew ever louder, until out of the woods, down the road, across the fields, came a host of blue-coated cavalry, a rider up front holding regimental colors aloft. The ground shook with the pounding of hooves.

"A thousand cavalrymen at least," Joel said. "Robert Henderson won't need to worry anymore about the cotton crop. It will be trampled. Your observations, Selena?"

"Horses well-fed, rested. What can Joe Johnston put up against them? Not much, I imagine."

Again Susannah was surprised at this kind of judgment being made on a movement of military forces that left her stunned by its suddenness and frightened by its awesome power. Apparently the Devereux viewed things with a cool detachment. The galloping cavalry slowed down, began to form into orderly lines, and then moved forward again.

"The cavalry will be on the flanks of the main force," Joel

said, "so you may not see any Yankee generals after all."

A small detachment of mounted men cantered down the road, and Joel trained his glass on them.

"However, there are your generals, Selena. All rehearsed?"

The clustered group of horsemen drew up at the entrance to the drive to Devereux Hall. A rider galloped forward until he was at the foot of the steps. Without dismounting, the Union officer addressed Joel.

"This is Devereux Hall?"

"Yes, it is, Major."

"You are Mr. Joel Devereux?"

"Yes, I am."

"General Sherman would like to know if it would be appropriate for him and his staff to rest here for a few hours."

"You'll have to ask the owner, Major," and Joel indicated Selena, "Mrs. John Coffee. The name may be known to your commander."

"Ma'am?"

"It would be appropriate for General Sherman to take rest here."

"Thank you, ma'am." The officer galloped away.

"A bit more than you bargained for, Selena?" Joel said.

"Actually, nothing could be better."

The Union horsemen, generals, colonels, and aides, drew up in front of Devereux Hall. A man in general's uniform got down from his horse, removed his hat, and mounted the stairs. He was of medium height, his dark red hair and beard short and unkempt, his face deeply furrowed and burned by the sun.

"Mrs. Coffee?"

"Yes."

"Your husband and my brother are old colleagues, I believe."

"I have met Senator Sherman on many occasions. Please do come inside, and let me order some refreshments for you and your staff."

"Most welcome, ma'am."

"This is my brother, Joel Devereux . . ."

"Well recommended by my old friend William Devereux."

" . . . and his fiancée, Miss Susannah Goode."

"A pleasure, ma'am."

General Sherman stopped in the doorway as his blue-clad staff trooped up the steps. "Gentlemen, please remove your spurs. I would not want to see these beautiful mahogany floors damaged."

Selena showed them into the dining room, and soon Fraser and his helpers were putting out on the long table bottles of whiskey, various brandies and liqueurs, pitchers of water and tea, glasses, even a large bowl of ice, on this hot July day. Fraser was as phlegmatic as if his liberators had worn gray rather than blue. Maids arrived with trays of hot biscuits and ham and blackberry and quince jelly. An aide rolled out a large map on the table and secured its corners with pieces of silver taken from the sideboard.

Selena, Joel, and Susannah withdrew to the piazza, but the windows were open and they had no difficulty hearing what was being said inside. Fraser served them iced tea, and Selena took out a fan. Inside, General Sherman lit a cigar.

"Here is my plan, and if you see flaws in it, do not fail to speak up. Generals Schofield and Thomas are to begin marching the Armies of the Ohio and Cumberland along this road to Atlanta, keeping abreast. General McPherson will take the Army of Tennessee, as he did in crossing the Chattahoochee, and swing wide to the north and cut the Augusta railroad at the town of Decatur.

"We have had enough experience with the rebels quickly

151

repairing rail lines. If enemy forces can be held off with comparative ease, then McPherson's men will take the time to render this impossible. Using the method our engineers have developed, the cross ties will be taken up and used to make fires to heat the rails until they are red hot and can be wrapped around trees. Then there's no way on God's Earth that they will ever be used again."

While General Sherman was speaking, a wagon pulled by two mules came up the drive, paying out copper wire as it came. The wagon stopped beneath the oak tree where they had had lunch. The men with the wagon took down a desk with pigeonholes, a large battery, and various other pieces of electrical equipment. Within minutes one of the men was operating a telegraph key. Within a few minutes more one of the men came up the steps with a piece of paper and entered the dining room. General Sherman read the telegram.

"We have intercepted a message from Jeff Davis to Joe Johnston. He is being relieved of his command for failing to hold us at the Chattahoochee and is being replaced by General John Bell Hood."

There was a murmur of excited comments from the men in the room.

"Mac, you must have been at West Point at the same time as Hood."

"I was."

"What's he like?"

"Not much going on upstairs. He's no thinker, but you can count on him to act, to the point of rashness. If it's a fight you want, you'll get one from John Bell Hood."

"Then Jeff Davis may have done us a favor. As you know, I'm very parsimonious with the lives of my men, but we are at a point where one pitched battle just might yield us Atlanta. I have no intention of trying to take the city by storm. The defenses are far too strong. But if we can get the enemy holed up in Atlanta, we may be able to cut all of the rail lines into the city. Sixty thousand men can't be sustained for more than a few days without resupply by rail."

The meeting continued, but the attention of the three on the piazza was interrupted by a rider galloping up the drive. A Union officer halted at the steps and dismounted.

"Where may I find General Sherman?"

"Just inside, in the dining room."

The officer hurried in and returned in a few minutes with Sherman.

"Mrs. Coffee, I am faced with a painful dilemma. One of my regiments has occupied the textile plants in the town of Devereux. Are these also your property?"

"I can show you the deed."

"That will not be necessary. I take your word for it. The problem is that all of the cloth being readied for shipment is uniform material and has the letters C.S.A., Confederate States of America, woven into it."

"I do not doubt it."

"I have standing orders to destroy all factories producing war materiel for the rebel cause, which those textile plants are unquestionably doing."

"Then burn them. I have no intention of entering the textile business after the war."

"I shall so report in a personal message to President Lincoln, and he will be most gratified by your patriotism. Shall I also send a message from you to Senator Coffee?"

"No, let him hear from the President that I am well and doing my patriotic duty."

"I will certainly ask the President to do that."

Sherman took a scrap of paper from his jacket, held it up against a column, and wrote a few words on it. He handed the paper to the officer, who saluted, remounted his horse, and galloped away.

Sherman approached them again. "Mrs. Coffee, may I ask one additional favor of you? If you could provide beds for my senior officers, I would like them to rest before we set out. I expect the Confederates to turn and fight at any hour."

"I'll have beds prepared."

"You wouldn't have as many as twelve beds, would you?"

"More, if you need them."

"General, may I ask a favor of you?" Joel said. "My fiancée and I must get to Catesville, which is in Confederate-held territory. It is a matter of great urgency. Would it be possible for you to provide me with some kind of pass?"

"I'm afraid a pass won't be of much use once the shooting starts. But if you need to reach Catesville is so great that you are willing to take the risk, I can allow you to travel with General McPherson's army into rebel-held territory."

"I'll have to discuss it with my fiancée."

"Very well. Let my aide know what you decide."

When Sherman had gone back into the meeting, Joel turned to Susannah.

"I saw an opportunity and took it. There was no chance to warn you."

"It's Elam Scroggins, isn't it?"

"Yes."

"If by going back to Catesville you can prevent his hanging, of course I will go with you. I won't have his death on either your conscience or mine."

"I won't ask what this is all about," Selena said. "I've got enough to cope with as it is. Now I'd better see about having beds prepared for the generals."

While Selena was gone, Susannah and Joel discussed what they would need to do to be ready to leave on short notice and then returned to eavesdropping on the council of war inside.

Selena came out on the piazza again and sank heavily into a chair.

"This has to be the most eventful day of my life."

"And it isn't over yet," Joel said. "Look."

In the direction of Devereux a column of black smoke rose into the sky. But for the extreme good fortune of Selena Coffee and General Sherman arriving simultaneously, smoke would be rising at this moment from Devereux Hall. That column of smoke reminded Susannah forcefully that in agreeing to travel with General McPherson, they would in the coming hours be entering a world of unchecked violence and death. Now, for the first time, she was truly afraid.

III

The Coming of the Night

13

By the time the Union generals and colonels and their aides had had their rest, a number of telegrams had arrived and several couriers waited on the piazza for replies to messages they carried. These were dealt with one by one, as General Sherman and his staff partook, standing, of a cold lunch Selena had ordered laid out for them on the sideboard in the dining room. Joel and Susannah joined them, and Joel noted the many admiring glances in the direction of Susannah, in boots and breeches and one of Joel's collarless riding shirts. She had braided her dark hair, exposing the graceful curve of her neck.

Then one by one the officers, their faces tense, put down their plates on the dining room table and filed out, picked up their hats from the long table in the entryway, and went out to where their horses were waiting at the foot of the piazza steps. The most crucial, and perhaps most bloody, phase of the Atlanta campaign was about to begin.

While Sherman and the other senior generals made their farewells to Selena, Joel approached Fraser, who was standing in attendance.

"Well, Fraser, did you ever think you would see a day like this?"

"No sir, I sure didn't. I kept waiting for one of those Yankee generals to tell me I was free, but nary a word."

"They've probably got other things on their minds right now."

"That may be, but they didn't leave no tips neither."

As the generals started down the stairs, Joel walked over to Selena.

"You saved the house, sure enough, and were even the perfect hostess. How're you going to explain that to the neighbors?"

"They will be given to understand that it was done under duress."

"But in Washington you will be considered a heroine for so graciously acquiescing in the burning of the Devereux mills."

Selena smiled. "Which should be helpful in keeping John Coffee on a short leash."

"Well, I'll be off now."

"Don't get yourself killed, Joel. You're the only member of the family I could ever abide."

He laughed. For Selena that bordered on the sentimental.

"I'll do my best."

Susannah approached brother and sister.

"Thank you for your hospitality," she said to Selena.

"My pleasure. You should really dress as a boy more often, Susannah. It becomes you."

Joel and Susannah went down the steps, mounted their horses and galloped forward to catch up with the party of Union officers, who were already down the drive, their horses at a trot. They rode together, thirteen men and a woman, to the crossroads, where the cavalry units protecting them waited. Most of the party took the road to Atlanta, while General McPherson, an aide, and Joel and Susannah took the road north to Devereux.

Some of the mills were already burned out, others were

still in flames. There were five in all, two cotton mills, a woolen mill, a flour mill, and a paper mill. Joel had apprenticed at them all, to learn the trades, before his father had concluded that his son's views made him unfit to be his successor. Then he had sent Joel up north to Princeton to get him out of sight and mind for a while.

Near Jenkins' livery stable, hundreds of women were gathered, their clothes cheap and dirty, and some were even barefoot. They were ringed by twenty or more Union troopers on horseback. He recognized some of the women. These were the mill workers, who ran the looms and other machinery. They were preferred to men because they could be hired more cheaply. Some had been taken off the streets of London and Liverpool. He had heard their stories, and improving their situation had been one of the first points of conflict between him and his father. Now, of course, the hands at the mills were almost exclusively female, the men of the county all off at war.

One of the women stepped out from the crowd, raised a fist to Joel. She was still young but worn down by work and visibly pregnant. She had the pallor of workers who passed all their daylight hours at the looms, and the blackheads around her nose and eyes of women who seldom if ever bathed.

"So, mister high and mighty, you now know what it's like to be a slave. I'm glad that at least one of the Devereux will be made to pay."

Joel searched for words but could find none. She thought he was a prisoner of Sherman's army, as well he might have been but for his Uncle Willy.

"You thought you tricked us, while you was working alongside us, by pretending to be our friend, but we all knew you was but a spy for your father, trying to find out what we was thinking, so you could keep us in our place."

"That's not true," Joel began, but boos and hisses from the women drowned his voice.

"I would like to help," he said.

"Well, ain't that nice," the woman shot back. "Maybe you could give us some of that scrip we got paid in, in place of real money, scrip that only could buy food and things at your company's store. Well, God bless the Yankees who burned down your store."

The women raised a cheer. There was nothing he could do to help them. He turned his horse and brought it alongside the fine mare of General McPherson, a tall, handsome man with a beard as luxuriant as Sherman's was scraggly.

"What's going on here, General?"

"The mill workers were brought together here to keep them from injury while we burnt the mills."

"And what will happen to them now?"

"I doubt that much thought has been given to that."

"This is barbarous. These women were doing nothing more than trying to keep bread in their children's mouths. You will just leave them like this, standing in the road, poorly clothed and unfed? They will starve."

"If you think this is harsh, imagine what would have been the punishment that would have been meted out to the owner of these mills."

"By now my father is well on his way to Savannah."

"And we may pay him a visit there before it's all over. This is war, Mr. Devereux. If more people of your class, like you and your uncle, had taken up the Unionist cause, we might not have come to this pass."

"My Uncle William is certainly a Unionist. I am not. I love this land and its way of life. My sole quarrel with my family and my class is that I will not compromise in my belief that one man may not own another man."

"As I said, Mr. Devereux, it's too bad that more members of your class did not recognize that this is at the heart of this conflict that has torn a nation apart. In any case, I am directed by General Sherman to see you safely into rebel-held territory. You and your fiancée cannot ride with my army, which may soon be engaged in battle. I propose to send my aide here, Lieutenant Bancroft, to ride with you a mile or so to the left flank of the army, accompanied by two experienced men. In the event of trouble, they should be able to see you out of it. If not, they can call up additional force."

Joel reined in his horse until he was alongside Susannah, who had been riding just behind them.

"Did you hear that?"

"I did. These women are being treated like this just because they worked for your father? It's worse than barbarous. And Sherman seemed such a courteous and proper man."

"Perhaps none of these women is married to a confidant of President Lincoln."

There was a vast army bivouacked in the pine woods beyond the Sidley mansion. Joel had meant to stop there to inform the Sidleys of the fate of their daughters. As he was swept along with an advancing army, this was clearly now impractical. The Sidleys would have to learn about their wayward girls another way.

In a ring of tents where General McPherson's senior officers awaited him, Joel and Susannah were no longer of interest to anyone but Lieutenant Bancroft. He left them for a quarter-hour and returned with two grizzled troopers with carbines slung over their shoulders.

"Sergeant Morris, Sergeant Palmer," was the lieutenant's perfunctory introduction. He was clearly incensed that he was being taken out of the action to serve as nursemaid to two civilians.

"I feel a lot less anxious with those two old sergeants along than with just that young lieutenant," Susannah said in a whisper.

Four men and a woman mounted their horses and rode away from the Army of the Tennessee. They were soon several hundred feet above the assembling army, riding along a ridge that separated two long valleys. In the distance a train was puffing along the Atlanta-to-Augusta railroad, those aboard oblivious of what was about to descend on them.

On the horizon a granite mass glowed in the afternoon sun, as smooth and rounded as a cabochon jewel to be set in a ring.

"Stone Mountain," Joel said. "After Elam Scroggins and I jumped from the train on that railroad you see below, we saw Stone Mountain at twilight the second night out. He thought it was the moon rising and couldn't understand why it didn't move."

"Conscience aside," Susannah said, "isn't it madness to go back to Catesville to try and save the life of this mountain man you have known only a few days, and with no way of knowing how it might be done?"

"Yes, but it is the honorable thing to do, and there's the conundrum. Were it not for this sense of honor that eats away at the soul of the South and has become so entwined with the issue of slavery that the two cannot be separated, this awful conflict could have been avoided. Yet I appeal to honor as the reason I must try to save Elam. Why?"

"Because you are an honorable man."

They looked at each other, riding abreast, and Joel thought, *How fortunate I am to have my fate linked to that of this woman who has a sense of honor of her own, who has said she will*

164

never leave me, will never fail me. How fortunate.

As the sun began sinking behind them, casting the shadows of five horses and riders down the trail ahead, the Army of the Tennessee emerged from the wooded land into open fields. Several columns of infantry, regimental flags fluttering in the breeze, were flanked by cavalry, artillery pieces and their caissons, supply wagons bringing up the rear, all the apparatus of war. Night came and this vast array was transformed into an archipelago of campfires.

"I've felt like a gypsy," Joel said to Susannah as they looked down on the spectacle below, "ever since I left Savannah, wandering back roads, living off the land, avoiding the forces of the established order that I once was part of. We are like gypsies in medieval times, watching the armies of crusaders move back and forth across the land, fighting for a cause. The South's cause is lost, but we will fight on in the name of honor."

They made their own fire, and Joel brought out sugar-cured ham and biscuits, pickled green tomatoes and okra, and other things that Fraser had packed for them. He passed around a bottle of old cognac that Fraser had brought up from the cellar of Devereux Hall.

"I must allow," one of the sergeants said, "that this is about the smoothest whiskey I ever tasted."

"Old cognac," Lieutenant Bancroft said. "You people lived well."

"Yes," Joel said, "we lived well. Where're you from, Lieutenant?"

"Ohio."

"General Sherman's state."

"That's right, and I'm a West Pointer, too."

"What made you attend West Point?"

"My father knew a congressman who said he could get me

an appointment. My dad thought it would be good for the family's standing. Trouble was, the army, before the war, was small and promotions hard to come by. You could enter as a lieutenant and retire after thirty years as nothing more than a captain. Both General Sherman and General Grant found this out, so they left the military for a time. I was about to do the same when the war came along, and everything changed. I thought if I could be at the right place at the right time, I just might be a colonel in a year or two. I wouldn't call where I am now the right place and time."

From below a band struck up a sentimental tune. Shouted commands were followed by a silence punctuated during the night only by the challenges of pickets on the edges of the sleeping army. Before dawn, however, the activity had begun again. By the time it was light, couriers were riding into the camp one after another.

"Palmer," the lieutenant said, "get down there and find out what's going on."

"Yes, sir. Something is for sure."

A half-hour later Sergeant Palmer galloped back up the hillside.

"C Corps has done taken the railroad and is tearing it up. They said the few rebel troops that was around was chased off like you would flies with a fly switch."

"So, you haven't missed any action after all, Lieutenant," Joel said.

The lieutenant only gave him a sour look.

They were saddling their horses when there was a great commotion below. Soldiers were grabbing their guns, officers were mounting their horses. From the edge of the woods beyond the encampment came ragged, then steady gunfire. A solid wall of gray-clad soldiers emerged, bayonets gleaming in the early light, flags flying.

"What the hell!" the lieutenant cried. "They must have marched all night from Atlanta."

He put on his sword belt, drew his sword. To the left of the Confederate line another mass of men in gray emerged from the trees. The lieutenant slashed with his sword, cutting down a stand of pokeberry and Joe Pye weed. A third line of Confederate troops appeared at the far left.

"It must be a whole army."

Then the three masses merged into one and began to move forward, and as they did the blood-curdling rebel yell rang out.

"Well, that's it. I'm not staying up here watching. Come on, men, let's go!"

The Union officer and the two sergeants mounted their horses and rode off at a gallop, without a word to Joel and Susannah or even a backward glance. Halfway down the slope a shot rang out, and Lieutenant Bancroft flew out of his saddle as if plucked by a giant invisible hand. The two sergeants, close behind, gave their officer only a passing glance as they veered away from the battle below.

"The poor man," Susannah said softly.

"The poor fool."

Union troops had begun to take defensive positions. A field had recently been cleared, and blue-coated men knelt behind stumps and fallen trunks. Some took shelter in a large brick farmhouse and began firing from the windows. Others fired from behind upended farm wagons. Confederates began to fall, but the long gray line moved forward like a wave rolling up on a shore.

As Joel and Susannah watched in fascinated horror, a Union cavalry detachment attacked the Confederate flank, raking the lines of men with carbine fire. Cannon had been brought out, and canister was fired point-blank, opening ragged holes in the Confederate line. But still the line moved forward until the two sides were fighting hand-to-hand. A pall of smoke began to form over the whole hellish scene.

"Joel, what are we going to do?" Susannah said in a voice that cracked.

"Stay put for now. Who knows what other Confederate forces may be out there."

He looked down the valley to the other side of the ridge, but there was no sign of activity. Perhaps the Confederates had put everything they had into this one charge, which had the Union forces in retreat. The ground that they gave up was strewn with Union dead. A dozen separate battles now raged across the valley floor. Mounted messengers rode up and down newly formed lines, carrying orders. General McPherson had to be evolving some tactic to halt the Confederate advance, but in the confused scene below it was impossible to know what that might be.

"So this is war," Susannah said. She was crying.

Joel put his arm around her. There was nothing he could say to console her over the horror she was witnessing.

"This is war."

From out of nowhere a large mass of Union soldiers struck the Confederate left flank with rifle fire and then bayonets, as the two forces clashed together. The screams of the wounded and dying could be heard each time there was a pause in the firing. The Confederate advance had been at least temporarily halted, but in places the dead were piled two and three deep.

There was another attack on the Confederate right flank, while Union cavalry struck here and there. Joel looked at his watch. It seemed that only a few minutes had passed, but to his astonishment the battle had been raging for nearly three hours. He went to his saddlebags and cut off some pieces of ham and put them on dried biscuits. They ate and drank from the bottle of cognac, while they watched John Bell Hood's last desperate gamble to save Atlanta fail. An hour more and the Confederates had been driven back almost to the woods from which they had emerged.

Then the bugles began to sound, and the Confederates abandoned the field of battle. There was no attempt to pursue them by the exhausted and battered Army of the Tennessee. But if the Union losses had been large, Confederate casualties must have run into the thousands. The valley floor was carpeted with their dead.

"Oh, how I wish I had not seen it," Susannah said. "I will have nightmares for the rest of my life. Those poor men."

"And for every one lying there, there is now a new widow and children without a father, parents without a son. 'We'll lick those Yankees in three months,' my friends said. They talked a lot about the glory of war. Well, there you see it."

14

They had been forgotten in the slaughter and its aftermath. The Army of the Tennessee was gathering up its wounded, preparing to reverse its direction of march and rejoin the main body of the Northern forces. They were being left alone with the dead in what had been Confederate territory but now was no-man's-land. Already the vultures were beginning to circle, the sinking sun casting their fleeting shadows over the battlefield.

"Let's get away from here," Susannah said. "I can't bear this sight any longer. I just want to be alone with you and pretend this never happened."

"But where are we going?" Joel replied. "To save the life of one Confederate deserter—if that is even possible—while thousands of his comrades lie dead on the field below? It is almost ludicrous."

"Perhaps it is even more worth doing now. To put one life in the balance against all these deaths is better than nothing at all."

She knew that he was as shaken as she, and she did not want what they had seen to cause him to lose his idealism, to become cynical like the honorable men who had brought this war on them.

"In any case, we must move in the opposite direction from the battle line. But I don't even know exactly where we are.

We do know that the Atlanta-Augusta railroad line is beyond that next ridge. No trains will be running now, and we could follow the line toward Augusta. We might even find food at one of the stations along the way."

"Then let's go quickly," she said.

As they rode through woods and fields toward the railroad, the sun set in a blood-red sky, a fitting ending for this day. Luckily they reached the railroad before it was dark. A train stood on the track, undamaged by the fighting but abandoned by passengers and crew. Excess baggage and clothes were strewn along the track where the fleeing owners had dropped them. They too were headed in the direction of Augusta, on foot.

"We should catch up with them soon if they stay on the track. I wouldn't mind a little nonbelligerent company. There'll be precious little law and order hereabouts now."

Oddly, Susannah welcomed this thought. Better something to fear in the future than to dwell on what they had seen. There was enough moonlight for them to easily follow the track through a deserted landscape, and they moved along at a good pace. In a large open field ahead they saw several fires burning.

"Must be the people from the train, camping out for the night."

They slowed their horses to a walk and cautiously approached the fires. A number of people were gathered in a cluster. A half-dozen red wagons were lined up in a kind of protective circle. Then she saw it.

A woman was standing with her back to a large tree, her arms to her sides. Ten paces in front of her a man stood, a large knife in one hand. He drew back his arm, and the knife gleamed in the firelight as it sped through the air, lodging in the tree trunk not two inches from the woman's face. What the crowd was watching was a woman being put to death.

Susannah was unable to suppress a scream, but Joel reached over and clapped his hand upon her mouth. With the other hand he pointed at one of the red wagons, on which was painted in large, curving letters: "Locatelli Bros. Circus." It was only an act. A second knife struck the tree near the woman's other cheek. There was a burst of applause.

"Just in time for the show," a mulatto with a curling waxed mustache said, with a touch of Creole accent. "Who are you?"

"Just two travelers trying to escape the fighting."

The man eyed Susannah.

"I thought it prudent to dress my wife in men's clothes."

"Indeed," the man said. "This morning someone rode up to the train we were traveling on and told us the track was being torn up behind us, and our train might soon be attacked. Naturally, we distanced ourselves from it. All day we heard cannon and musket fire. Do you know what's going on?"

"There's been a big battle. The Confederates were badly beaten."

"That's fine with me."

"The Union army is probably now headed back in the direction of Atlanta."

"That's also fine with me."

"Who are you?" Joel said.

"Slaughter McCain is my name. Inappropriate a name as it is for a barber, it is the one I was born with. I am leading a party of free Negroes to the Land of Goshen."

"Land of Goshen?"

"It is a valley in the North Carolina mountains, entirely owned by free Negroes. We plan to seek refuge there until the fighting is over. While our sympathies are, of course, with

Lincoln's army, General Sherman can't free us, for we are already free. But he can kill us. He is beginning to rain down shells on Atlanta, and it would be entirely too ironic to be killed by the army of emancipation."

"And the circus?"

"We found them camped in this field. They were fleeing Atlanta for safer parts. The circus owners decided it wasn't worth the game and abandoned the performers and the animals. The local people shot the animals, and the performers have no money with which to buy food. The good Lord must be watching over us. They have transport and we have money. We quickly struck a bargain."

"May we join you?"

"Do you carry side arms?"

"We do."

"What we are short of is weapons. If you are prepared to help us defend ourselves, if need be, we can strike another bargain."

Joel looked at Susannah.

"Of course," she said. It was the most bizarre story she had ever heard.

There were six of them around the dying fire: a Negro man with ebony skin, a colored woman with skin like polished maple wood, an Italian couple with dark hair and eyes, and Joel and Susannah. Divided by oceans of race and culture, what could they possibly have to say to each other? Joel began.

"What role do you perform in the circus?"

"Did perform," the Italian man said. "Clowns."

"Actors then. It is a long and honorable tradition, dating back hundreds of years in Italy."

"You have been in Italy?"

"Yes."

"More than hundreds of years," the dark-eyed Italian woman said. "The tradition is that we were first performers in the Roman arenas, and when Rome fell we took to the roads, jugglers, rope walkers, knife throwers, bear trainers, clowns, and we wandered all over the earth until the circus was born again. I do not know whether this is true."

"It is true," the Italian man said. "My name is Toto, and there was such a name for comedians, they say, back in the ancient days."

"Your family name?"

"Family name? Actors and circus performers have no family names. To have a family name is to be part of the church, and we are always and for all time excommunicate. When we die we have no hallowed ground because, they say, we have no souls."

"Then you are like slaves," said the Negro man, who had been listening intently. "When the slave dies he is buried in a place apart, with no name on his gravestone. If he has a family, the white man won't recognize it. You can't go to heaven if you ain't baptized, they say, and they wouldn't let us be baptized. But that's all going to change now."

"There's others who don't have no last names," the colored woman said. "Whores don't. If you have one, you leave it at the whorehouse door. And don't expect no decent burial neither."

"Worse than that where I come from," the Italian woman said. "In my village when a prostitute died, according to my grandfather, the man who collected trash would come get the body, unclothed, and tie a rope to the feet, and drag it behind his horse to the trash heap."

"What do you live for, then, when you are treated like trash?" Susannah said. Something was stirring within her that she did not understand.

174

"You work at your trade as best you can for as long as you have life," the Italian man named Toto said.

"Yes," the Negro man said, "that's all you can do, but sometimes it leads somewhere, and in this land, North or South, we don't throw nobody's corpse on the trash heap. I was trained as a cabinet-maker, worked for a powerful rich family that could afford their own cabinet-maker. I got to be real good at my trade, so good that they let me do cabinet work for the other planters in my free time, and I saved up enough money to buy my freedom, set up shop in Atlanta and made enough more to buy my wife's."

"Since we are confessioning, I'm going to have to tell you that all you say is true," the colored woman said. "If you ain't born to money and have no respect from the gentry, then you have to make your way by being good at your trade. You may not think that whoring is like acting or making cabinets, but there's as many little things you have to get right as there are, I suppose, ways of making wood joints. I earned my freedom by knowing exactly what men wanted. You have to know how men feel about color, too. There are four degrees of how much Negro blood you have in your veins, and men want to know which degree you are, oftentimes."

"In fact," Susannah said, "there are eight degrees—at least in New Orleans," and she proceeded to enumerate the eight degrees in Creole parlance. *"Mulatto, quadroon, octoroon, mustee, mustefino, griffe, sacatra,* and *marabou."*

When Susannah awoke, the sun was already above the horizon, and a ribbon of mist hung over the stream that ran alongside the field in which they had camped. Everyone else still slept, including Joel by her side. Fear had given way to exhaustion, and they had all sunk—certainly she had—into the depths of sleep, where war and its horrors were only troubled dreams.

Slowly, one by one, the sleepers in the grass, lying scattered like fallen on the field of battle, arose, stretched, and began the routines of the day that they now must face. Slaughter McCain was everywhere, exhorting his charges to take heart, return to the road for the Land of Goshen, where they would be safe. The ladies were encouraged to take advantage of the nearness of a wide stream to bathe before returning to the dust of the road.

Susannah joined a dozen other women in disrobing and descending, behind a thicket of river birches, into the cool water, passing bars of soap from one to the other. The eight degrees of color that she had enumerated the night before, to the astonishment of those in the circle around the fire, seemed all exhibited here. For the first time in her life she realized that her white skin was part of this spectrum, just one more shade that a body might display. Yet it made all the difference in the world which shade you were born with, and there was nothing you could do about it.

Once the women had dressed, some of the men, including Joel, bathed. Afterwards he took their horses to the stream, washed them down and examined their hooves. Then she helped him groom their coats with curry combs. As they were currying the horses' legs, Joel felt the muscles.

"Their cannons are sensitive. That means they are sore, and pretty soon, unless they get some rest, one or both of our mounts could start to go lame. What we should do is hitch them to one of the wagons, without harness or rider, and just let them walk along behind, for at least today."

Joel went away and spoke with one of the circus people, and soon they were side by side on the high driver's seat of a circus wagon.

"Our worth to our companions went up considerably when they found out I could drive a four-in-hand. Not many people can."

Joel cracked a whip, and the four white draft horses hitched to the circus wagon moved forward. Susannah was fascinated with the effortless way in which he managed the four sets of reins he held in his large, strong hands, the touch of which, she recalled with a shiver, her body knew so well.

Their wagon was loaded with free Negroes, some inside, some sitting on top. There was enough space alongside the now deserted railroad track for the wagons to move in single file, and they made good time. Soon their passengers began to sing hymns. If you didn't know, Susannah thought, what lay behind this exodus, you would have imagined it was some kind of holiday outing.

"Last night you rattled off the degrees of color, which startled me—and everyone else," Joel suddenly said. "Why?"

"I don't know. It just came out. Maybe, I think, I wanted to show myself part of their world, that I spoke their language. I was really struck by the fact, which I had never considered, that performers, slaves, and whores all have no last names, and that marks them as being outside respectable society. They only exist to serve respectable society. I, of course, learned the degrees of color—the Creole French are very precise about such matters—at my mother's establishment. I learned many other things that a twelve-year-old should not know. I never had an age of innocence."

"That is sad. I hope I can help make up for it."

"You already have by not letting my past make any difference. I thought that when you found out, I might lose you. Your father was right, of course, that I was a threat to the order of his society, one of those with no last name that must be kept out. I don't even know my father's name, and probably my mother doesn't either."

They rode on in silence. She would have very much liked to know exactly what he was thinking. As the old order unraveled, she supposed that most people were rethinking what the peculiar society that they had created in the South was really about.

They came abreast of about a dozen Confederate soldiers, ragged and without their weapons, walking the rails away from Atlanta.

"Would you men like some food?" Slaughter McCain called down from the wagon ahead.

"I ain't taking no food from slaves," one of the soldiers shot back. "If it wasn't for you people, we wouldn't have had no war."

"Oh, shut your mouth, Yancey," another said. "We'll take your food, mister, and we thank you."

"By the way, we are not slaves," McCain said. "We are free Negroes."

"Where're you boys from?" Joel said.

"Mostly White, Rabun, and Cate counties. Yesterday there was nearly forty of us. You see what's left."

"Pretty bad fighting."

"The worst I ever seen, and I was at Missionary Ridge. We was whupped, that's all, though the generals and politicians will say we killed a lot of theirs, which is true enough. Even got their head man."

"Who's that?"

"General McPherson. He was riding up and down the lines giving orders, and he ran into two of our boys in a piney wood, and they told him to get up his hands. Instead he tried to ride off, and they shot him dead."

A basket was handed down containing the usual staples:

ham, corn bread and sweet potatoes, and the caravan moved on.

"Yesterday we were riding with McPherson," Joel said, "and today he's dead. If one thing has been proved, it is that war is no respecter of rank."

"Yes, look at your father, fleeing in a caravan no different in reality from ours. Tell me, Joel, how did this enmity between your father and you begin?"

"I think Uncle Willy was mainly responsible. He did not take the responsibilities of his class with sufficient gravity, showed his distaste for slavery. Wouldn't conform. Even when he and Auguste were young there was sufficient money for a young Devereux to indulge himself. He spent several years in Europe and returned with a French "housekeeper." He also returned with a precise knowledge of how one traded in cotton and other commodities on the European markets. So he became a very successful cotton broker, using other people's money to support the life he lived.

"He indulged me, I think even tried to corrupt me, in the sense that he lured me away from the plantation way of life. He mocked Southern honor and would certainly have been killed in a duel, had he not refused all challenges, content to be scorned as a coward. In short he was a thorn in the side of the planter class. He gave me gifts, the very things that would encourage my interest in nature—a fowling piece, a fly rod, and other things that could not be condemned as unmanly. But at the same time he gave me scientific instruments. It was he who arranged with Professor Arnold at Princeton for my entry into the faculty of science there."

"Yet in the end he betrayed you."

"What do you mean?" Joel said, turning toward her, speaking sharply.

"There, in the Gun Room at Devereux Hall, when he told

you that he was cashing in his winnings and going to Europe with his French mistress, you felt betrayed."

"Yes. How did you know?"

"Because from that moment on you never mentioned him again. He had led you down an inviting path toward freedom from all you despised, and then he wouldn't take that path himself."

"Yes."

"So now you are alone, feeling somewhat abandoned and betrayed."

"Except that now I have you, which trumps all the cards of all my family, damn them."

"I think this is immensely amusing," Susannah said and laughed.

"What is?"

"Our 'confessioning', as that colored prostitute said last night. Here we are telling our innermost secrets, the daughter of a brothel madame and the son of a *grand seigneur,* while riding a circus wagon."

"War has a highly developed sense of irony."

The circus wagons had, one by one, come to a halt. People were getting down and running forward, shouting unintelligible things.

"We had just as well satisfy our curiosity," Joel said.

They got down from the wagon and walked to where the entire company had gathered beside the lead wagon, on the edge of an abyss. The bridge across a gorge had been blown up. Aside from a few smoldering pieces of wood on each side of the chasm, the rest of the bridge lay in a heap far below, where a swift torrent ran through the timbers. The rails that had crossed the divide had been ripped apart, and the metal ends hung down, twisted like strands of taffy.

15

The trail came out of the woods at the rocky end of a ridge. It was not yet dawn and below, Catesville lay blanketed in ground fog. They had made it this far without incident, but the real danger to them might lie in this sleeping little town. It was with great reluctance that he had separated them from the protection of their traveling companions, but the circus caravan had turned south to find the Augusta road, and their destination was to the north.

They had headed their horses north along the stream that the bridge had spanned, and this turned out to be an old Cherokee trail. It had never been developed as a road, but was frequently enough used by drovers to keep it from returning to brush. This they had learned from a man driving a flock of geese to market in Catesville. They also passed drovers of cattle and pigs, but for the two days of their journey had not seen a single house.

"Well, here we are, about to begin our adventure. I feel like Don Quixote."

"Then I am Sancho Panza," Susannah said and laughed. "I am here to keep you from doing foolish things."

"This whole business is foolish, but like Don Quixote I am driven by a code of honor—one that I don't even believe in."

"As you said, Joel, war has a highly developed sense of irony. What do you propose to do?"

"Try to reach Amos Boggs before the town wakes up. He'll know what's going to happen to Elam, who's probably being held in the sheriff's jail."

They rode down off the ridge and followed the road into town. At the Cate Springs Hotel the only light came from the kitchen. At the town square there was a light in the telegraph office in George Malik's store and in Sheriff Boggs's room above the jail. They crossed the square and confronted a gallows from which the bodies of two young men hung. Neither was Elam Scroggins.

"Oh, my God," Susannah said in a low voice.

"They're desperate now, desperate enough to hang some deserters to stop the mountain boys from taking off for home. It's too late for that, but they won't have heard here about the battle outside Atlanta."

They tied their horses out of sight and mounted the creaking stairs to the sheriff's room. Amos Boggs stood at the top of the stairs in a flannel undershirt and red galluses, a pistol in one hand and a bulls-eye lantern in the other.

"Last people I expected to see. What you folks doing here?"

"We need to talk to you."

"Well, come on up and have some breakfast."

The room was furnished with three wooden chairs and a table, and a narrow bed in one corner. On a woodstove bacon was frying in a skillet.

"I'd like to offer you some real coffee, but there ain't none, and I can't abide that stuff made from chicory and acorns and persimmon seeds. There's bacon and eggs, though. The Yankees can't blockade pigs and chickens. There's also biscuits and jam, courtesy of Jessie."

Amos Boggs paused, as though he had just remembered something. He looked at Joel.

"You've just got to Catesville?"

"Only a few minutes ago."

"Then you most probably don't know about your brothers."

"Know what?"

"One's dead, the other's run off, they say, for South America."

"Who's dead?"

"Junius. Kicked in the head by his horse."

"I'm sorry to hear that."

What else could he say? Junius had lived a life in which nothing had happened, always under the thumb of his father, Auguste. He had never married, so there would be no heirs to remember him. In a few years he would be forgotten. When the history of the family would be discussed, someone would say, "Wasn't there another brother?" And an old party would say, "Why yes, there was Junius." And when the old party died, it would be as if Junius had never lived.

"How did it happen?"

"They wouldn't come into town for fear they would be snatched up and put in gray uniforms. I told them the Black Band might swoop down on them, knowing that your father was rich, and there might be some loot to be had in Cherokee Rose, and then the Band did descend on us. Your brothers got a little warning. They went to get on their horses, and when Lamar rode into town, he said that Junius had been injured, he thought, and someone might ought to go out and see about it.

"I sent Dorsey out, and what he found was that your brother was cold stone dead in the stable. Dorsey figured that what happened was that Junius had got so excited that while he was getting down his saddle, hung up behind his horse, he forgot to pay attention to the way horses do, and his horse kicked back and hit him square in the head, done him in."

"What about Lamar?"

"You'd better talk to George Malik about that, but as I understand it, Lamar rode on down to Traveler's Rest, where he took a boat to Savannah, having quite a bit of gold on his person. He was headed for Florida, and from there he planned to sail for South America—he said—and never come back.

"The Black Band did come riding in, took all the silver they could lay their hands on at Cherokee Rose—and at the Mission too, Miss Goode—and got away fast, not doing much damage to either place, probably having heard there was regular Confederate troops about, not knowing that these were only a couple of dozen with a captain in charge."

"From the Provost Marshal's in Atlanta?"

"That's what was said, but I'm not sure. This captain said he wasn't having nothing to do with having boys hanged for desertion, wasn't why he was sent up to Catesville."

"Then why was he sent?"

"He didn't say. Well, enough of that. Why don't I fry those eggs so we can have some breakfast?"

As they were eating the sheriff said, "You wanted to talk to me about something."

"Elam Scroggins. Is he still alive?"

"Oh, yes. He's my guest downstairs."

"When's the trial?"

"It's going on now. What a dang fool thing to do, deserting with General Johnston's military codes. Colcock Stiles would have had him swinging from a rope by now, were it not for his lawyer. But he'll hang in the end, you can be sure."

"What's Colcock Stiles got to do with it?"

"Well, when this captain said he wasn't having hangings on his conscience, the lieutenant under him, who was next in line for the honor, telegraphed Atlanta and got Judge Stiles sworn in as a military justice in the cases of these deserters. And Stiles ain't got nothing against hangings at all. Don't even blink an eye.

"But when people saw these two boys hanging out front of the jail, they wasn't very happy. So they went to old Ellsworth, who's pretty much quit lawyering, and asked him to come forward and offer to defend Sergeant Scroggins. Well, it turns out that Ellsworth was an army lawyer during the war with Mexico and knows military law inside out. He's got the judge tied in knots, and since there's spectators at the trial, Stiles has to be a little careful. But in the end Scroggins is going to hang, because that's what Atlanta wants."

"I'm going to try and stop it."

"Good luck to you, but why you?"

"If it weren't for me, Scroggins wouldn't have been handed over to the military police. Who can I trust here?"

"Me for one and George Malik for another. There's others you could trust, but none that could do you any good."

"Are they going to indict you for stealing the gold that disappeared?"

"They are."

"Why would Stiles want that?"

"There's a rumor that Stiles, and maybe Givens Crenshaw, are involved themselves in what happened."

"When do you expect to be indicted?"

"Right now they need me as a jailer, but as soon as the Scroggins case is disposed of, I reckon I'll be indicted the next day. The grand jury's in session. Judge Stiles may even deny me bond so they can put me in my own lockup, but I ain't planning on letting that happen. I guess I forgot to tell you that me and Jessie got married yesterday. I couldn't go to the courthouse for a license, of course, but the Congregationalist minister agreed to marry us anyway. As soon as there's a verdict in the Scroggins case, me and Jessie are riding out of Catesville."

"You may not have to do that. When you took a posse out and found the trunk from the bank, it was empty."

"Right."

"You know what was in that trunk? Nothing but rocks."

"Are you sure, Joel?"

"I am. The gold was stolen long ago, but recently Jeff Davis asked Governor Brown to turn over the gold to the Confederate treasury. Then it would have been discovered that the gold wasn't there. So the real robbers staged a fake robbery to cover up."

"Who are these real robbers?"

"My father, with some help from Lamar and Junius, who got a cut. I'm sure Stiles and Crenshaw were involved and probably got a cut as well. What do you think Joe Brown would do to them if he found out."

"I don't know, but I wouldn't want to be in their shoes."

"Exactly. When does Stiles arrive at the courthouse?"

"He's already there cooking things up. He wants this trial over with by tomorrow."

"Then I think I'll pay a call on him. I have a couple of favors to ask."

"Joel, no! Don't do it," Susannah cried out.

"It's the only way."

"Can you prove what you just told me?" Amos Boggs said.

"Junius and Lamar have confessed to me. Of course Junius is dead and Lamar is planning to leave for South America. Does Stiles know that Lamar is about to leave the country?"

"I wouldn't think so."

"You found out from George Malik, who got it from

reading telegrams that passed through his hands, didn't you?"

"Well, yes."

"And then there's Auguste Devereux. He hasn't admitted in so many words that he was behind the scheme, but if he feels threatened he will sacrifice Stiles in a second."

He turned to Susannah. "I'll be careful. There's no need to worry."

There was a pretty but sullen-looking young woman behind a desk in the outer office. He went past her toward the door to the judge's inner chambers.

"You can't go in there. The judge is . . ."

He didn't hear the rest as he went through the door and closed it softly behind him, throwing the bolt. It was several seconds before Judge Stiles, in close conference with Mayor Givens Crenshaw, looked up. He was already in his black judicial robes. With his high polished forehead and dark red beard, he reminded Joel of an ancient statue of a satyr he had seen in the Vatican museum. His small, cunning eyes only added to the impression.

"Why, Mr. Devereux, how good to see you," and without even the slightest pause, "and please accept my condolences on the death of your brother."

"I need to talk to you, Judge Stiles."

"It would be a pleasure, but as you can see I am about to hear a case, a serious one, a capital offense. So, if we may postpone . . ."

"No, I need to talk to you now."

"Did I hear you correctly, sir," Stiles said, drawing himself up magisterially.

"You heard me correctly. It's about the gold."

"The gold?"

Joel did not reply.

"Oh, you must mean the gold taken from your father's bank."

"Gold from my father's bank?"

"The gold from the U.S. mint that was put there for safe-keeping."

"Until very recently, I wasn't aware of any gold from the U.S. mint being stored there. Apparently you have been."

Too late, Stiles realized he had fallen into a trap. But he regained his composure in an instant.

"As chief magistrate of the county, it was necessary that I be informed."

"Very well. I am concerned with the gold's disappearance."

"I can tell you nothing there. Perhaps Sheriff Boggs can when he testifies before the grand jury."

"I'm not talking about that incident, which in any case involves only the taking of a trunk filled with rocks."

The judge winced but Crenshaw, whom Joel had been watching out of the corner of his eye, turned as white as the tropical suit he was wearing.

"I am baffled as to what you are driving at," Stiles said, speaking less assuredly than before.

"What I am driving at is that the gold was taken some time ago and that you are a party to the crime."

"That is a monstrous accusation, sir."

Stiles had risen from his chair with a great show of indignation.

"As you wish, but I am prepared to go to Governor Brown with my 'monstrous accusation.' "

"With what proofs, if I may ask, sir?"

"I have already discussed the matter with my late brother Junius, with Lamar, and with Auguste Devereux himself. I think you know my father well enough to realize he would sacrifice anyone to protect himself."

He waited for a reply, feeling somewhat like a commander of cavalry, sword drawn, ready to give the order to charge the weakest point in the enemy lines. He could almost have predicted what would happen next, and it did.

"How much do you want?" Givens Crenshaw said in a trembling voice.

"Want? From whom?"

"Leave this to me, Givens," the judge said. "But the question is well-enough posed. What do you want, Mr. Devereux, barging in here while we are in conference?"

"Nothing for myself. Only two favors for others."

The judge's eyes revealed nothing, but he did not break off the exchange.

"Go on."

"If there was no gold in that trunk, an indictment of Sheriff Boggs would be inappropriate."

"The second favor?"

"The case against Sergeant Scroggins, a capital one as you said, is out of all proportion to any offense he may have committed and should be dropped."

"May I ask," Stiles said in a sarcastic voice, "what interest a Devereux might have in the fate of this miserable mountain man?"

"Noblesse oblige, Your Honor. I would see justice done."

This statement of the obligations of aristocrats was like a slap across Colcock Stiles's face.

"I will take your requests under advisement, but may I remind you that you and your family have spent your shot."

"And may I remind you that not only might you, and your creature here, go to jail for an extended period or, for misappropriation of vital war resources, might even hang. Not to speak of what action the federal government will take when they inquire—after they win the war, as they surely will—as to

189

the whereabouts of the gold that was in the U.S. mint in Dahlonega."

Joel went to the door, threw back the bolt and passed into the outer office, where the young woman stared open-mouthed as he nodded to her and went down the courthouse stairs. His confronting a man as ruthless as Colcock Stiles was reckless to the extreme, but how else were Elam Scroggins and Amos Boggs to be saved? He had told Susannah that there was nothing to be worried about, knowing it might not be so, and now he knew it wasn't. *But, goddamn it,* he said to himself, *I am a Devereux despite myself, and honor must be served. Besides, I'm pretty sure I won.*

That evening Joel and Susannah dined at Cherokee Rose on what dishes the local market could provide, but at least with a bottle of fine wine from the Devereux stock. As he poured the last of the wine, looking forward to a night in Susannah's arms after too long an interval, there was an explosion, a pane of window glass flew to pieces, and a black hole appeared in the wall beside Joel's head.

He pinched out the candle flame between thumb and finger and shoved Susannah beneath the table.

"Stay there. Don't move."

In a few long strides he went to the bedroom, snatched up one of the two pistols that lay on the chest, dampened the oil lamp that burned on it, and in no more than ten seconds he was crouched beside Susannah.

Whoever had fired at them had not left. There was the creak of footsteps on the front porch, the creak of the door opening, and dim waves of light rippled down the walls. Whoever was in the next room had lit a lantern, and the light from it spilled through the dining-room door. A lean, tall man stood there, dark-haired, with several days of beard, his white shirt that of a gentleman. He held the lantern up, and his eyes swept the room. As he looked toward the far dark corner of the room, Joel stood up and fired his pistol. A red stain spread over the right shoulder of the white shirt, and the pistol the man was holding dropped from his hand.

The assassin turned and staggered through the door, still holding the lantern. There were cries outside and then the sound of the hooves of horses, two or three of them, fading away into the night.

As they sat on the floor in the dark, Joel said, "I should have known better. It never occurred to me that Judge Stiles would try to have me killed. But of course, I threatened his reputation, his wealth, even his life. With me dead he would have been safe."

"We have to get out of here."

"Yes, but not tonight, Susannah." He began to shake and had difficulty in speaking the logical words he had meant to speak. "Stiles will now have to do what I want, or at least hire a more capable assassin, more likely the former. But for tonight we are safer here than leaving. We can sleep in the slave quarters."

"Joel, my darling, are you all right?"

"It's just that I had never shot a man before tonight. Like Uncle Willy, I always managed to avoid duels."

16

They reined in their horses at the crest of the hill to look down into Nacoochee Valley, serene in the afternoon light. It was said to be the most beautiful valley in the North Georgia mountains, if not the entire Blue Ridge, and it was certainly the most beautiful Susannah had ever seen. With her were Jessie Finch and her son Johnny and Sheriff Boggs's deputy, Dorsey, who was along for their protection. It had not been an arduous ride from Catesville, and they were all still fresh.

Dorsey, a large, affable young man, was in a particularly good mood, whistling and humming. Amos Boggs had alerted Dorsey that he and Jessie were leaving Cate County for good. Whether the indictment against him was now quashed or not, he knew too much about what had happened to feel safe in the same county with Colcock Stiles. This meant almost certainly that Dorsey would replace him as sheriff, since nobody else in the county knew anything about law enforcing.

"This valley is sacred to the Cherokees," Dorsey said, "and the mountain too, Mount Yonah. Yonah means bear in the Cherokee language. You ladies can breathe easy now. We're in White County."

For Susannah it would have meant more than just breathing easy, it would have meant the end of all their troubles and dangers—if Joel were with her. But he and Amos had stayed behind to make sure that Judge Stiles released Elam Scroggins and dropped the charges against Amos. When Joel arrived in Nacoochee, and only then, could her real life at last begin.

"Where is this house we are going to?" Jessie said.

"You can't see it from here," Dorsey replied. "It's at the far end of the valley. It belongs to some rich doctor in Atlanta, and wouldn't you know that George Malik has some connection with him, so that we can stay there for a night or two."

They descended into the valley, a mosaic of pasture and cornfields and vegetable gardens. Along one side of the valley ran the Chattahoochee River, its banks lined with river birch and sycamore. Along the other side, the homes of farmers and the summer cottages of planters, these distinguished by their gingerbread decoration, were half hidden in the shade of oaks and black gum and red maple.

Last rose a two-story white house with a shingled roof, flanked by several large magnolias and outbuildings that would appear to be kitchen, washhouse, smokehouse and ice store. This was Dr. Robinson's summer place.

A middle-aged Negro man, tall and well built, stood on the piazza, his arms folded. He wore black trousers and a white shirt. They dismounted and tied their horses to a long hitching rail, which indicated that Dr. Robinson had many guests. The Negro came down the steps to meet them.

"Sheriff Dorsey?"

"That's right."

"Then you would be Mrs. Boggs and Miss Goode."

"That's right, too."

"I have received a telegram from Dr. Robinson that I should expect you. He will arrive himself day after tomorrow. It seems that General Sherman is shelling Atlanta, and he believed he would begin his summer sojourn in the mountains earlier than usual."

The bombardment of Atlanta was mentioned as though it were something to be expected from time to time, like a thunderstorm.

"My name is Solomon Williams, and I am Dr. Robinson's butler when he is in residence and caretaker of The Magnolias when he is not. I should mention that I am a freeman and do not stay here unless there is entertainment in the evening. I have a small farm of my own in the Bean Creek settlement over the hill. My wife, Betsy, is Dr. Robinson's cook, and she has prepared some iced tea, if you would care for refreshments."

"That would be lovely," Jessie said.

"Shall I serve it in the parlor, or since there is a nice breeze down the valley this afternoon, perhaps you would prefer the piazza," and he indicated a row of rocking chairs.

"Let's sit outside," Susannah said.

Solomon Williams went inside the house, softly closing the screen door behind him.

"He talks like a college professor," Dorsey said.

When Solomon Williams returned, it was with a tray of glasses of iced tea, into each of which was stuck a sprig of mint and a glass stirrer. Also on the tray was a plate of sesame-seed cookies, as thin as wafers. While they drank their tea, Williams stood alongside, his hands joined behind his back. Susannah had noticed that the collar of his tieless starched shirt was held together by a heavy gold stud, as were his cuffs.

"What are those mounds out in the pasture?" Dorsey asked.

"Ah," Williams replied, "those are Cherokee burial mounds of great antiquity."

"I thought maybe that's what they were."

"When Dr. Robinson's father first came south, the Cherokee nation had just been driven from these lands and marched off by the U.S. Army to the Oklahoma Territory. Their lands were distributed by lottery to white men, and those who won a parcel of land soon sold it off to men with the money to put the land to good use, such as Dr. Robinson's father."

"It was all because of the gold that was found," Dorsey said.

"The gold was first found just there," Solomon Williams continued, "beyond the mounds. On the other side of the Chattahoochee there is a stream, Duke's Creek, you could walk there in a few minutes, and it was there that gold was discovered and there that the Cherokee nation lost their ancient hunting grounds."

"There must be a lesson in it," Dorsey said.

"There is, that the love of money is the root of all evil. First Timothy, chapter six, verse ten."

Solomon Williams's voice was as rich and resonant as a bass violin. Not a college professor, Susannah thought, but rather a preacher on Sundays as well as farmer, butler, and caretaker.

"Why did Dr. Robinson's father come south?" she said.

"The consumption. His doctors told him that he must seek a more salubrious climate, and being a rich Boston merchant, he could afford to do so. He built this house and settled down in Nacoochee Valley. He had need of a servant, so he bought my father and the next day set him free. He taught him to read and write and gave him money to buy the small farm that I now own. He was a most generous man. These studs of gold that you see at my throat and wrists were fashioned from a nugget found in Duke's Creek and given by him to my father."

Later, at Williams's suggestion, Dorsey took Johnny Finch down to the river for a swim, leaving Susannah and Jessie alone on the piazza in the lengthening shadows.

"I have some rather momentous news," Jessie said, "at least for me momentous."

"What is that?"

"You know I am from Florida originally?"

"I seem to remember that, yes."

"I grew up on a citrus farm that was owned jointly by my father and his brother. It was an idyllic life for a child, and it also provided a good income. There was enough to send me to normal school in Pensacola, and that's where I met John. He was, as you know, a land surveyor, and he had work in the Pensacola area for a few months. After we married we lived in several places in Georgia, and I could always find work as a schoolteacher. When he was killed at Chickamauga, I had at least that income to fall back on, but it wasn't enough.

"My parents died some years ago, and my uncle, who never married, became the sole owner of the orchards. I never gave it much thought, but I guess it wasn't a total surprise when I got a telegram a few days ago from a lawyer in Florida. My uncle had died and left me all of his property."

"How wonderful for you, Jessie."

"You recall that not too long ago I asked your advice on how I should reply to Amos's proposal, and I admitted that support for Johnny was a consideration. You asked if I loved him, and I said I thought I could learn to. You said, then say yes, and I did. Oh, I'm so glad I did. I was not made to live alone."

Susannah stole a glance at Jessie. The smile on her face and her heightened color said what she had left unsaid.

"I told Amos that the orchards are my dowry. We're going

to make our way to Florida, which has pretty much been left out of the war, and Amos and I and Johnny are going into the citrus business. You know Amos loves to grow things.

"I can see him now, rising early to check on the irrigation, the little runlets of water, cool and clear, that weave their way through the grove like some kind of puzzle. There's deep shade beneath the orange trees, broken up by splashes of light. The oranges weigh down the limbs of the trees, and in the dim light they look like round paper lanterns of the kind put up for dances and such.

"There'll be a lot of hard work, but neither of us will mind that; and with a little time there'll be a living to be made from the oranges and lemons and grapefruit and tangerines. Amos says he's never seen a tangerine. The tangerines are down at the end of the orchard, up against a swampy place of reeds and red-winged blackbirds."

"You should write poetry," Susannah said.

"I did once. There was this teacher at the normal school in Pensacola who encouraged me. I showed some of my poems to John, but he couldn't understand them. After we got married I didn't write any more poetry. John was a good man, but he wasn't one for sentiment and such . . . Life is strange, Susannah."

"Yes, it certainly is."

"Who would have thought that I would end up married again and to a man of no education, a county sheriff, but a man who was meant for finer things." She laughed. "He's reading *The Count of Monte Cristo* now, and he can't put it down."

Susannah put her hand on Jessie's wrist and had to bite her lip to keep from crying.

"God go with you, Jessie. It's good to know that some happy endings may come out of this war."

Dorsey and Johnny Finch returned from the river at sunset. Johnny had taken off his shirt and filled it with cherries they had picked from a row of trees that ran from the road to the river. Williams put the cherries into a bowl of ice water, and the four of them sat on the piazza in the twilight and ate the cherries. *If only Joel were with me now,* Susannah thought, *what a perfect evening this would be.*

But Joel was not there. He was in Catesville, as was Amos Boggs, dealing with a man who had shown himself ready to commit murder to protect his interests. She had congratulated Jessie on being one of the few to survive the war with a happy ending. She should not have said that. There were no happy endings until they happened.

That night Susannah lay awake for a long time, the windows open, listening to the monotonous call of a whippoorwill, following the course of the moon over Mount Yonah. Everything in nature was steady, predictable, except for the lives of men and women. Even these, she supposed, were for the most part predictable. The people around here were born, grew up, married, farmed a piece of land, raised their children, grew old, and died.

There were others whose lives followed an unpredictable course, like that of the comet that had just shot across the night sky between the moon and the dark silhouette of Yonah. Look at Solomon Williams, who would be a slave today except for a consumptive merchant in Boston. Look at her. A childhood passed in a whorehouse in New Orleans, then years as the ward of a strict Calvinist missionary, and then the leap across a fiery chasm into the arms of a man who was born into a life of wealth and privilege but was now as much of an outcast as she.

It was a time of choices, as the South and its way of life began to crumble, or gambles would better describe what people were being forced to. Jessie and Amos had calculated the odds and made their choice. She and Joel had not yet even thrown the dice. Where they would go and what they would do she was content to leave until Joel had settled the matter of honor involving a mountain man who tonight was either dead or alive. Joel, she forced herself to admit, might be dead himself.

Nothing could hasten the rising of the sun, and as she did on nights like this, too often, she retreated from the war into the sanctuary of sleep. But this night the doors of the sanctuary were closed, and she tossed and turned through a night of terrifying dreams.

There was a pounding on the door. Something unintelligible was being shouted. She opened her eyes to full daylight. What terrible thing had happened?

17

Joel slipped into the courtroom, nearly filled with the spectators that a hanging case always drew, squeezed himself into the last row, up against the wall, just in time for the "Oyez! Oyez! All rise."

Judge Colcock Stiles entered the room, followed by the clerk of court, arranged his bulky form on the bench, and pronounced the ritual words that transformed a roomful of people into a place of judgment. Joel caught a glimpse of Elam Scroggins as he sat down; he looked like a man who considered himself already dead.

Stiles surveyed the courtroom with his beady eyes until his gaze froze on a man in the back row intently staring at him. After a judicious pause the judge summoned to the bench a lieutenant from the Provost Marshal's staff in Atlanta, who found himself cast in the role of prosecutor, and Sergeant Scroggins's elderly lawyer. There was considerable mumbling, and then prosecutor and defendant's attorney returned to their seats.

"I wish to inform the court," Stiles said in a resonant voice, "that I have just received a telegram from military headquarters in Atlanta withdrawing this case from my jurisdiction. The authorities in Atlanta wish to question the prisoner further regarding certain matters of a sensitive military nature that I am not at liberty to disclose. The prisoner will, therefore, be transferred under military escort to Atlanta. Case dismissed."

The gavel fell, and there was a sigh of disappointment from the audience.

"I have one further announcement to make. The grand jury of Cate County for this session, having completed its work, is herewith also dismissed. Court adjourned."

"All stand," the bailiff intoned as Judge Colcock Stiles exited through the door between his bench and the Confederate and Georgia flags. This time a buzz of puzzlement ran through the spectators, among whom only one understood what had just happened.

He rode down the street with the uncomfortable feeling that his back was exposed to anyone with a rifle in a second-story window. He reasoned that it was not likely that Stiles had had the time to set up another attempt on his life, or was it even likely that he would do so. He had kept his part of the bargain and could assume that Joel now had no compelling reason to reveal to the authorities what he knew about the missing gold.

All of this was reasonably sound logic, but how often did logic drive men's actions? He would have liked to keep riding on out the Unicoi Turnpike and not stop until he reached Nacoochee, towards where Susannah, Jessie and her boy, and Amos's deputy Dorsey had left early that morning. However, he had a thing or two he must do before he would feel free to go to Susannah. He took the fork in the road that led to the Cate Springs Hotel.

He tied his horse to the cast-iron hitching post in the form of a Moorish boy and went up the steps. Only then did he notice the figure at the end of the piazza. It was that gallant lady, Harriet Read, who had ridden in a carriage with the dead body of her murdered friend for most of a day. He approached her.

"Good morning, Mrs. Read. All goes well with the ladies?"

"Good morning, Mr. Devereux. All goes as well, I suppose, as can be expected, given that we all know in our hearts that the Atlanta we will return to will be occupied by the Yankees, if indeed we are allowed to go back at all. I gather that you have run off with our housekeeper."

This last unexpectedly blunt remark was accompanied by an ironic smile. He returned the smile.

"Not a spur–of–the moment decision, I assure you. Susannah Goode and I are old friends."

She surprised him again. "God, would that I had done the same, followed my heart when I was young rather than convention and my parents. Now it is too late. To leave my husband and run away with the man I loved would, at my age, only make me a laughingstock."

"I'm sorry you are unhappy," was all that he could think of to say.

"If you would like a metaphor for hell, Mr. Devereux, it is an unhappy marriage. Why am I speaking so frankly with you? I hardly know myself. Perhaps because you don't give a fig for convention. I envy you that. I envy Susannah Goode. Now you had better leave before I say something even more unacceptable."

It was only as he walked away that Joel realized that Harriet Read had had her own amorous designs on him.

He found the two boys, Elias and Leander, sitting on the kitchen steps scrubbing pots. A large tree beside the steps had recently been cut down, and Joel seated himself on the stump before the boys could rise.

"What you doing here?" Leander said, as though affronted by Joel's presence.

"I've come back to Catesville to settle some accounts," Joel said.

"Where's Miss Susannah?"

"She's staying with friends. She wanted me to see about you. You like working at the hotel?"

"It's all right," Elias said, "but they say that when the Atlanta ladies leave, they're going to close it again."

"I expect that's right. What are you going to do then?"

"I'm going back to my people."

"You're going to the Oklahoma Territory?"

"No, they say it's hot and dusty out there. I'm going up into the Snowbird Mountains in North Carolina, where there are Cherokees who ran away when they tried to take them west."

"What about you, Leander? What are you going to do?"

"I'm going with Elias. I'm going to become a Cherokee."

He almost laughed at this juvenile fantasy, but, as he remembered well, at age fourteen you expect to be taken seriously.

"I ain't got no other place, Massa Joel," Leander said, reverting to his subservient manner. "I don't fit in with colored folks no more, and I sure don't fit in with white folks. I'm going to become a Cherokee."

"Then you'll have to stop calling people 'massa,' Leander. Suppose the Cherokees won't have you, Elias?"

"They've got to take one of their own people," Elias said.

"Suppose they won't take Leander."

"Because he's black? That don't make no difference. The chief of the Cherokees in North Carolina now is a white man."

"I never heard that."

"That's what Reverend Goode told me. He got lots of reports about my people. They elected this white man they

203

traded with as their chief so they would have someone to parley with the white government."

"What do they want from the government?"

"They want not to be sent out to the Oklahoma Territory. They want to be left where they are and be able to own land."

"And then what would they do?"

"Farm like everybody else."

"What would you do?"

"I've got some education and speak good English. Maybe I could help our chief."

"What about you, Leander? You'd never see your family and friends again."

"Ain't got no family, ain't got no friends except Elias."

"What about April, your mother?"

"She don't care nothing about me."

Leander lowered his eyes and looked down at his pale brown hands. Did he know that Auguste Devereux was his father? All of the other house servants would know. If he knew, or suspected, that Joel Devereux was his half-brother he certainly didn't want to acknowledge it. It was one of those things that no one wanted to talk about. On plantations all over the South, young white men and young light-skinned slaves passed each other in the fields with averted eyes.

"How are you going to get to the Snowbirds? You'll need horses."

As he said this he realized he had just accepted the boys' scheme. Why not? What place was there for either of them in the new Georgia about to be born?

"We haven't quite figured that out yet," Elias said.

"Hm," Joel said. "You're going to have to. You can't do anything in this life without money."

Money had not been a consideration for him when he was young. Now he knew.

"There'll be dangers in riding up into the Snowbirds," he added.

"We know that."

In the back room of the Emporium, George Malik was sitting with Amos Boggs and Elam Scroggins, an open bottle of brandy on the desk.

"I wouldn't mind a bit of that," Joel said, settling into a chair.

"Have we done it?" he said after a good long swig of brandy.

"It seems so," George said, "provided all of you get out of Cate County before the sun goes down."

"The lieutenant from the Provost Marshal's thinks I'm holding Elam in the jail and that he's taking him to Atlanta tomorrow," Amos said. "We've got to move before he figures out what's going on."

"Did Stiles actually get a telegram from army headquarters in Atlanta ordering Elam's case to be dismissed?"

"No, of course not," George Malik said. "Givens Crenshaw snuck over here and asked me to fake that telegram. He said that the judge would see to it that I had my reward."

"I'll be eternally grateful," Elam said, "for your saving my poor neck, Mr. Devereux. Anytime you want anything from me that I am able to give, just call on me."

"I just might. George, I need three horses and I'm low on money. Is a Devereux still good for that much credit?"

"Need you ask? When do you want them?"

"Now."

"It can be arranged."

"Good. Elam, how would you like to ride out for Hiawassee in about an hour?"

"Nothing would suit me better, but I'd have to stay off the

turnpike. I don't want to get jailed again."

"How would you do that?"

"There's an old Indian trail across Tray Mountain, comes out above Helen. From there on I'm in home territory."

"Could you take a couple of boys with you, a Cherokee and a colored boy?"

"Oh, those boys. 'Course I could. Where're they headed?"

"The Snowbird Mountains. How far is that from Hiawassee?"

"About a two-day ride, that is if you don't get bush-whacked."

"They say they understand that. Now that leaves you and me, Amos. Why don't we get over to Nacoochee tonight, and our women, before that lieutenant discovers the truth?"

"Before you go," George Malik said, "there are two tele-grams you should know about. The first is addressed to Lamar, but since he's left and Junius is dead, it's rightfully yours."

Joel took the telegram. "My father's had a stroke."

"Yes. I'm sorry."

Joel did not know what to reply, so confused were his emo-tions.

"And the second telegram?"

"This Captain Fordyce, who accompanied the unit from the Provost Marshal's headquarters, has sent a telegram to Atlanta, but it's in code. The only reason I mention it is that Captain Fordyce has been asking questions about you and Susannah ever since he arrived."

"Might I see that telegram?" Elam said.

He looked at it for a while, and then said, "You wouldn't happen to have a pencil and piece of paper would you, Mr. Malik?"

George brought pencil and paper, and Elam began writing

down groups of two or three letters, apparently at random.

"Why, this is an easy one," Elam said, lifting his head. "It's often that way with the higher-ups. They're too high and mighty to bother with double cyphering and that sort of thing. Give me a couple of minutes and I'll tell you what this here thing says."

It was more like ten minutes, during which the room was silent except for the breathing of the other three men, before Elam looked up again and handed the piece of paper to Joel, who read it aloud.

"Eyes only for Colonel Alexander. Devereux and the woman traveling with him have returned to Catesville. How long they will stay and why they are here is not clear. Shall I arrest them now or just have them followed, including if and when they leave town? Captain Fordyce."

"Alexander," Joel said, looking at Elam. "A name familiar to you?"

"Well, yes. Same name as the one who stopped them from shooting us when we jumped off that train."

"I know. You told me that he didn't take orders from the commander of the troops on that train and that he had a leg shot off at First Manassas but only limped a little because he wore some special false leg made for him in Paris."

"That's what they said, these boys in Colonel Drake's regiment."

"What else do you know about him?"

"Nary a thing."

"What do you make of this, George?"

"Only what I can deduce. If he had a false leg made for him in Paris, where they are known for such work, and got it sent to him through the Yankee blockade, then he is obviously a man of money and influence. Since he appears to be outside the chain of command, this Colonel Alexander is probably on a secret mission and—I would hazard the guess—comes from army headquarters in Richmond, where such missions usually originate."

"Ah," Joel said. If George Malik guessed correctly, and the Lebanese merchant was one of the shrewdest men Joel had ever met, then this Colonel Alexander who had countersigned the pass from stationmaster Marcey in Savannah allowing him on the troop train to Atlanta, and then saved his and Elam Scroggins's life, had been on his trail all along.

"I can't make anything of it," Joel said, quite truthfully. "Come on, Amos, we'd better get moving."

He paced the doctor's study while he waited for Susannah to come down. Jessie had said she was in a nervous state, had been awakened from a bad dream. But still, what was taking her so long? To distract himself from the aching he felt until she was once again in his arms, he examined the contents of the study. There was a long desk with a leather top embossed in gold along the edges, on it a basket filled with correspondence, a microscope, a medical text, several pages marked with slips of paper. A human skeleton hung from a hook in one corner of the room. There were two chairs and a sofa covered in a tobacco-colored velvet. One wall of the study was filled with books, many medical and scientific, but also books on history, even some texts in Greek and Latin. The doctor was also a scholar.

He took a volume from a shelf, the *Anabasis* of Xenophon. He had read it at Princeton. As he flipped through the pages he came upon a piece of folded paper and opened it. On it was a continuous string of meaningless letters printed in a neat hand. The bottom half of the sheet had been torn off. Curious, he held the paper to the light. There was a watermark: "Brevard and Sons, Atlanta, 1859". Hearing footsteps on the stairs, he put the book back and went out into the hall.

"Joel!"

She ran to him and he enfolded her in his arms. She smelled of laundry soap and her body was slimmer than when they had begun their adventures. He found this slimness exciting, and under her dress she apparently wore no undergarments.

"I'm sorry to have taken so long, but once again I had no clothes and no Selena to steal from. But the cook did find me an old work dress of the doctor's late wife. There were also shoes but too small for my feet. So, here I am in a country frock and barefoot."

She was laughing now, breathless. He held her tighter.

"You look like a shepherdess from a bucolic poem."

"Where are the others?" she said.

"Amos and Jessie are upstairs, and Johnny is out in the workshop making a bow and arrows under Dorsey's direction. Elam is headed for Hiawassee with Leander and Elias, who are going on to the Snowbirds, they say, where Leander swears he's going to become a Cherokee."

"Jessie says you freed Sergeant Scroggins and brought Amos to her. You are a hero."

"I doubt that, but you and I have much to talk about, Susannah."

"First a stroll."

"As you command."

She led him out and across the lawn to a walk that led into the trees under whitewashed latticed arches entwined with white roses. The walk ended in a deeply shaded circle of grass with a fountain in the middle and around the edges statues of Pan playing his pipes to three dancing nymphs.

"The shepherdess's grotto," she said, and in one smooth movement pulled her dress over her head and threw it on the grass, revealing the body, shade-dappled, that he had so ached for. She came to him, and before he could do or say anything she had undone his belt and pulled down his breeches.

"You have no shame, do you?" he said, running his hands down her bare back.

"Consider my upbringing."

They fell onto the grass together, and he entered her slim white body under the eyes of Pan and his troupe.

Afterwards, lying on his back and looking up at the statues, he said, "An enchanted pagan place."

"Did you hear the pipes? I did."

They dined around a long dark table at the canonical Southern hour of two in the afternoon. The linen was starched and the silver polished. A bowl of white roses adorned the table, as though a tribute to their hour in the grotto. Betsy had prepared a meal of fried chicken, rice with milk gravy, and side dishes of yellow squash, slow-cooked beans, and pickled peaches. The Reverend Solomon Williams of Bean Creek Baptist Church said the grace before serving the diners.

Jessie Finch looked embarrassed, as if everyone knew that she and her new husband had spent the entire morning in her bedroom, as of course everyone did know. Susannah, it seemed to Joel, felt not the least embarrassment, glowed with satiation and pride in having skillfully given a man everything he could desire. She had seen and heard many things as a child and had told him that she knew pretty much everything there was to know about the act of love. Somehow this knowledge had been a kind of vaccination, she said, against playing the wanton. There were no forbidden byways for her, and consequently she could, without any regret, give herself to one man and one man alone. He need have no fear of her straying.

After dinner there was the traditional Southern siesta, leaving Joel and Susannah alone on the piazza, far too keyed up to contemplate sleep.

"You told me your father has had a stroke," she said. "How did you find that out?"

"A doctor in Savannah sent a telegram to Lamar, and since he has decamped and Junius is dead, George Malik gave it to me. The doctor says Auguste can neither speak nor write, and it is unlikely he ever will again. Poor Auguste, toppled from the heights. His factories burned, his plantation in the hands of a daughter married to a confidant of the hated Lincoln. Two sons dead, a third has exiled himself to South America, where he will sooner or later die of drink or disease, and the fourth son estranged. In fact I am now the last of the Devereux. It's a queer feeling."

"Yes," she said, "the last Devereux and no place to call home. You can't go back to Devereux Hall and there is no more Cherokee Rose."

"As well, the gold I brought back from Spain is almost exhausted. The final irony is that somewhere there is a vast amount of gold from the U.S. mint in Dahlonega. Auguste Devereux knows where it is, but now he can't tell. So only Colcock Stiles knows. The saga of the Devereux is over, and we are alone and soon penniless. What do we do?"

"We'll make a new life together, Joel, you and I."

"I'll have to find work, but what, with the economy of the South in ruins?"

"You had an offer of employment from that professor at Princeton."

"But no way to communicate with Professor Arnold until the war is over."

"Could we not make our way into the North?"

"It would be hard and dangerous."

"I wouldn't mind, after all we've gone through . . . What on earth is that?"

He turned. Coming down the road, pulled by a single horse, was what looked like a delivery van, except that it was painted all black.

"It must be a hearse."

The van turned up the drive to Dr. Robinson's house.

"Not a very good omen for our new life," Susannah said and laughed nervously.

When the vehicle drew near, they could make out, lettered in gold leaf on the side, "Michael O'Leary, Photographer, Portraits & Views," and in smaller letters beneath, "Daguerrotypes, Collodion Method, Albumin Prints." The van was driven by a young man in a billed cap, his face and forearms much bronzed by the sun.

"Might this be Dr. Robinson's house?"

"It is, but he's not here. He is, however, expected tomorrow."

"In that case, I'll go back to the little inn down the road for the night and return tomorrow. But before I do, might I impose on you for some refreshment."

"There's iced tea."

"Possibly even whiskey and spring water?"

Joel laughed. "I shouldn't be surprised. Would you like something to drink, Susannah?"

"Nothing, thank you."

He went into the house to find Williams, and there was indeed whiskey and water to be had. Joel wanted to engage the young man in conversation. He was curious to know what kind of business an itinerant photographer could have with Dr. Robinson that would make him willing to wait a day to see him.

When he returned to the piazza with two whiskies—his to promote conviviality—he found Michael O'Leary already ensconced in a rocking chair, his cap hung on one arm of it. The cap had concealed dark red hair, thick and coarse, parted down the middle. With his green eyes he was the picture of an Irishman.

"To your health."

"And yours. You know Dr. Robinson?"

"Never met him. But I'm told he may be interested in some photographs I have."

"Portraits?"

"In a way. Photographs of a medical nature. You're kin of the doctor's?"

"No, just house guests. Joel Devereux. My fiancée, Susannah Goode. The doctor was delayed in joining us. Photographs of a medical nature?"

"Pictures taken on the battlefield. Dr. Robinson is a renowned surgeon, I'm told, and he has been engaged by the Confederate government to train army field surgeons. My informant believes he would be most interested in acquiring some pictures I have."

"I see. You're a war photographer, then?"

"By default, though I've never done better business." O'Leary took a sip of whiskey. "Before the war I had a portrait studio in Memphis, and to supplement my income I started to do views, of monuments and mountains and steamboats, things like that. But to do views you have to take your darkroom with you. You know anything about photography?"

"Not much."

"Well, there used to be only daguerreotypes. I still do a few for old-fashioned folks, but the problem with daguerreotypes is that you can't make copies from them. With the wet collodion method you can make as many prints as you want. The drawback of collodion plates is that you have to make them up in a darkroom right before you shoot. Once they dry off they're no good. Then after you take your picture you have to go back to the studio and develop right away. That means if you are going to work outdoors, you have to take your darkroom with you. That's what this rig here is, a darkroom on wheels."

"Ingenious. But aside from special cases like Dr. Robinson, how do you make money out of photographing the war?"

"That's what I asked myself at first. But with all the men off soldiering, my business in Memphis dried up. Then I read about this fellow up north, Matthew Brady. They say he has twenty photographers in the field. Why couldn't I become the Matthew Brady of the Confederacy?

"To answer your question, I mostly make money by getting together soldiers from a unit, and they're usually from the same city or county, and posing them, getting their names and addresses. When I have enough of these poses, I travel to where these boys come from and sell copies to their families. What mother or wife wouldn't want a photograph of her loved one? Nine out of ten buy."

Amos Boggs and Dorsey walked out on the piazza.

"Mr. Boggs and Mr. Dorsey. Michael O'Leary. He's here to see Dr. Robinson."

"Pleased to meet you."

O'Leary put down his empty glass on the floor and stood up. "Well, I'd better be going. If you wouldn't mind telling Dr. Robinson when he arrives tomorrow that I'll be around to see him in the evening. About six o'clock."

"What does that fellow want with Dr. Robinson?" Boggs said, as O'Leary drove away.

"He has some battlefield photographs to sell him, probably of war wounds. It seems our Dr. Robinson is a surgeon in the employ of the Confederate government."

"Hm. Joel, Jessie and I have decided to start out for Florida while it's still possible to get there. Williams says there's a weekly stagecoach tomorrow for Traveler's Rest on the Tugaloo, and there we can get a boat for Savannah. I thought I would go in to the county seat and see if I can get tickets for it and do a little shopping for Jessie and Johnny. Dorsey here's going on back to Catesville, before they get suspicious of him too."

"Thank you for everything you've done for us, Mr. Dorsey," Susannah said.

"My pleasure, ma'am."

Boggs and Dorsey went out to the stable to get their horses, and Joel and Susannah sat down on the piazza steps.

"You know," Joel said, "I think we'd better get moving too, or the war is going to catch up with us. To keep heading north may be the best course."

"Then let's do it, Joel. I know there are dangers involved, but so are there any way we turn."

18

The sun was setting when Amos Boggs rode up. Joel and Susannah were sitting on the piazza steps again. Boggs tied his horse to the rail and sat down on the steps beside them.

"Did you get the stagecoach tickets?"

"I did. I also saw that photographer fellow that was out here this afternoon."

"Oh."

"In jail. I paid a little call on Sheriff Chastain of White County, who I've known for twenty years or more, and we had a whiskey in his office. It seems some Confederate officers—not the fighting kind, you know, the kind that ask questions like they are from higher-up—were here looking for a man selling photographs, and they grabbed him when he drove into town this afternoon.

"After another drink Chastain told me 'in great confidence' that they had searched that contraption the photographer drives and found what they were looking for. It was some photographic plates of dead soldiers, dead Union soldiers, all of them Negroes. No weapons to be seen, and some of the corpses with hands tied. In the background two Confederate soldiers grinning like idiots. You wouldn't have to be a genius to understand that these Negro soldiers were shot after being captured. Now wouldn't Abe Lincoln love to have those plates?"

"Why?" Susannah said.

"Chastain said he heard these Confederate officers talking among themselves. They were saying the peace party in the North is on the rise, and that old Abe had pretty much decided he's going to lose the election in November—save some big Union victory, like taking Atlanta—and proof of the Confederates having killed unarmed Negro Union soldiers would be like a tonic to the war party."

"I can't believe that that innocent-talking photographer," Joel said, "is part of a Northern spy ring."

"Well, from thirty years of law enforcing, I can tell you the most innocent-talking are the ones you have to be the most suspicious of. And there's more. You won't get to meet Dr. Robinson. They arrested him leaving Atlanta, and they are looking for the rest of the 'Yankee spy ring.' Does anyone know that you met that photographer fellow here this afternoon?"

"Not as far as I know," Joel said, "except Solomon Williams and his wife, of course."

"Because they found a card on this O'Leary with Robinson's name on it and directions to his summer home, and on the back of it was penciled in the names of you two. Now, they may make O'Leary talk—spies don't have much in the way of legal rights—or they'll find out in the course of things that this is where you are."

"What are we going to do?" Susannah said.

"First, let me tell you the worst part. Sheriff Chastain had just got a telegram from the Cate County court, which had been sent to law officers in all the surrounding counties, advising that an army deserter, who had stolen secret Confederate codes, had escaped from custody with the help of two accomplices, and that the authorities were offering a large reward for the apprehension of these fugitives, the two accomplices having the same names as those written down by that photographer. He showed the telegram to those Confederate officers, and they was mightily interested."

"Colcock Stiles doesn't waste any time, does he?" Joel said.

"He's not slow-witted, that's for sure," Amos replied. "Now, of course, the Confederate authorities ain't offering any reward, not having yet heard about all this, but I reckon the good judge has put some of his own money on the table."

"But what does he gain by having us arrested?" Susannah said.

"Well, I'd be remiss if I didn't tell you what I think. He don't want you arrested as much as dead."

"What do we do?" Joel said.

"Get out of here fast, is what I would advise. Be on the road before the sun is up. You'll be on your own. Me and Jessie and the boy are riding into town before it gets full dark. We'll spend the night there, because the stagecoach comes through real early in the morning and don't wait if you ain't there."

Now Susannah had the desire that she had expressed to herself before drifting off to sleep the night before, to be alone with Joel in this lovely place. But life never gave you just what you desired, it always put some condition upon happiness. Now they had to flee before dawn. Solomon had gone to the kitchen to ask Betsy to prepare an omelet for them. Then he and his wife would leave for their little farm on Bean Creek, and she and Joel would be all alone in this large house belonging to a Dr. Robinson, whom they would probably never meet . . .

The sound of hoofbeats rang out in the night, three or four horses ridden fast up the long drive from the road.

"We'd just as well stay put," Joel said. "Our pistols are in the saddlebags out in the stable, ready for taking off before dawn tomorrow. I was ever too organized for my own good. Are you all right, my love?"

"I would die with you if I had to, but most of all I just want to be free of all this, free to live with you."

She knew that this would be small comfort to him, or to her, but more and more she had to speak the truth, however bleak. Their journey, it seemed often to her, was doomed to end tragically.

Joel did not reply, just rose and damped down the wicks of the two lamps that lit the room. They went to the window together. The bare-swept earth around the hitching rail was lit by moonlight almost as bright as day. Four Confederate officers dismounted, hitched their horses to the rail, stood together and looked up at the darkened house, hesitated, conferred together. Deference was given to a tall black-bearded officer. Moonlight twinkled in the gold braid on his collar.

"They're wondering whether, if they come up the steps, they might not be met by a barrage of gunfire. It's enough to make you pause. Uniforms well-cut, sons of good family, the kind who are assigned to the staffs of generals, to do the subtle things that officers in the field don't know much about or want to know. The tall one limps, probably from a war wound."

"You've certainly learned a lot from one glance," Susannah said, reassured, in this moment of great danger, by the confident opinions of her lover.

"They're of my class," he said.

She sensed there was more that he had not said. It had to do with the tall black-bearded officer, whose face, as he raised it to look up at the window where they stood, appeared to her as a skull, the shadowed eyes empty sockets.

Somewhere behind them another presence had entered the darkened room. Were there more of them, who had come in from the back of the house? Joel whirled around.

"Come with me," a deep, resonant voice said.

So they followed Solomon Williams through the house, dark but for beams of moonlight here and there. They went into the kitchen, where the odor of a recently cooked omelet could still be detected. Williams lit a lamp, opened a door and led them down stairs to an earthen cellar where root vegetables were stored in bins. Behind these was a curtain of heavy canvas, which when pulled aside revealed a brick-lined corridor. They were walking fast now, and the underground corridor seemed to go on and on.

Susannah felt as if she were in an ancient tale she had read in *Bulfinch's Mythology*, pursued by the dark forces of the underworld, Orpheus and Euridyce, perhaps, or Kore and Persephone. She must not look back, she thought, almost believing her illusion.

Then more stairs, up this time, and they emerged in the moonlit circle of statues of Pan and his nymphs, where she and Joel had made love with abandon. In the moonlight Pan's lips were still poised on his pipes. And then the spell was broken.

"Follow that path," Solomon Williams said. "You will find your horses tied to a post some hundred yards from here. Continue along the path and you will come out eventually on the Unicoi Turnpike at Helen. You'd best take the road north."

"Our eternal thanks," Joel said.

"Not to mention it. You are the first white folks I have set on the road north."

They rode through the little town of Helen, still asleep, and after that there were few houses. The Unicoi Turnpike followed the Chattahoochee River, near its headwaters hardly more than a stream, for a few miles, and then began to wind up into the higher mountains. They were in uninhabited forest by the time the sun rose.

"Now for the first time I feel safe," Susannah said, "though I know that may be an illusion."

"Just keep alert. I'd put my pistol in my belt, if I were you."

She reached into a saddlebag and did as he said. They rode on at a steady pace, and within an hour were high enough to look down on the hills and the Piedmont beyond. Even Stone Mountain was visible, a dot on the horizon.

"I still find that whole business of Michael O'Leary and Doctor Robinson fantastic," Susannah said. "If it's true, George Malik could be implicated."

"It has the ring of truth to it. You heard what Amos said he overheard. The peace party in the North is in the ascendancy, and they say that Lincoln is resigned to losing the election in November unless there is a major Northern victory—such as taking Atlanta. Proof of a Southern atrocity would give supporters of the war in the North a boost."

"Still, a renowned surgeon . . ."

"Remember that Doctor Robinson's father was from Boston and didn't move South voluntarily, and the first thing he did in the South was free a slave. Boston is the abolitionist stronghold. It's plausible. If you need further proof, there is that hidden staircase. Doctor Robinson's house is without question a stop on the abolitionists' underground railway, transporting runaway slaves to freedom in the North. And then I found a coded message in a Greek text in the doctor's library, which is decidedly odd. I borrowed the book, by the way. I figured he wouldn't be coming home for a while. It's Xenophon's *Anabasis*, which is the first Greek I read at Princeton."

"I don't know it."

"It's about a Greek mercenary force that helps Cyrus the Persian overthrow his brother, Artaxerxes, and take the throne. Cyrus is defeated, and the Greeks find themselves on their own out in the middle of Asia Minor. They start marching upcountry, looking for a way home, going further and further into the mountains and meeting all kinds of adventures and hardships along the way. Sounds a bit like us, doesn't it, substituting Jeff Davis and Abe Lincoln for Cyrus and Artaxerxes."

"What does Anabasis mean?"

"Going up country or just upcountry . . . Now what's that?"

She looked to where Joel pointed. A metallic light ran through the trees.

"It looks like a field telegraph wire," he said in a concerned voice.

At that moment they rounded a bend in the road and confronted a barrier.

"Damn. I forgot this was a toll road, but why the telegraph . . ."

A few paces more and they saw a shack, half a dozen unshaven men in rough clothes sitting around a fire where they were cooking something, and half a dozen large dogs lying in the dirt, sleeping or scratching, chained to a heavy wire. One of the dogs saw them, and in an instant all of the dogs were barking, straining at their chains to get at them. One of the men picked up a whip and laid it several times across the dogs' backs until they became quiet.

"Goddamn dogs."

"Good morning. How much is the toll?"

"Ain't no more how much, it's whether you got papers. This here is a controlled military road . . . Why I do believe one of you gentlemen is a lady. You wouldn't happen to be a Mr. Devereux and a Miss Goode, would you?"

Another of the men got up and went into the shack. Out of

the corner of her eye she saw Joel take the pistol out of his belt and she heard it being cocked. The man came out of the shack raising a double-barreled shotgun, but Joel already had his pistol aimed at him.

"Now you do as I say or I'll blow your brains out. Break that gun and throw the shells as far as you can."

The man did as he was told without hesitation. The others sat motionless around the fire.

"Now let up the barrier."

In a low voice he said to Susannah, "Follow me as fast as you can ride your horse."

As the barrier rose Joel's horse sprang forward as if it were coming out of a starting gate. Susannah spurred her horse forward. In seconds they were around the curve, and then around another, riding dangerously fast, Joel leaning forward like a jockey. Without warning Susannah's mare slid in loose gravel. As the horse went down she was unable to pull one foot from the stirrup. *She's going to land on top of me and break my back,* Susannah thought. But when they hit the ground she was thrown clear, striking a blow to her head that left her momentarily unconscious. She stood up. Blood was running down her cheek from sliding across the gravel. Her horse was unable to get to its feet, whether stunned, as she was, or from a crippling injury.

She walked toward her horse, reeling around in the road like a drunk. Joel jumped from the saddle and caught her as she fell. In the distance could be heard the baying of dogs.

"They've let the dogs loose," he said. "We haven't much time. Get up behind me on my horse."

"I can't. I've done something to my ankle."

"I'll lift you."

The baying was growing close. The only quick way he could get her up on his horse was to put her foot into the left stirrup, but this was her injured foot and she screamed with pain. The dogs now seemed just around the bend.

"Too late! They'll tear us to pieces before we can get mounted. There's only one thing for it. That laurel thicket."

He picked up her pistol and shoved it into her belt, and they plunged into the thicket. The limbs of the densely growing mountain laurel bushes were too thick to be pushed aside, and she dragged herself under them on her one good leg. As the laurel grew thicker, she stooped lower and lower until she was down on her hands and knees. The barking of the dogs was close now, but whether they had entered the thicket she could not tell.

The cover of leaves above had become so thick that it was almost as dark as night. She could no longer see Joel. Some distance away there was a gunshot and the howl of a wounded dog. The barking continued. She dared not go back to where the men would now be, but crawling forward was becoming more difficult. Soon she was inching ahead on her stomach. There was another gunshot, and the barking ceased.

"Joel!" she cried, knowing that this might draw those vicious dogs in her direction, but without him she was a frightened twelve-year-old alone in a world of cynical debauchery. He had saved her, but she had always known that her salvation was provisional, that one day a dark angel might hover over her and intone, "Susannah, abandon all hope. You are damned. I have come for your soul."

Suddenly, the dark angel became the Confederate officer who had looked up at them as they stood at the window at Dr. Robinson's, his face a skull in the moonlight, his shadowed eyes empty sockets. What was left of her reason dissolved in mindless panic.

"Joel!" she cried again. There was no reply, and then she called repeatedly, in an ever fainter, ever hoarser voice. Each time she was answered only by an echo, a derisive rejection from out of the darkness to her appeal for help. Finally she gave up.

She had no idea how much time had passed and, unable to see the sun, in which direction she had been moving. She was too exhausted to crawl any further. *I'm going to die here, she thought, this is the destiny planned for me from eternity, and Joel, nor anyone else will ever even find my remains. So, I was damned all along.* There was a ringing in her ears and she lost consciousness.

She awoke with a start. Had she heard a voice?

"Susannah! Susannah!" The voice came from far away, Joel's voice?

"I'm here! Help me!" How could anyone hear this weak call from the depths?

"Susannah!"

"Yes! Yes, I'm here." But where was here?

"Susannah!" The voice was closer now, a human voice. "All right then. Can you move forward?"

"I'll try."

"You don't have far to go."

She pulled herself forward by grasping onto roots, the laurel branches scraping her back, one painful pull of an arm after another, one more scrape or cut after another. But inches at a time she did move ahead. The darkness grew less and less, and finally she saw splashes of sunlight on the ground ahead of her. She was again up on her hands and knees. The laurel thicket ended as abruptly as it had begun. She came out into full sunlight, tried to get to her feet and fell to the ground. Joel was running toward her.

"Are you all right?"

"As ever I have been. I'm not going to die. I'm not going to hell."

"Certainly, you're not going to die. As to hell, that is a place outside my ken."

He helped her to her feet and held her in his arms. Whether he or she was shaking the most she could not tell. She kissed him hard on the mouth with bloody lips.

"I was sure I had lost you."

"I was sure I was going to die."

"What can I do for you?"

"Water, I just need water."

"There's a spring over here. Come."

She knelt by the spring and greedily drank the ice-cold water. It was the best thing she had ever tasted.

"Now let's clean you up a bit."

She looked down at herself. Her shirt was in tatters and even her riding breeches were torn. She had bled from a dozen cuts and scrapes. Her cheek was so swollen from falling off the horse that it half-closed one eye. But these were hurts to her body that would heal. Her spirit was whole and free.

"It's not as bad as it looks," she said, glorying in what she had endured and survived. "No broken bones. My ankle hurts, but I don't think it's sprained. It's just that I don't have the energy even to put one foot in front of the other."

"Then I'll carry you."

"To where?"

"I climbed those rocks, and from there you can see a mountain village. There should be food there, maybe even fresh mounts."

She realized for the first time that the sun was low in the sky.

"How long was I in there?"

"Nearly seven hours."

"That was hell."

"You are not the first to observe that. The mountaineers call these thickets 'laurel hells.' Many a hunter has got lost in one and never been heard of again, but I figured it was the only way that we were going to save ourselves from those dogs. Once in the laurel they could only get at me one at a time. I shot two, and the rest turned tail."

"They were huge."

"Bear-hunting dogs."

"You've saved my life twice today."

"I consider myself the luckiest man on Earth to have had that privilege."

As day turned to twilight they followed a path that led toward the village. Susannah was walking now with the help of a tree branch serving as a crutch. Her head began to ring again, and she imagined that it sounded like singing. She feared she might have a concussion from her fall, but her eyesight seemed normal.

"Do you hear singing?" Joel said.

It was dark enough now to see the lights of many fires in an open meadow. The singing had stopped, and a man's voice rose and fell. There were huge tents and a kind of platform, around which were gathered hundreds of people.

"What's going on?" she said.

"It's a camp revival meeting. They last for several days, sometimes a week. There'll be plenty of food. Let's just walk right in."

As they proceeded toward the lighted area, it was clear that other things than saving souls were going on at the edges of the revival meeting. Behind some bushes a couple were making love, and a little further on several men were sitting on the grass passing around a jug.

They entered the lighted area and were seen by several

people who nudged others. Soon all heads were turned in their direction. The preacher on the podium, in galluses and a collarless striped shirt, stopped in mid-sentence.

"Now why does Saint Paul tell us . . ."

A white-bearded elder sitting behind the preacher on the podium said in a loud voice, "Bring them down front."

A man led them to the podium.

"What in tarnation happened to you?" the elder said.

Joel spoke up. "We were attacked by robbers, who took our horses and all our money and possessions. My wife became lost in a laurel hell and is lucky to be alive."

"Mysterious are the ways of the Lord," the preacher said. "He has brought you forth from the wilderness to salvation." He fixed Susannah with a fiery gaze, "You have been saved, haven't you?"

"Indeed, I have been saved." Although meant in a different sense, she had never said truer words.

"Praised be the Lord."

He turned to Joel, "And you, sir, have . . ."

But at this point a large middle-aged woman came forward and took Susannah by the arm.

"Reverend, first let me put some decent clothes on this child."

"Yes, by all means, Sister."

What must have been apparent to anyone on the podium was that Susannah's shirt was so torn to pieces that her breasts were mostly exposed.

The woman took Susannah to a stream, sat her down on a rock and took off the remains of her shirt. Joel stood a discreet distance away while the woman washed her cuts and scratches with a piece of wet flannel.

"He was about to start preaching over you and he would have gone on for the better part of an hour, with you standing there in front of everyone half-naked."

Then the woman applied an ointment to each cut with a fingertip.

"Bear grease," the woman said. "Best thing for healing cuts." She handed Susannah a clean man's shirt to put on.

"Thank you so much. Would you be able to let us have a little food? We haven't eaten all day."

"Lord, girl, there's enough food here for an army. The kitchen's under that tent over there. You just tell them Mrs. Tompkins said to let you have anything you want."

That night they slept in the open field with the revivalists. It turned out that the camp meeting was on the edge of the little town, and the next morning, just as the others were beginning to awaken, Susannah and Joel made their way into town. There they bought back their own horses, with saddles and tack, which the road guards had sold to the local livery stable. The saddle bags were, of course, empty.

"Damnation," Joel said, "all my prized possessions, my fly rod, my fowling piece, telescope, compass, everything but that Greek text. I can see why they wouldn't have much use for that. Damnation . . ."

"You ungrateful man. We're not only alive, we have our horses back, and yet you complain."

He laughed. "You're right, of course. Let's buy some food and at least a compass. The man at the livery stable said there is another barrier on the road at Unicoi Gap, but there's a back road, a path really, directly to Hiawassee. I'm almost certain that Elam and the boys were not allowed past that first road barrier. They will have to find another way. But at least we can look up Elam's wife in Hiawassee and let her know he's safe."

"And then?"

"Now that we're wanted as spies, we've got yet another reason to head north. So, I guess we just keep moving up-country, if you agree."

"I go where you go, my love, but don't take it as criticism if I say that we are going to have to decide soon on a final destination. Time is not on our side."

IV

The Way Upcountry

19

The little town of Hiawassee was the last outpost of upland Georgia. Just beyond was the North Carolina border, circumscribing the high mountains, first the Nantahalas, then the Snowbirds to the west, the Pisgahs to the east, and finally the towering citadel of the Great Smokies, wreathed in cloud in summer and often hidden by fog in winter, with its unexplored and unmapped reaches. It was here, as a young man, that Joel Devereux had in solitude thought out his life, and thereby the way to Susannah Goode, as lovely and strange as one of those green coves hidden in the high mountains, available only to a man who had journeyed there and tasted the cold, clear waters of paradise. So he said to himself as they rode out of Hiawassee to the Scroggins property, the townspeople having been strangely vague about which, if any, of the Scrogginses might be found there.

What they found was a gorge cut in the forested landscape by a fast-flowing little river and a swinging bridge spanning it. At the other end of this frail, ramshackle construction was a house, several times added to, scoured by wind and rain of any paint it may once have had. The supports of the bridge carried a cord across to a tarnished brass bell. Joel pulled the knotted end of the cord, and the bell on the other side rang improbably loud and clear. After a few seconds the front door of the house swung open, and Elam Scroggins ventured out onto the swaybacked, rotting piazza that ran the length of the house.

"Where have you folks been?" the army deserter, who had just escaped the gallows, called across the chasm in a cheery voice.

"It's a long story," Joel called back.

"Well, come on over and tell it to me, but mind the boards in that bridge. Some of them are right rotten."

When they reached the other side, after having crept gingerly over the creaking contraption of rope and wood, Sergeant Scroggins vigorously shook both their hands, his wide smile revealing two missing teeth.

"I do declare, you are a sight for sore eyes."

"Elam, how did you get past the guards at the turnpike barrier?"

"Nothing much to it. I know all those boys. We growed up together. That counts for a lot up this way, even let me take the colored boy and that Indian on up the road, which I reckon they weren't supposed to do. Those boys are on their way to the Snowbirds now. I gave them an old pistol of my pa's, more to buck up their spirits than for any good it's going to do them."

"Where is your wife?" Susannah said.

"Asa? Why, she's inside. You all come on in and meet her. I've told her a lot about you, Mr. Devereux."

Just at that moment a woman came out on the piazza. She wore her light brown hair in a bun and was skinny as a rail, the fall of her plain calico dress to her ankles broken only by the slight swell over apple-sized breasts.

"You must be Mr. Devereux and Miss Goode. You're just as Elam described you."

"We are," Joel said. "We stopped by to let you know your husband probably wouldn't be able to make it to Hiawassee right away, but I'm glad to see I was wrong."

"Only because you saved him from hanging. We'll be eternally grateful to you, Mr. Devereux. Could you set a spell?"

"Actually, would it be too much bother for us to stay with you for a night or two? We need to rest up. Did the road guards tell you they set their dogs on us?"

"They did not," Elam said.

"Well, I suppose they wouldn't talk about it, since they stole our horses. We had to buy them back from a livery stable."

"And then I got lost in a laurel hell," Susannah said.

"That can happen, and there's some don't ever get out. I reckon you folks do need a rest, and you're welcome to stay as long as you want."

"Take a seat," Asa said, gesturing to the row of rocking chairs that adorned every piazza in the South. "I'll bring some refreshments. I'm afraid cider is all we have."

They went to bed with the sun that evening and slept until midmorning of the next day.

As they lay in bed, Joel said, "Today we do nothing. We don't get lost, we don't have dogs set on us, we don't get arrested as spies . . ."

"And we don't get chased by outlaws," Susannah added, "or join a circus, or have lunch with General Sherman, or get shot at by assassins."

They laughed quietly, just glad to be alive.

When they stopped laughing, Joel said, "By the way, Elam told me who the would-be assassin is. For a while the man was in the cell next to his in the Catesville jail, a gambler from Charleston who had killed a man during a card game. He was apprehended in Georgia and was being held in Catesville awaiting return to Charleston to stand trial. One night Givens Crenshaw came with some kind of paper, and the man just walked out of the jailhouse. It was the night I was shot at through the window at Cherokee Rose. I suppose Stiles had him released in return for his silencing me."

"Oh, how I wish Judge Stiles would get his just deserts."

"He well may. When Union forces occupy Catesville, as they soon must, I imagine there're going to be a lot of old scores settled, and Stiles is the only slave owner of any consequence in the whole county. I wouldn't be surprised to see Stiles and Givens Crenshaw decide to take up residence elsewhere. Who knows, if George Malik is part of a Northern spy ring, he might even replace Crenshaw as mayor."

"I would enjoy that a lot," Susannah said.

That afternoon Susannah sat in the kitchen and helped Asa peel and pickle a bushel of overripe peaches that she had bought cheap at the Hiawassee market, while Joel and Elam walked the Scroggins farm.

"It was once a fine farm. The soil's real good, but my grandpa bought it cheap because there was no way of getting to it without going three miles downstream or two up to cross the river. Then he built that swinging bridge, and the fellow that sold it to him so cheap wished he hadn't.

"Grandpa put in apple trees and raised corn, wheat, and barley, kept pigs and a few cows, built the house and added to it two or three times. He was an industrious man, and I guess we would be right prosperous now if my pa hadn't taken to drink. It would need a heap of work to bring it back to what it was. I don't know. I can't see taking up farming again when the war's over. I've been to the city, learned a trade, married a town woman. I just don't know. What do you think, Joel?"

They stood beside an empty hay barn, its roof partly fallen in. It was the first time Elam Scroggins had used his Christian name.

"I think it's going to be hard making a living by farming

after the war. The South will be dirt poor. They'll have to break up the larger plantations. There's no profit in plantation cotton without slave labor, and they'll have to find some other way of raising it."

"Well, I sure ain't sharecropping, that's one thing I know."

"They're going to need telegraphers again. They'll be stringing wire everywhere, but the good jobs, I suppose, will mostly be up North."

"That's what Asa says, and she's smart as a whip. She says I ought to go to Canada, but I don't know. It's awful cold up there and I wouldn't know nobody."

"Canada?"

"Right before the war started a fellow came to Atlanta from some big telegraph company up North, looking to hire some really fast operators to work the American end of this cable they was laying across the Atlantic. They tested some of us, and I was the fastest. I said that ain't all, and I took the telegraph wire and stuck it in my mouth. You get little shocks that way, and I just read off the Morse code from my tongue. This fellow said he had never heard of anyone who could receive a telegram on his tongue, and I was as good as hired. High pay too.

"They got the cable laid, it come out at Halifax in Nova Scotia, but then it broke, and then the war come along. Anyway, a couple of months ago, Asa sent this fellow a letter, asking if there might be a job for me after the war. He remembered me because of that trick I done with my tongue, and he said there would be work in Halifax once they got the cable laid again. They figured that would be within a year of the war being over.

"Asa is all for me taking the job, says there would be more than just my pay. She was trained as a bookkeeper, and before we married worked mostly for cotton brokers. She knows all about the trade, and she says that when that cable across the sea is working, there will be real money to be made in trading cotton futures by telegraph.

"She says the winters up there ain't all that bad—not even as bad as Hiawassee—because of something called the Gulf Stream, but there's lots of fog. She's found some pictures of this place in newspapers and magazines and cut them out and pasted them in a scrapbook, and it does look all right. Lots of ships in the harbor. She has this idea of buying a house, with a pretty little garden, up on the cliffs, where we could watch the ships sail into the harbor."

"She may be right," Joel said, hoping very much that she was. "My Uncle Willy did well in cotton futures before the war."

They were walking through an orchard of gnarled apple trees, and Joel stopped in his tracks. Something had just dawned on him.

"Your wife sent a letter up North?"

"Yes, to New York."

"How did she do that?"

"Oh, there's ways. I guess there's ways of doing pretty nigh anything if you want to bad enough."

"Tell me about it."

"One way, the one Asa used, is to send a letter up to this place on the North Carolina–Tennessee border, out in the middle of nowhere, where there's this kind of open-air market where they trade stuff, Northern goods, things like coffee and tea that you can't get in the South, for valuables, mostly silver, that folks down South that needs the money have sold or that have been stolen from homes by deserters and outlaws.

"You can take a letter there and pay to have it mailed at the U.S. post office in Knoxville, Tennessee. Then when there's a reply they bring it from Knoxville to this market. You have to pay a pretty penny, of course."

"Could I just go over there and send a letter up North?"

"You could. Better still a telegram, and you wouldn't have to wait a week or two to get a reply. Now, it's a three-day ride to where this market is, and you would have to be a mite careful. The folks who run it are of the roughest sort."

"I'll have to talk to Susannah."

"You think I should take this job in Halifax?"

"I do. Everybody's going to have to learn new ways after the war, Elam. Those who try to go back to the old ways are going to end up just where you said you didn't want to be, as sharecroppers."

"You may well be right. I'll study on it."

That evening Joel and Susannah found themselves alone on the piazza while Elam sat in the kitchen talking to Asa as she prepared supper. It was the first chance Joel had had to ask her whether he had done the right thing in letting the boys go off into the Snowbirds and become part of Elias's people.

"I see things from a different viewpoint," she said, "partly because I'm an outsider to Southern society myself, partly because I've had a good bit to do with the Cherokees. One or two would come right regularly from the mountains to talk with Philander, tell him the latest developments, and seek his advice. If these Cherokees are not sent west—and at this late date that isn't going to happen—they're going to have to find a place for themselves among the mountain people. I know the boys' idea sounds a little crazy, but Elias might really be able to help his people. How proud that would have made Philander. About Leander, you would be the one to know."

"I don't. I just had this feeling in my gut that this might be the only way that had any chance of working for him."

"Sometimes how you feel is better than what you know."

"How was your afternoon?"

239

"Asa confided in me a lot. I guess she hasn't had a female friend to talk with. I pretty much know her life story."

"Tell me a little."

"She comes from Rome, Georgia, a sleepy sort of town, except that it is where a branch of the Western and Atlantic Railroad ends at the docks on the Coosa River, from where steamboats take bales of cotton to the Gulf ports; and so there are a number of cotton brokers located in Rome.

"Asa's mother died when she was young, and her father, a hardware merchant, raised her. He was a man of decided views, and once decided, unchangeable. He decided that Asa was too plain and too shy ever to attract suitors and she would therefore have to make her own way in the world. He enrolled her in a bookkeeping course, though women weren't generally welcome in the profession at that time.

"Asa shared her father's view of her lack of attractiveness to men. About this time the war began, and women were no longer excluded from commercial positions. She worked for several cotton-brokerage firms and learned all the ins and outs of buying and selling cotton. She lived at home with her father and had a life so dry that the most exciting thing she knew was her office routine.

"This included taking telegrams down to the local telegraph office each noon. The telegraph operator at that time was a Mr. Scroggins, who had been assigned temporarily to the Rome office by his superiors in Atlanta. After a few weeks it became apparent that Mr. Scroggins did not share her opinion, and that of her father, as to her unattractiveness. Time spent at the telegraph office grew beyond the demands of commerce. One day she informed her father that she was bringing a young man home for dinner.

"Three weeks later they were married, and about this time Elam was called back to Atlanta and she went with him. Another three weeks and Elam was called up to the newly formed Confederate Telegraph Corps."

"And now perhaps on to Halifax, Nova Scotia," Joel said.

"Yes, Asa told me. She sees no future for Elam, or herself, in the South."

"The war sweeps all before it," Joel said. "Elam and Asa, Jessie and Amos, off on their way to become citrus growers in Florida. You and I. What common thread is there in all this? I'll tell you what I think. Those who were not part of the great movement for Secession have had to make new lives. Those who were will return to the old ways, will grow embittered, will forever be justifying to themselves how their great enterprise failed, will withdraw into the dream world of Dixieland."

Susannah looked out to where the sun had set among the mountains, leaving a scattering of red clouds in the afterglow. She played a bit with the dark strands that had escaped from her pinned-up hair and tumbled down her neck, ivory in the twilight.

"Yes," she said, "three men and three women removed from the great movement of Secession, that illusion that now takes down the South with it. No question about that. But there's more to it than that, Joel. Three couples that have put their love for each other above all else and perhaps would not have had the war not come along, like some great dark man-of-war, aflame, sinking, and too few boats to put down for those that would save themselves."

"That's very eloquent, and also true."

"It's all in books, the books that kept me from madness when you were lost to me in Spain."

"Yes," he said, "but what about us now? The others have played their cards, taken their pieces off the board. We alone remain. What are we to do?"

"That is a man's decision, yours. But I will not press you now. This is our day of idleness."

After supper Joel lingered a while with Elam and Asa. When he went up he found Susannah lying on the bed, illuminated by candlelight, her dark hair streaming over the pillow, her slim white body punctuated by pink nipples, the dark triangle of hair where her sex dwelled.

"Does this mean that our day of idleness is over?"

"No, it means that now we slow down. We have been throwing ourselves upon each other like wild animals, which is understandable. We are both passionate by nature, were separated for a long time, and have had to find moments for love when and where we could."

"And now?"

"Now it is time for you to make love to me as slowly as possible and for as long a time as you can bear."

"And then?"

"You will no doubt be resourceful."

In her invitation to savor her fully, he knew, there was also a challenge. The winning of her was not quite over.

Their brief idyll ended abruptly the next morning. Elam returned from Hiawassee with their horses, which he had taken to the livery stable the evening before for grooming and feeding. He wore a worried look.

"They say in town that two fellows have been asking after you by name, claiming to be law officers. We don't have much use for law officers up in these mountains, so nobody told them a thing."

"What did they look like, these two?"

"Well, I didn't think to ask that. But I suppose you folks would be smart to get over into North Carolina right away."

"As soon as we can get our horses saddled," Joel said.

They rejoined the turnpike on the other side of Unicoi Gap, skirting the last guard post at the pass.

"Who do you think the two men looking for us are?" Susannah said.

"Well, they could have been sent by Colcock Stiles."

"To kill us."

"Yes, or to collect the reward he's offering. Or they could have been sent by this Colonel Alexander who's been on my trail ever since Savannah. I think I recognized him looking up at the window at Nacoochee. The one who limped."

"Yes," Susannah said, "with the moonlight on him his face resembled a skull . . . or some kind of demon."

Joel turned, looked at her, concerned.

"You're not going back to that kind of thinking, are you?"

"No, but sometimes you can't help seeing what you see . . . or think you see. I'm all right, Joel."

They reined in their horses at the crest of a long ridge bristling with the trunks of giant oaks and chestnuts.

"This may not look like much more than ordinary woods," Joel said, "but it's on the Eastern continental divide. Back of us the rivers, the Savannah and all the others, flow into the Atlantic. Ahead they flow west toward the Mississippi and the Gulf of Mexico. That little creek you can see down there is the beginning of the Hiawassee River, which flows into the old Cherokee lands in North Carolina and Tennessee. Beyond is the United States of America, even from the Confederate point of view."

"So, we are at a watershed," Susannah said.

"Yes."

"Then here is the point at which you must choose, Joel. I will go with you whichever way you choose, but choose you must."

"I cannot go back," he said, "however much I love the land where I was born and its way of life, but it is a life built on the servitude of others. I am not seduced by the way of life in the North, but it is there I think we must head. Would that there was something in between."

"Then we cross over into the North?"

"Yes."

The war had turned the mountains of North Carolina and Tennessee into a kind of no-man's-land, and they passed one dwelling after another that had been burned to the ground. They met few travelers on the road. Of each, however, Joel asked whether any of the marauding bands for which the area was notorious had been seen. The answer each time was that there had been no raids recently. These bands claimed to be Union or Confederate irregulars but were only interested in loot, as they swept down from the mountains into the valleys, burning, raping, and killing as they went.

At noon they stopped for a lunch of cold chicken and biscuits provided by Asa, which they ate under a willow tree at the edge of the water. In the distance the first range of mountains, the Nantahalas, was now visible, and above them white thunderheads were building up.

"It looks like we're going to have a storm later," Susannah said.

"This time of year, there's a thunderstorm in the mountains nearly every afternoon. The clouds build up all day, then in late afternoon the storm comes. By sunset it's clear again, with clouds just on the peaks, a beautiful sight."

"Without war this place would be a paradise," Susannah mused. "The cause of the South is lost, and even those who won't admit it know it's true. Why can't the killing just stop?"

"These mountains once were a paradise," Joel said. "From the Nantahalas on is some of the most beautiful scenery on earth. As to why the killing can't stop, you'll have to seek your answers in Richmond and Washington."

20

After lunch they continued along the turnpike until late afternoon, when they reached the trading post that Elam had told them about. It was a sprawling structure built beside a dam, serving also as a mill, general store, and inn. A waterwheel turned lazily. A large, white-bearded man emerged from the dark doorway. He wore steel-rimmed glasses, and his blue apron was dusted with flour.

"A good afternoon to you."

"Good afternoon, sir. Would you have a room for the night?"

"I have six rooms, all of which are empty. You may take your pick."

A tall, handsome Indian woman with graying hair came out on the porch.

"My name is George Smithson, and this is my wife, Frances. Her father was a Cherokee chief. When I bought this land from him, he threw in his daughter as part of the bargain."

Smithson's wife smiled in a manner that suggested she had heard this feeble joke hundreds of times. A tall, husky young man, who appeared to be part Indian, appeared around the corner of the building.

"This is our son, Oliver. We have two other sons, but they're up in the mountains on a trading expedition. Oliver will tend to your horses. Now do come in."

The room they entered was large and well lighted. There were a number of comfortable chairs and a long table with a dozen straight chairs drawn up around it.

"Would you care for a glass of my wife's Catawba wine?" Smithson brought a bottle and four glasses.

"May your journey continue to be both pleasant and safe."

"Are there any bushwhackers about?" Joel asked.

"Not recently, but in any case they give us a wide berth. It is well understood that if any harm came to me or, especially, my wife, her people would track down whoever was responsible."

"No regular troops about, either Union or Confederate?"

"None. Although North Carolina is part of the Confederacy, there has not even been an attempt to enforce conscription up here. Should there be, I would send my boys up into the mountains. I am a Quaker, and I would not see my boys off to war. Both sides in this conflict are convinced they are right, but it matters not to me which side is right. War is not God's way to settle differences."

After they had drunk their wine, Smithson said, "Would you like to see the mill?"

They went through another room filled with merchandise.

"On this side store goods, rope, nails, axle grease, pulleys, anything a farm could use. On the other side trade goods for the Cherokees, axes, blankets, beads, mirrors, powder, and shot."

"What do the Cherokees trade in return?"

"Mostly hides and furs, sometimes gems, even a little gold they pan up in the mountain streams."

"What's this?" Susannah said, picking up a dried root.

"That's sang."

"Sang?"

"Ginseng root," Joel said. "It grows in the forests and is supposed to be good for all kinds of ailments. You have to know where to look for it, and those that do, don't want others to know, so they always work alone. After a while some of them get sort of funny in the head. I've met them from time to time in the Smokies. They're as shy as wild animals."

"They know my boys, though," Smithson said, "and they'll come to them with their sang. It fetches a right smart price. A dealer comes by a couple of times a year and buys my sang. They say a lot of it ends up in China."

They passed into the next room, which was the mill. The wide floorboards were worn smooth as glass by feet treading in spilled flour and cornmeal. A giant millstone was turning on top of another, driven by the waterwheel. Flour flowed out into a bin below. There was a warm, comforting smell in the air, promising bread to come.

"You can adjust the stones up or down, and if you set them for the coarser grind, it's for cornmeal. Whether wheat or corn, you dump it into that chute above, and the mill works all by itself. God must have a special place in Heaven for whoever first thought up this way of making bread."

That evening they sat with Smithson and had another glass of wine while he smoked a pipe and his wife prepared supper in the kitchen.

"Rabbit with prunes, one of my favorite dishes," Smithson said. "Frances is a fine cook. That's why our boys grew up strong and healthy."

"You have a good life," Joel said.

"It suits me. Folks around here are used to marriages between whites and Cherokees. Didn't matter to my family either. Quakers are very tolerant, as you may know, when it comes to matters of race. I make a decent living and will stay on, if I still can, when this abominable war is over. If not, we'll go to Pennsylvania, where I come from."

"We're thinking about going up North ourselves," Joel said, "but there's something we need to know before we make that move. I hear there's a kind of barter market up on the Tennessee border where it's possible to hire someone to ride into Knoxville and send a telegram."

"I know the place. My boys go up there from time to time to do some trading. I should warn you, though, if you are thinking of traveling there—particularly with a lady—that many of those involved in this trade are desperate men, if not criminals."

"Is there not someplace nearby where I could stay while we wait for a reply to our telegram?" Susannah said.

"I'll ask Frances. She has kinfolk up that way."

"If I can find someone to send and receive a telegram, how do I pay?" Joel asked.

"U.S. dollars. Confederate money's not accepted, which is small wonder. Let's say you agree on twenty dollars. To guarantee that the man you hire comes back with your reply, you tear a twenty-dollar bill in half. He gets the second half on delivery, and he can take the two pieces to the national bank in Knoxville and exchange them for a whole one."

A distant sound outside grew into that of horses' hooves, and Smithson went to the door. His wife came out of the kitchen in an apron, a wooden spoon in her hand.

"It's the boys, Frances," Smithson said.

Two tall, dark-haired young men in buckskins entered the room and embraced their mother. The third son came in from the mill.

"It's a good thing I cooked two rabbits," she said, "and even that may not be enough."

The two sons, Monroe and Sammy, went out to stable their

horses and wash up, and then they all sat down to supper.

"Well, how did you do?" Smithson inquired, after saying grace.

"We have good news," Monroe said. "We came across a miner with some excellent gemstones, amethysts, topazes, sapphires, that he's been holding for a long time. But since his regular customers aren't buying and don't seem likely to as long as the war goes on, he sold them to us at a very good price."

"Those will have to go North," Smithson said. "No market in the South for jewels at all anymore."

He looked at Joel, and Susannah was pretty sure she knew what he was thinking.

"There's news," the other son, Sammy, said, "that's not so good. A really bad gang is on the loose up there, Indians. They'd been serving as scouts for that Colonel Kirk's Yankee raiding party and had been issued repeating carbines. They deserted with these and are riding through the countryside looking for loot."

"Not Cherokees, I hope," Frances Smithson said.

"No, Catawbas. We heard this one story, that last week they raided a rich farmer who they were sure had silver that he had buried. So they tied his wife to a tree, piled up some brushwood, and said they were going to burn her unless this man told them where the silver was buried. He said he didn't have any silver. They lit the fire, and he kept saying he didn't have any silver. By the time these Catawbas realized he must be telling the truth and cut the wife's ropes, she was so badly burned she died."

"Sammy, don't speak anymore of this in front of our guests, and 'specially at table."

"Sorry, Ma."

The high spirits Susannah had been feeling all day faded

away, and once again she was seized by the dark premonition that somewhere upcountry a terrible fate awaited them.

This gloomy thought was punctured by an unexpected question from Joel to George Smithson.

"Tell me, Mr. Smithson, has there been a mule train, or something of the sort, passing this way in the last year or two, something you wouldn't normally see?"

"Only once, and I suppose it would have been unusual in peacetime. But with the war on, you see a lot of things you wouldn't normally. Mule train? Yes, carrying wooden boxes of ammunition up into the mountains. Don't know why, but people running wars aren't likely to explain themselves."

"How do you know it was ammunition that this mule train was carrying?"

"Plainly marked on each and every box."

They went to bed that evening in a room scented by the cedar chips that filled bags hung in the large plain armoire. After the candle had been snuffed and they were lying alongside each other in the moonlit room, Susannah spoke.

"Mule trains?"

"This whole story of the Dahlonega gold began with a bank robbery. Rocks were substituted for the gold that a trunk originally contained, hundreds of thousands of dollars' worth, maybe even a million, though I don't believe that. Something about this has been nagging me, to the point that I did some calculations on how much gold a trunk could hold. Nothing like a million dollars' worth. Four, five, six trunks is more like it, a whole mule train to carry it away. Ammunition being taken up into the high mountains? I don't think so."

They rode off soon after dawn, Susannah and Joel and two of the Smithson boys, Oliver and Monroe. They were heading away from the Snowbirds towards the Pisgahs and what lay beyond.

As soon as they were around the first bend in the turnpike Monroe said to Joel, "You have side arms?"

"We do," and Joel exhibited the dueling pistol he carried. "Fully loaded when we started out, but three shots spent along the way. That leaves me with a fully-loaded pistol, and Mrs. Devereux with two chambers loaded, for emergencies."

Susannah understood that Joel had decided that with the Smithsons it would perhaps not be a good idea to describe her as his fiancée. She rather liked the sound of Mrs. Devereux.

"What did you spend those three shots on?"

"One on a man."

"Kill him?"

"No. The other two on dogs attacking us. Killed them."

"Well, we've got a bit more gun than that toy you have," and Monroe pulled a large Colt revolver from his buckskins. "Pa don't approve, being a Quaker, but on the other hand he wants us to go on living, and there's no way you're going to do that upcountry unless you're armed. So he don't ask whether we're carrying guns, and we don't tell him that we do."

The road had become not much more than the Cherokee war path that, Monroe said, had been there since before even the oldest stories of war with the Creeks, that being long before the first white man had journeyed into these mountains. Susannah remembered the story of the ancient Greeks, mercenary soldiers, moving always upcountry, not knowing where they were, which way was home, and almost despairing. They were now riding into the high mountains, mostly still unexplored, wearing clouds like wreaths, as Joel had said. These mountains had a strange fascination for him, and she vaguely understood that it was in some way like his passion for her. If she could figure that out, perhaps she would be able to understand him better.

Around a bend in the old Cherokee war path a wagon lay on its side in the undergrowth. The Smithson boys dismounted and examined it, speaking in low voices in Cherokee. It was only then that Susannah looked up from her musings to the sky, which was thick with circling turkey vultures. And then her eyes returned to earth and the place, a half-overgrown, abandoned farm plot, where the black-winged vultures with red-skinned heads were beginning to land.

"We'd better have a look," Oliver said with a sidelong glance at Susannah.

He and his brother went toward where the vultures were coming to earth and by throwing rocks drove them, clumsily flapping their wings, into the branches of the surrounding trees. The two of them stood, looking down for only a few seconds, and returned silently.

"What?" Susannah said.

"You don't want to know," Monroe answered.

"I must know," she said, and got down from her horse.

"Don't, Susannah," Joel said.

"I must," she repeated. The dark forces had her in their grip again.

In the little clearing four bodies lay. Two were adults, a man and a woman, and where their hair had been there now was only clotted blood and patches of bare skull. The other two were half-grown, a boy of about sixteen and a girl of about twelve. The girl's long blond hair made a graceful swirl in the grass. Her unseeing eyes were open to the sky.

Susannah staggered back to where the others waited, desperately trying not to throw up. The three men stopped talking in low voices.

"I told you not to," Joel said.

"Four ordinary people murdered, two of them scalped. And then a little girl of twelve dead. Why must the universe be filled with such horrors?"

"I'm sorry," Joel said, and turned to Oliver and Monroe. "Indians."

"Or those who would like it to look that way. Anyway, not too long ago."

"Whoever did it, then, must be close about," Joel said.

"Most probably," Oliver said. "We'd better move along."

That night they slept in a grove of chestnuts, but there was little sleep. The three men took turns standing guard, and the horror of what they had encountered that day kept Susannah from sleeping at all until it was nearly dawn. The next day they continued on along the old war path, meeting no one. Toward sunset they came upon a fork in the path, one branch going up into the higher mountains, the other heading down into a valley from where a column of smoke rose.

"That's the market down there," Monroe said and took a telescope from a saddlebag. "Well, they ain't lacking for business."

He handed the telescope to Susannah. She put it to her eye and surveyed the scene below. The goods for sale were spread out on a carpet of pine needles, an immense amount of silver, tea sets, knives, forks, spoons, and much more, twinkling in the setting sun. There were musical instruments, a violin, a harp, a silver flute, a lady's riding saddle and boots, a sewing machine, copper cooking pots, Oriental carpets. Men milled about, some in pieces of Confederate or

Union uniforms. She noticed several were missing an arm or a leg, casualties of the war reduced to bartering. She handed the glass to Joel.

"All the paraphernalia of the good life of the old South," Joel said, "soon to grace sideboards in Cincinnati or Chicago. When the war's over there won't be much of the good life in the South for a long time to come. The Secessionists sowed a whirlwind, and now the reaping has begun."

"We'd best spend the night here," Oliver said. "We don't want to venture amongst that crowd after dark, nor do we want to announce ourselves by starting a fire. So, I guess it's going to be hardtack and dried beef for supper."

As the evening passed there came from below cries and shouts, singing, a gunshot.

"No," Oliver said, "no place to be tonight. They're well supplied with liquor. And you sure don't want to take your wife down there tomorrow, Mr. Devereux. I'll ride with her to my auntie's place up on the mountain, and then join you and Monroe. I've got a little trading to do on my own account."

"I don't even want you to go down there," Susannah said to Joel.

"He'll be all right if he's with me," Monroe said. "I do a lot of business with those folks."

"Will you be able to sell your gemstones?" Joel asked.

"Easily. Something valuable that you can conceal on your person is what they want the most."

Susannah thought of the gold coins that Joel had concealed in his vest. There were only a few left, and one of those would have to be used to buy U.S. dollars to send the telegram to Princeton. If there was not a positive answer, what were they to do? Cross over into the North and look for work? And they would be considered rebels.

255

The next morning she kissed Joel goodbye, hiding her tears, and she and Oliver watched Joel and Monroe as they descended the mountain. Then they turned and took the path leading upward. *I may never see him again,* Susannah thought, *and I'll be all alone with an old Indian woman out in the wilderness.* She felt the darkness closing in around her. No, she said to herself, you've got to quit that crazy way of thinking, about the powers of darkness and hell, or you really will go mad. *How ashamed Joel would be of me, and I am going to see him again.* She turned to Oliver.

"This is your mother's sister's place we're going to?"

"Yes. It's a little farm she and her husband work. He's a kind of part-time preacher, too."

"Preacher?"

"David, that's his English name, went to a mission school in Georgia and was studying for the ministry when the removal to the Oklahoma Territory took place. He ran off to the mountains like a lot of Cherokees, like my ma and auntie. He doesn't really have a license to preach, but I guess that doesn't matter. He's the only preacher people around here got."

"Where was this mission in Georgia?"

"I don't know exactly."

The farm was a clearing in the forest high up on the mountain, the house a log cabin chinked with mud, the chimney of fieldstone, the roof of oak shakes. A fire burned down under a big black cast-iron pot. In an open shed to one side of the house hams hung, tobacco dried. The shed was decorated with deer antlers. In a garden on that side of the house sunflowers grew, beans, tomatoes, squash, melons. From the other side of the house rows of corn extended to the edge of the forest. On the porch a tall man in buckskins stood, white hair to his shoulders, his skin the color of an old penny, his nose sharp as a hawk's beak.

"Is that you, Oliver?"

"Yes, sir."

"You have your mother's features, but it's hard to be sure after so many years. You were eight when I last saw you."

"This is Mrs. Devereux," Oliver said. "Ma wants you to put her up for a couple of days."

"On this piece of earth, what your mother wants will be done, as ancient custom demands. Your servant, ma'am, David Goode."

Susannah could feel the hairs stand up on the back of her neck. The powers of darkness might not rule the world, but those of chance and coincidence often did.

"I'm very pleased to meet you. I won't be staying long, and I will explain why I've been brought here."

"You are not required to explain anything, Mrs. Devereux. You are our guest, that's all."

A tall, gray-haired Indian woman, who much resembled Frances Smithson, emerged from the field of corn carrying a wooden bucket.

"Your sister sends us a guest, Mary," David Goode said to her.

"And a welcome one," the woman said. "We have no one to bring us news of the outside world from one month to the next."

Before Susannah could even get her bearings, Oliver, after exchanging a few words with his "auntie," rode away, and Susannah found herself alone with David Goode and his wife, the daughter of a Cherokee chief.

"Would you care for some refreshment?" Mary Goode said.

Susannah barely repressed a laugh. On every front porch

in all the South, whether the hosts were white, black, or Indian, that was always the first question asked. What the Cherokee woman brought her was an herbal tea, strong, bitter, and delicious. After she had explained her situation with the minimum of lying—how she hated the lying!—she turned to David Goode, whose wife addressed him by some unintelligible Cherokee name.

"Oliver told me you were educated in a mission school in Georgia."

"Yes. The Mission to the Cherokee Nation near the town of Catesville in North Georgia. But time was not on our side. My teacher was a young Presbyterian minister, Philander Goode, whose name I took for my name with white people. He was a dedicated man, full of hope and zeal. He had learned Cherokee even before he came to Georgia, from Elias Boudinot, himself a student then in the north."

"Yes, I have heard of him."

"Boudinot founded the first Cherokee-language newspaper, using the script devised by the great Sequoia to allow the Cherokees to put their words down on paper."

"Yes, I know."

"I, too, was full of hope, but both Doctor Goode and I were to see our hopes dashed, all because of the discovery of gold."

"In Duke's Creek."

"My, you are well informed, Mrs. Devereux."

After a supper of a kind of stew of squirrel meat, corn, peppers, and beans, Susannah said she must find sleep.

"And while you sleep," Mary Goode said, "let me wash your clothes. Our one wash pot had been used today for making soap, but that's now done. I'll give you a new buckskin dress I've just made to wear."

And so Susannah went to bed on a mattress of sweet-smelling balsam boughs, and slept the sleep of the dead. She awoke in the morning refreshed, climbed down the ladder from the loft where she had slept, and went out on the porch. David Goode was sitting cross-legged, mending what looked like a fish trap.

"Good morning, Mrs. Devereux," he said.

"That's not really my name," she said. "It's Susannah Goode."

"Goode?" His brow wrinkled.

"I am Philander Goode's niece. I was too tired and confused yesterday to explain."

"How odd that you should come here."

"It's a long story, or rather many things have happened in a short time to bring me here."

"Doctor Goode . . ."

"Is dead. He died just a few days ago." So much had happened that she couldn't even remember how many days had passed.

"I'm sorry to hear that. He was a Christian gentleman, kind and gentle."

"He was all those things."

"I am so sorry . . ." He looked as though he might cry. "If you would like to wash up," and he indicated a rickety table with a bucket and a metal basin.

She dipped a gourd into the bucket, poured some water into the basin, and washed her face with her hands.

"There's porridge with dried fruit in a pot over the fire."

She came back out on the porch with a bowl of porridge, stood, and looked out over row after row of blue mountains. The clouds were already building up for an afternoon thunderstorm. This little farm was an oasis of peace up above the horrors that the death agony of the South brought in its train.

"I don't suppose Doctor Goode had many Cherokee pupils these last years?" her host said.

"Hardly any in the eight years I lived at the Mission. The last was a boy who was found in the forest. No one ever learned where he came from, except that it was somewhere up in the Snowbirds. Philander named him Elias after Elias Boudinot."

"So the name lives on. Elias Boudinot was himself named for the president of the Continental Congress, who brought him up north to be educated as a white man. And for that his own people murdered him out in the Oklahoma Territory."

"Yes. I brought the new Elias with me when I left Catesville. By now he should be back in the Snowbirds with his people."

"So many odd things all at once. Dr. Goode encouraged me to run away when the army came to take my people to the territory. His good friend was a Cherokee chief, and he sent us to him. The chief had two daughters. After some time I married one and George Smithson the other. I shall have to look up this new Elias when the troubles are over. We can form a Cherokee Mission old boys' club, a very small one. Now what else can I do for you? My wife is already out in the field, weeding the young corn."

"May I help her?"

"You needn't, though you can if you like."

So for that day and the next and the next she worked in the fields beside Mary Goode, with few words passing between them. Of Joel and the Smithson boys there was no sign. The more anxious she became the harder she worked, so that she could lose her worries in sleep. She hoed the young corn, working in her bare feet, her face and arms reddened by the sun, brought heavy buckets of cool water up from the stream for the mounds of ripening squash. The stream had been dammed, and once or twice a day Susannah would slip out of her buckskin dress and dive into the pool, float in the cool, clear water. How few material things one needed to be content.

21

They rode away from the market, each with the results of his venture. Monroe had sold his gemstones for a good price, Oliver had bought two Sharp repeating rifles that must be sold without his father's knowledge, and Joel had, to his surprise, a reply to his telegram, a reply that he dreaded showing to Susannah. His other concern was that in paying for the telegram he had sent and the one he had received, the few gold coins that remained to him had spilled out on the ground. He had quickly covered them with his hand, but not before several of the gaunt, bearded men in pieces of Confederate and Union uniforms had seen them.

As he rode along Joel felt a happiness, despite the discouraging telegram. He and Susannah were still alive, untouched by the violence that washed over the South like a hurricane-driven wave, taking all before it who were unlucky enough to be in its path. Now they were deep into the mountains of western North Carolina, of little interest to the generals and presumably beyond the reach of Judge Stiles or the mysterious colonel.

Riding ahead of the Smithson boys in his eagerness to be joined again with Susannah, he suddenly found two men on horseback blocking the road. One held a rifle in the crook of his arm. If it was the few gold coins they wanted, they were welcome to them. He had too much else to live for. Joel began to raise his hands when he realized that this might not be just a robbery. The man with the rifle slowly raised it. He looked like the kind of worthless white that hung around the Catesville courthouse. The other was a half-breed, a long knife in his belt. Just the types that Judge Colcock Stiles would be able to hire if he wanted someone killed.

Joel spurred his horse off the road and across a half-grown-up field, headed for the woods beyond. Two shots rang out. The first grazed his neck, and he could feel blood flowing. The second creased his skull and threw him off his horse. He hit the ground so hard it knocked the breath out of him. He lost consciousness, for seconds or minutes, and came up from the dark to hear more gunshots, but he was not hit again. Horses' hooves rumbled as the riders maneuvered their mounts, shouts rang out, more gunshots, and then the sound of horses galloping away.

"Goddamn," a voice said, "two Sharp rifles and them both unloaded. Had they been loaded, I would have knocked their asses right out of the saddle."

"Well, that's the way it was," another voice said. "Now we'd better tend to this one before he bleeds to death. The shot to the head looks the worse, but scalp wounds always bleed a lot. It's the one to the neck that's worrying, nicked a blood vessel."

"We'd better get him to Auntie fast. She'll know what to do."

Joel felt himself being lifted to a saddle, felt the moving off, with someone riding beside him so close that their knees knocked together, felt something being held against his neck.

"He's looking awful pale," Monroe said. "I reckon we ain't got much time."

Joel felt warm and comfortable and supposed he was dying. He had studied a little medicine at Princeton and learned a bit about the circulation of the blood, had heard a professor say that death by losing blood was a relatively painless way to die. But what of Susannah? What would become of her? And then he felt himself descending into a bottomless pit.

When he awoke Susannah was smiling down at him. He tried to get up, but he was so weak he could not even lift his head.

"What time is it?" he said.

"About ten o'clock in the morning."

"It can't be. We only left the market at nine."

"It's not the day you left the market. You have been unconscious, my love, for three days."

"I have?"

"I was sure I had lost you. If it hadn't been for Mary Goode, you would have died. Somehow she stopped the bleeding. Cherokee medicine, preparations made from plants."

"Mary Goode?"

"I'll explain later. For now, just rest."

"I'm hungry."

"I'll bring you some soup."

She returned with a bowl of clear broth and fed him with a spoon, but after a few spoonfuls he felt himself drifting off to sleep.

When he awoke again it was late afternoon. His bed was by the window, and he could hear Susannah talking to someone on the porch, a man.

"But what do you do for money?"

"Don't need any. We grow everything we eat, and I make everything needed to run a farm. Mary weaves the cloth for our clothes or makes them out of buckskin. If there's something I can't make, like nails, I barter for it with skins and furs, cured hams, the like. I need powder and shot, of course, for hunting, fishhooks and cork floats for fishing. But that's about it. Corn whiskey, of course, is like money, and that's why we grow more corn than we need ourselves."

"Why not just sell the corn?"

"Stop and think about it. You would have to have several mules to carry to market the corn that makes up a couple of gallons of moonshine. Yes, corn whiskey is the money of these mountains, always has been. But why are you interested in all this?"

"Because we don't have any money. We thought we might get some, but it seems not. I was trying to find out if it would be possible to live in the mountains with little or no money."

"It is, but it takes a lot of hard work, and you have to learn how to do things, like weaving baskets and splitting shakes off an oak log and making soap out of hog fat and ashes."

"I could learn," Susannah said.

As he lay in his bed, Joel cried, partly from the trauma of being snatched from death, partly from his pleasure in hearing Susannah searching for ways for them to stay together and survive. She had said that she would never fail him, and she never would.

She had obviously found the telegram from Professor Arnold confirming that there would be a position for him once the war was over, but that telegraphic transfers of money were prohibited by wartime regulation to any place within a hundred miles of the front, such as Knoxville or Chattanooga. Arnold had said that if Joel had funds of his own he could resume work, and he would be compensated after the war was over. He had exactly six five-dollar gold pieces left, and no prospect of getting any more.

He looked up at the ceiling of the cabin, where bunches of

dried plants hung, some of which must have made up the preparations with which the Cherokee woman, now tending a black iron pot hanging over the fire, had stanched the flow of blood that had been taking with it his life.

The next day he was sitting on the porch himself, talking with Susannah and David and Mary Goode. He who had found little Elias in the mountains and taken him to Philander Goode at the Mission, David who had begun his studies there with Philander, Mary who had fled the removal to the Oklahoma Territory, as had David at Philander's urging, and Philander's niece and ward, Susannah Goode.

"Mary thinks you'll be able to travel soon," David Goode said, "not that you aren't welcome to stay as long as you want."

"No, though it's very kind of you to offer. We should move on north."

He looked at Susannah. How beautiful she was, barefoot, in a buckskin dress that came only halfway down her thighs, Indian fashion. She wore her dark hair braided in a pigtail down her back. Her arms and legs and face were flushed from working in the sun.

Suddenly he wanted her badly. He wanted her naked, to enter her, to hear her moans of pleasure. The feeling was so immediate that it sent a shudder through his body. She smiled. She knew what he was thinking.

"Yes, we have to leave as soon as possible," Joel said. "There's a danger to you as long as we are here. Besides, we have to let the Smithson boys go home. They've been camped down at the bottom of the mountain ever since they brought me here."

David Goode said something to his wife in Cherokee and she replied, laughed.

"Mary said that if their mother found out that her sons had

left you unguarded, she would skin them alive."

The sun was lower in the sky now, and the Goodes went back to their farm chores. He and Susannah were left alone on the porch. The afternoon clouds were gathering, and cloud shadow covered her face and hung there but could not conceal the tears running down her cheeks. He went over to her, sat down next to her, put his arm around her.

"What is it, my love?"

"I nearly lost you. That first day you lay there, white as chalk, and I thought that it was the end, and had we not been with a woman who knew Indian medicine, it would have been. What incredible luck. I could see the spirit ebbing away from your body, and I was like a demon, moving back and forth frantically with the things that Mary needed. Finally, the blood stopped flowing. Mary looked up at me and said, 'It is good now.' It was then that I at last saw the truth about myself, always thinking about only me. Now it was love for another that drove me, and it set me free."

He took her hands in his, too overpowered with emotion to speak, but then he did.

"I learned the truth about myself lying in bed with Manuela, in a hunting lodge in the Pyrenees, at dawn. I had betrayed you and felt loathing for myself. I knew I had to get back to you at any price."

"I know that," she said simply. "But that is the past, and now all we must be concerned with is to survive. Without each other, what life would either of us have?"

"When I came out of unconsciousness and saw your face, that was my first thought."

"When you came up to me from whatever dark place you had been," she said, "you kept muttering something about 'the sea.' What does it mean?"

"The sea, yes. When I got the telegram from Professor Arnold saying he could not provide any money until the war was over, I folded it up and put it in that Greek text I've been carrying with me. When I opened the book it was at the page where the Greeks are saved, and I thought about you and me. That was only minutes before I was shot."

"How were the Greeks saved?"

"Could you bring me the book *Upcountry*?"

She brought him the slim volume, and he turned to the page where he had placed the telegram.

"At this point the Greeks under Xenophon are in the high mountains of Asia Minor, they are lost, being attacked by hostile tribes, have almost given up hope, and then . . .

" 'The shout kept getting louder and louder, and those behind began to run toward those ahead, and the shout grew even louder as the numbers grew greater. Xenophon leaped into the saddle and rode ahead. It was then that they heard the soldiers shouting, "The sea! The sea!" passing the word back. The rearguard troops broke into a run, the pack animals, the horses. When they reached the summit they saw the sea and began embracing each other, even captains and generals, with tears in their eyes.' "

"The sea?"

"They were Greeks. The sea was their home. Once on it they could find their way to their native towns and villages from any place."

She looked at him thoughtfully. "It's about home, isn't it."

"Yes."

"I've never had one, and Devereux Hall is certainly not yours anymore."

"No."

"Home for you is the high mountains, isn't it?"

"Yes."

"And from there you could find your way to the future, wherever it may be."

"Yes."

"Joel, I'm taking charge, for now, of our expedition upcountry. When you're strong enough, I'll relinquish command."

"Yes, ma'am."

Sometime in the hours between sunset and midnight Susannah came to him, sat down on his bed, took his hand.

"You wanted me mightily this afternoon, didn't you?"

"Yes."

"Well, I'm of the same persuasion. While I know it's probably not prudent, there are times when you have to say yes to life. If you precisely obey me, I think we can safely do what we both need so badly."

She led him down the rows of corn in the moonlight, the shadows of the cornstalks passing over them like bars. At the end of the cornfield, there was a swath of thick, moist grass, along the path where buckets of water were brought up from the mountain stream to water the crops.

"Lie down," she said.

She unloosened his clothes, slipped the buckskin dress over her head and stood, a slim nymph, in the moonlight. She kneeled down beside him.

"Now, you must not move. I'm not having you break open your healing wounds by throwing yourself around. This time I'll do the work."

"I believe you said you had assumed charge, ma'am."

She giggled, and then she straddled him, and he felt himself entering her with astonishing lubricity. Her cool body lay lightly on him for a while, and then she began to move slowly.

"Remember," she said, "don't move."

He had to think of everything else but what they were doing, from sharpening pencils to shining his boots, to avoid moving. Her hips rose and fell in luxuriant curves and rhythms. He was sweating with the effort not to anticipate her. When she did begin to come, he grasped her firm behind in his hands and held her close to him while they both came.

After an interval she rolled off him and lay on her back in the damp grass.

"Oh, God, oh God," she gasped. "Tonight leaves nowhere to go on to."

"We'll see about that," he said.

After a while he said, "Did you know that the ancient Greeks believed that if you made love in a cornfield, you'd have a better harvest? Is it the same with the Cherokees?"

She laughed. "I've no idea. It's not exactly the kind of discussion Philander and I would have had."

"Anyway, we can remember this as our house gift to the Goodes."

"I'll remember it," she said, "as the best I've ever had."

22

Next evening Mary said that Joel's wound had healed enough that travel was possible without great risk—not without any risk, but with a risk less than if they stayed in the area, with the remnants of Colonel Kirk's scouts on the loose with repeating rifles and on the rampage in twos and threes. That was enough for Susannah. Her task now was to move them ahead while the odds were still on their side. Besides whoring, she knew a lot about gambling, having hovered around the green baize tables in her mother's establishment, peeking into the hands of the cigar-smoking, cologned and pomaded men who played at cards there, finally understanding the odds better than most of the players, and that at age twelve.

As she rode north with Joel, Susannah kept looking behind her. The men who had tried to kill Joel could reappear at any time.

"How goes it?" she said to the man who rode beside her, their horses kept to a slow walk.

"I'm doing fine," he said, "just fine."

She did not believe that, of course, but she judged that he would be able to sit a horse for the rest of the day, until she could find some place for them to bed down for the night. It was a gorgeous day, the white clouds piled high, the air sweet with the scent of honeysuckle. Her horse moved at a pace that rocked her hips back and forth in a mimicry of the act of love.

As so many times before in the days and weeks they had been together, she felt what great joy might await her around the next bend in the road, if only they could escape the malevolent forces that swirled around them like a black fog.

"You are my good angel," he said.

"Mary Goode is your angel," she said. "It is her knowledge of the healing power of plants that saved your life."

"She and Tyche."

"Tyche?"

"The Greek goddess of luck, of chance."

"Then she is a good goddess."

"Good for some, bad for others. In my case, if my horse had moved in only a slightly different rhythm, if the finger on the trigger of the gun fired at me had been more—or less—steady, the second bullet that grazed my skull might have entered an inch to the left and into my brain."

"Good for some, bad for others. Those are words spoken to you by your Spanish mistress, Manuela, aren't they?"

He looked at her. "You surprise me again."

"A woman's eyes can look into the mind of the man she loves, even though she doesn't totally understand him."

Hour by hour they entered into the higher mountains, the forest ever denser and darker, the feeling that eyes were watching them ever growing. But these were real dangers, not imagined ones. She had not yet been able to explain fully to Joel the change that had come over her. The powers of spiritual darkness that had followed her all her life, like furies, had been driven away by her frantic efforts to save his life. She had told herself that she would put up her own life as security for his. Suddenly, with this thought, the powers of darkness fell back, as though struck by one of the mountains' afternoon thunderstorms, and she was left standing in possession of her own soul.

"Hello there, mister," a voice said, shaking Susannah out of her reverie.

A man of middle age squatted in the shadow of the pines, a dark, scraggly beard, skin so pale that he might never have come out into the sun, his clothes rags, a canvas sack slung over one shoulder.

"I know you, don't I?" the man said.

"I'm not sure," Joel replied.

"Well, I think so. You was up in the high Smokies a few summers ago, weren't you, with some perfessor, with telescopes and all?"

"You're right there. You're a sang man, aren't you?"

"You don't have to be a perfessor to figure that out. You know what?"

"What?"

"There was two fellows by here about an hour ago. They was looking for you, or at least I suppose they was, since there's few people along this road these days, and not many of them are a man riding a horse and a woman riding another and dressed in man's clothes. I said I hadn't seen nobody all day, and at the time that was surely true."

"Why are you telling me this?"

"They struck me as bad types, one a half-breed, one the lowest kind of white man, both with pistols, and those repeating rifles in saddle holsters, sort of like the kind you would expect to sign on with that Colonel Kirk."

"I certainly thank you," Joel said. "Is there any other way that we can pass other than this road?"

"Where you headed?"

"Toward the Smokies."

"Go back about half a mile and you'll find an old Cherokee trail, half grown-up, that goes north. That'll take you up on the ridge, and from there you'll overlook the road. If those fellows are still about, you ought to be able to spot them."

"I thank you again. Might I know your name?"

"Ain't got one," the sang man said.

She had supposed that the trail they were told to take by the ginseng gatherer would be high above the road. It was, however, only a hundred feet or so higher, and soon enough they spotted the two men. They were sitting beside the road sharing a jug. She and Joel quietly got down from their horses and walked them until the two men below were out of sight.

"I know this trail," Joel said. "I came up it a long time ago. I must have been about eight years old, with my father and some of his cronies, to the Raven's Nest."

"Raven's Nest?"

"A hunting lodge that Auguste had built when he was a young man, a place where he could get out of the public eye, he and his cronies, hunt, fish, drink, all those things that Southern gentlemen are addicted to. There were women too, who I was given to understand were the wives of my father's friends. Later I realized that this was not the case. The ladies were of a certain profession."

"My mother's."

"Yes. So, perhaps now we have the answer to our riddle. We know that the mule train carrying boxes of ammunition came up this road, and that the boxes likely contained gold rather than cartridges. What more logical explanation than that the destination was Raven's Nest, remote and well-guarded and, with the war on, virtually forgotten?"

"You think the gold's still there?"

"I would bet on it."

Half an hour later they were at the crest of the ridge, Raven's Nest just ahead, a dark, almost fort-like structure of logs at the point of a rocky promontory, overlooking endless ranges of mountains.

Below the lodge was a stone guardhouse that Joel said he remembered from his single visit at age eight. An elderly man improbably came out of the guardhouse.

"Why, Mr. Joel."

"Fletcher, what are you doing up here?"

"Got too stove in with arthritis for gardening and greenhouses. Your pa said, what with my wife dead and the children gone, maybe I wouldn't mind taking on caring for Raven's Nest. I said I wouldn't, and I don't. There's a certain satisfaction in living alone, with only the animals and birds and trees for company. It's not a bad way to end your life."

"No, I suppose not. How long have you been here?"

"Two years. July 4, 1862, to be exact, the day of independence of that country we used to belong to."

"Was there a caretaker here before you came?"

" 'Course there was, old Braswell, but he died that April, I think it was."

"So, there was no caretaker at Raven's Nest between April and July, two years ago?"

"Well, that's right, though I can't imagine why in the world that would interest you. In any case, it didn't make no difference. Nothing here was bothered. People are scared of your pa. He'd as soon set the law on you as look at you."

"Yes, I know. Fletcher, this is my fiancée, Miss Goode."

"My pleasure, ma'am."

If I hear "fiancée" one more time, Susannah thought, *I'm going to scream.*

"We're headed up to the Smokies."

"Where you used to pass your summers with that professor?"

"That's right. Would it be all right for us to spend the night here?"

"Not for me to say. It's your house, after all."

The sun was setting when they entered the lodge, opening the door with the big iron key the caretaker had given them. There was a huge stone fireplace with logs laid in it, six or eight feet long. On the walls of rough-hewn pine boards the stuffed heads of animals were set, deer and bobcat and panther, the pelts of foxes and beaver.

It was, Susannah saw instantly, a masculine kind of place, a view that was confirmed by the next room, with its billiard table, glass cases of fly rods, racks for guns, these now empty. All that was lacking was the boxes of cigars and the bottles of cognac, Calvados, and Armagnac: the gun room of Devereux Hall transposed to the wilderness, but now over all a fine coat of dust and pollen. Auguste Devereux might have had his way with men and with women, but time he had not been able to ward off. She took Joel's hand in hers. So it is with us all, she thought, a phrase taken like so many others, from a book in Philander's library. Until Joel had returned to her, the library had been all the life she had had.

Not long after dawn they began their search of the dusty rooms, one by one, some just as they were left at the end of the last hunting season before the war, others piled high with the paraphernalia of the last guests, returning to family and frantic preparations to defend home and honor. But nowhere did they find a trace of the Dahlonega gold.

"This place is vast," Susannah said, "so many rooms for what is just a hunting lodge."

"That's the way life was lived," Joel said, "with no limits. We shall not see its like again."

That too was a phrase from some book she had read, but

Susannah couldn't remember which it was.

By noon there was nothing left to explore, it seemed. She stood on the stone terrace and looked out over the grandest alpine landscape she had ever seen.

"Nothing left to explore," she said absently.

"Except the well. Why leave a stone unturned before admitting that I was wrong? It was a romantic idea I had, something the eight-year-old in me dreamed up. But the rope and pulley seem sound. Why don't you lower me down for a look?"

"I'm not lowering you down anywhere, my friend, not in your condition. You may lower me down for a quick look—I'm as light as a feather at this point—and then we move on fast, before those renegades come across us."

Joel lowered Susannah into the well, one foot in a bucket at the end of the rope, a lantern in her hand. The well was deep, the penetration of the noon sun, lighting ferns and lichen clinging to the rock walls, growing less and less, until all was dark but for a small circle of blue overhead and the circle of dim light around the lantern. The darkness held no fears or terrors for her. It was the dark natural for a shaft descending into the earth. In the days when all of her being was focused on Joel's survival, her spiritual sickness had been cured.

At the bottom, the shaft opened into a kind of cave through which an underground spring ran. And then she saw it.

"Joel!"

"What?" his voice echoed down the shaft.

"A box, broken open, with 'LIVE AMMUNITION. DANGER,' printed on it.' "

"That's all?"

"No. Up on ledges there are other boxes, but there's not

enough light to see much more than that."

"So. I'm going to bring you up now."

"Wait. There are gold coins in the water. Let me down a bit further."

The coins twinkled in the light of the lantern she held in one hand, her arm crooked around the rope, while with her free hand she scooped up a fistful of gold from the bottom of the swift-running stream. The coins were as cold as ice. She put them in a shirt pocket, picked up the rest of the coins, until all were gone and both of her shirt pockets full.

"Now you can bring me up."

She stepped out of the well into the light of day, poured the glittering contents of her pockets onto the well head.

He examined the coins. "All marked with a 'D' for Dahlonega."

While Joel sought out some clothes for them in closets and armoires and closed up the lodge, she went down to the remnant of pasture where they had tethered their horses, to find four horses there rather than two. She paused just a moment too long before bolting into the woods. Two men in buckskins had their pistols trained on her. She opened her mouth to plead, to explain, to threaten even, but no words would come out. There was no hope of mercy in their eyes.

"She's a beauty, ain't she?"

"She is that. It's almost a shame."

"Why don't we have a piece of her before we kill her?"

"You are some fool. Her boyfriend's about, most likely armed, soon to wonder why she hasn't come back with their horses. Now wouldn't you be in a pretty position when he shows up."

"So, we just shoot her."

"No cure for stupidity, I suppose. Now this Devereux

fellow hears a gunshot coming from down here and goes on the alert. Where is he, by the way?"

"Got no idea."

"Well, that's right. We'll do it my way. We'll wait till we can take them both."

"All right, but I get her scalp, with all that long black hair."

"You make me sick," the whiter of the two said.

All that Susannah understood was that she and Joel were going to die in just a few minutes. Her ears were ringing, her sight seemed to dim, as though her senses were being dulled, so that she would be spared the full horror of the last minutes before the shots rang out and they were no more. Her eyes closed, she lost all sense of time. Then there was a rustling of undergrowth, as of bushes being parted. Joel was about to fall into the same trap she had. It was all over.

The explosion came from somewhere beyond her, roared around her and faded away. She opened her eyes. One of the men lay on his back in the grass, his chest covered in blood. The other stood frozen, his pistol half-raised.

"Drop it," Joel said, and the man, the darker-skinned one, let his hand loosen, and the revolver he had been clutching fell into the grass.

"Susannah, get his gun."

She ran forward and scooped up the pistol from the grass, but the man grabbed her by the wrist. They struggled for the pistol, and she could smell the odor of the man, like rancid bear grease. He had the barrel of the pistol now firmly in his grip, but as the butt of the pistol slipped from her grasp her finger grazed the trigger. A blast of exploding powder erupted in her face, and now she smelled the odor of her singed hair and eyebrows. The half-breed rocked back and forth and then fell to his knees. Then slowly he twisted forward and lay down on the earth as if going to sleep.

Joel came to her and put an arm around her.

"Are you all right?"

"I will be all right . . . someday, but not for a long time. Right now I don't know whether I meant to kill him or it was an accident. Maybe I never will know."

"What I did, I had to do," Joel murmured into her neck. "Either him or you."

"What you had to do . . . yes. Somehow what we both did doesn't shock me as much as it should. I suppose war makes you hard and unfeeling in the end."

They leaned against each other for support, breathing hard. *We are near the end of our rope,* Susannah thought. *I don't think I can endure much more.*

Fletcher, the old guardian of the place, burst wild-eyed into the clearing carrying an ancient musket. He looked down at the dead men.

"What's happened, Mr. Joel?"

"These men attacked us. We killed them."

"Well, you did good. These mountains are full of the worst kind," Fletcher said, poking the dead men with his musket.

"Could you get rid of the bodies?"

"Surely."

"And you're welcome to their two horses, the pistols and the rifles."

"I do thank you."

Fletcher took the dead men by the ankles, one at a time, and dragged them into the woods. When he returned he was carrying a pair of boots.

"Thank you, Fletcher," Joel said. "We'd better be going now, before something else happens."

"Won't you stay for a minute or two? I don't get much company, and I should offer you some refreshment. All I've got is some mountain liquor, but I imagine after killing two men your nerves might be a tad raw. Excuse me, ma'am."

"Of course we'll stay for a while," Susannah said. "I might have a swallow myself. My nerves could certainly use it."

Susannah drank directly from the brown-and-cream jug, like the mountain men, the first time she had ever done a thing like that. The fiery liquid took her breath away, swirled up her nostrils, and within a minute or two she was giddy. But she was relaxed and quite willing to sit there quietly and listen to Joel and Fletcher reminisce.

"You remember old McCord, I suppose," Fletcher was saying.

"The Irish gardener? Of course I do."

"I was apprenticed to him at age twelve. My ma had run away and my pa got himself killed in a barroom fight, and so I was an orphan. Your father decided to turn me over to McCord, to see if he couldn't make a gardener and landscaper of me. McCord taught me just like he had been taught on some big English estate in Ireland. If I did things right, he'd just grunt. If I did things wrong he'd beat me. It worked, though. I got to be a pretty good gardener before McCord went north to work for some rich gentleman there."

"I remember the flowers that you grew in the greenhouses, especially in the winter, for the dining-room table and the sideboards."

"For your mother, yes. She was a fine lady. Your father was, well, he was what he was, and I don't need to tell you about that."

After the jug had gone around a second time and Susannah had passed her turn, they said goodbye to the guardian, got on their horses and rode away. For a long time they were silent, relaxed by the liquor, just savoring their escape from death. Then Joel began looking at her as though he were about to say something.

"What is it?" she said. "You're thinking of what we just did, aren't you?"

"No. There'll be plenty of time for that in the future."

"Who do you think these two men were?"

"My best guess is that they were working for Colcock Stiles."

"I would rather not have to tell you this, but the half-breed said that after they killed us he was going to take my scalp. So maybe they were the same people that killed that farm family."

"That doesn't mean they weren't also hired by Stiles. But let's not talk about it anymore. Whoever they were, they're dead."

"So, what were you thinking of?"

"I was thinking that now there is only one other matter to be settled."

"What is that?"

"Will you marry me?"

"What? Why, . . . I don't know. Let me think about it."

"I'll give you ten minutes."

23

They traveled the road to Waynesville, again silent. There were no clouds on the mountains this day, the temperature had soared, and the horses' hooves churned up fine road dust that settled on them like a coating of flour.

Finally Joel said, "You wanted a little time to think about it. Have you thought?"

"You know the depth of my passion for you. Why can't we just continue on as we are? Why would the last of the mighty Devereux clan marry a girl raised in a whorehouse? Can you reconcile that with your sense of honor?"

"My love, honor means doing what you know within yourself to be right, not conforming to what others may think. You and I, Susannah, don't give a damn what others think."

"Then why marry?"

"For your protection, if something happens to me. God knows we have tempted fate a dozen times over in the last few weeks. When I was recovering from that gunshot wound, I made up my mind that I would ask you to marry me. When this awful war is over, I may yet find in the wreckage of the family empire some bits and pieces of property I may claim as mine. How would you like to own Raven's Nest?"

"I would love it. It is the most romantic spot I have ever seen. My only hesitation was that I would bring dishonor to your name."

He turned and looked at her, a tired, emotionally exhausted young woman, her hair, eyebrows and lashes singed by gunpowder and coated with road dust, her clothes dirty and stained. Yet her remarkable beauty shone through, the long curved neck, the full lips, the deep blue eyes. He wanted to say that it was honor that she would bring to his name, but this seemed melodramatic.

"What dishonorable thing have you ever done? You see, you have no answer. What your mother has done—and I pass no judgment on that—has nothing to do with you, my grave, virtuous, and noble-spirited Susannah."

"Then I suppose I must say yes. Joel, what is it?"

"Just a little choked up, that's all. You have made me very happy."

"Anything so as never again to be called your fiancée. The other thing that I cannot endure much longer is the ham and cornbread that we seem to subsist on."

"I will see that you know fine things, however I manage to do it. A tour of Europe would make a nice honeymoon. But I am dreaming. All that we possess for now is a handkerchief full of gold coins."

"I will live with you in poverty if need be, Joel, but you are far too clever not to succeed at whatever you decide to do. Then you can indulge me in any outrageous way you choose."

They slept that night in the woods and entered Waynesville early the next morning. Waynesville was the largest town along the southern slope of the Smokies, but not much of a town at that: a central square boasting a lamppost at each corner, a single wood-frame hotel, a bank, a barber shop, a livery stable, a dry-goods store, and an open-air farmers' market.

"Waynesville was our base during the survey of the Smoky Mountains," Joel said. "When war came, Dr. Arnold left his scientific instruments with the proprietor of that dry-goods store. I suppose they're still there."

They took a room at the hotel, and Joel opened the bundle of clothes that he had brought from Raven's Nest.

"On the off chance you might say yes to my proposal, I brought this dress along, which looks to be about your size."

"To be married in."

"Yes."

"It is lovely. White organza with lace."

They both bathed in the bathhouse out back of the hotel, and Susannah washed her hair and rinsed it from the barrel of rainwater provided. Now properly dressed, they walked across the square to a red brick building where they were told a justice of the peace had his office.

"Well, I don't know," said the justice of the peace, a gray man in a threadbare suit. "There's certain legal requirements."

"There's also a war on," Joel said, spinning a gold coin on the desktop as he spoke. "We weren't able to bring birth certificates and such with us, but we are obviously of marriageable age, and we both are prepared to sign affidavits that we have no impediments to marriage."

The justice's eyes were on the spinning gold coin.

"Well, you have a point there. There is a war on, and it ain't all that easy to put your hand on family documents. Tell you what I'll do. Give me an hour to prepare the affidavits, we'll do the ceremony, and I'll give you the marriage certificate with official seal set in wax and all. That'll be five dollars—five U.S. dollars, that is."

The coin stopped spinning, and Joel handed the justice the five-dollar gold piece. They spent the next hour wandering about the square, and just before they returned to the justice's office, Joel bought Susannah a bouquet of pale pink roses at the farmers' market. Fifteen minutes later they left the red brick building, husband and wife, and dined on roast chicken, fried potatoes, and salad greens at their hotel.

"What now, my husband?"

"Why don't we go over to the dry goods store and see if Doctor Arnold's surveying instruments are still there. I'm curious."

"You would like to be back in the high mountains, wouldn't you?"

"I found myself there, and somehow that brought me to you. I learned there that my life would not be like that of others in my family, and that only a woman who was not like others would do for me. You should have seen the young women that my family threw at me."

"And eager they were, I am sure, to bed down with the handsome and rich scion of the Devereux family."

"I suppose so, but now it is you who are the last Mrs. Devereux."

"Yes," she said, and almost but did not say more. "Now let's look for your tools, which obviously mean so much to you."

The proprietor of Hood's dry good store had not changed in the least, a balding man who had become a merchant to escape the farm where he was brought up, farming being, Joel remembered him saying, the most hateful occupation God ever put on this Earth.

"Why Mr. Devereux, didn't expect to see you again until all this fighting was over. How's the professor?"

"I'm not sure, Mr. Hood. No way of communicating with the North."

"And it's a shame. Ain't nobody going to profit from this division of the country. I suppose you're here to take up your surveying again."

"I'm not sure that's going to be possible."

"Might be. Nobody's going to disturb you up in the Smokies. You and the professor and his other boys are about the only ones who know how to get around up there, other than Indians and sang men."

"Are Professor Arnold's instruments still here?"

"They are, and I would be glad to get shut of them. They must have cost a lot of money, and I was never too happy in holding them. I'll just give them to you if you want, if you're willing to sign a receipt."

He could feel Susannah's eyes on him.

"All right, why don't I just do that."

Back at the hotel he sat on the edge of the bed and Susannah sat cross-legged in the middle of it while he opened the musty leather case and took the instruments out, one by one, from their flannel wrappings.

"Theodolite," he said, exposing the brass optical instrument with all of its gears and scales, "for determining angles, from which, by triangulation, you can calculate distances, both horizontally and vertically . . . a mercury barometer for measuring air pressure, another way of estimating the height of mountains, a compass for finding true north, a telescope for getting your bearings, a spirit level for setting your instruments on the horizontal, a quadrant for determining the position of stars, a chronometer for recording time accurately, a plant press, and a microscope."

"You are in love with this business, aren't you?"

"It allows me to make my way in the wilderness."

"What is it about the wilderness you care about so much?"

"Its wildness, its lack of rules, of man-made order, of profit and loss, of social position and arrogance and carriages with matched horses and English shotguns and Cuban cigars and sixty-year-old Madeira. Now do you understand why the wildness of a seventeen-year-old girl in a darkened church seduced me?"

"A bit. Now let me tell you this. Were it not for that night and what it led to, what would have become of a girl who spent twelve years surrounded by luxurious depravity and eight in the most austere Calvinism? I think I might have gone mad."

As she spoke he wrapped each of the scientific instruments in flannel and returned them to the leather case.

"So we have come this far, Susannah, and now what next?"

"I would think that next we do what newlyweds customarily do on the evening of their marriage, and what a pleasure it will be to do it on a real feather bed. It took great concentration of mind to ignore that cornhusk mattress we sported on at the Scrogginses'."

"But you didn't mind the wet grass in the Goodes' cornfield."

"Mind? That was my celebration for seeing you back from the edge of death. It is a night that will live in my memory forever."

Sometime in the night the thunderstorm that a dry, hot summer day in the mountains usually provokes broke with particular violence. While Susannah slept on, Joel got up to watch one of nature's phenomena that he most enjoyed. The wind swept across the lamp-lit square, hurling tree limbs and all kind of debris ahead of it, until all but one of the swinging lamps was extinguished. Then with customary suddenness the storm subsided.

He was about to return to bed when into the light of the one remaining lamp a line of horsemen emerged into the square and crossed over to the entrance to the hotel. There they dismounted noisily and trooped up onto the piazza.

"What is it?" Susannah asked sleepily from bed.

"Confederate troops, half a dozen troopers and too many officers. Four or five. I think I'd better go down and see what this is all about."

"Be careful," Susannah said as he dressed.

In the entrance to the hotel the dozen or so Confederates milled about. The senior officer, a colonel, his back turned to Joel, was discussing lodging for the officers and men with the hotel proprietor. This was no ordinary contingent, it was something elite. The colonel's dress, sodden as it was, and his demeanor spoke of West Point.

Joel went into the parlor and sat in the semidarkness until officers and men trooped upstairs. Then he approached the reception desk.

"What's this all about?" he said to the hotel proprietor, whom he had paid in advance in gold.

"Don't know officially, but unofficially it seems these fellows have been sent up to do a survey."

"Survey?"

"Should Atlanta and Richmond fall, would it be possible to move the Confederate government to the mountains and continue the war from here."

"That should be good for your business."

"I'll say it would."

Joel went back upstairs and reported to Susannah on what he had learned. Then he lay down beside her and watched the one remaining street lamp's light undulate across the ceiling.

"You sound worried. Why?"

"These are staff officers, just the kind who would be informed on intelligence matters—on spies, for example. We've seen them before."

"Where?"

"By moonlight, at Dr. Robinson's."

"Colonel Alexander."

"Yes."

"Well, he's no demon. That I now know."

"That doesn't make him any less dangerous to us."

"But he doesn't know who we are."

"He will as soon as he sees me. And remember that the hotel proprietor, the owner of the dry goods store, and the justice of the peace are now acquainted with the name Devereux. It's only a matter of time before this colonel and his officers stumble on who we are, even if we hide ourselves."

"How much time?"

"About the time people are up and about tomorrow morning in Waynesville."

"Then what are we to do?"

She was sitting on the edge of the bed, putting on her nightgown, as though she were preparing to leave at a moment's notice.

"To do? I don't know. I've improvised so many times, always staying one jump ahead, but now I feel at the end of my rope, old and tired and with no ideas."

"That's when a man should take a young and frisky wife."

"What do you mean?"

"May I make a suggestion? If we were to flee into the high mountains, where that Mr. Hood said only you and your surveyors and Indians and sang men could find their way, would they be able to find us?"

He laughed. A young and frisky, devoted and loving wife.

"Find us? Not in a thousand years."

"Is there some place up there we could hide for a while?"

Too much tension for too long, he thought. *I've ceased to think clearly.*

"There's a place, if it still exists, where we could hide out until this bloody war is over, if need be. Professor Arnold had a cabin built up in the high mountains where we all stayed."

"Well, then?"

"It's too far to walk, and horses can't take you there. Not surefooted enough. They tend to fall off mountains. We would need mules."

"There's a livery stable here, and as far as I know, you won't have a problem trading two saddle horses for two mules."

"We would need three mules."

"Even three."

"Suppose the cabin's no longer there?"

"I wouldn't be afraid. Your wife has unbounded confidence in you, Mr. Devereux."

He walked across the square littered with the debris of the storm, the one street lamp still burning. There was not yet even the first hint of dawn in the sky, but the livery stable blazed with light. He was not surprised at this. Travelers came early for their mounts, anxious to be on the road by sunup. The man who owned the stable was of a type, bent, gray and wiry, like Jenkins at Devereux and many another he had met. His and Susannah's horses had been well groomed, their jaws even now moving with the crunching of the oats their feed bags held.

"Come for your horses," the man said to make conversation, since why else would Joel have shown up at the stable at four in the morning.

"Could be, but maybe I might want to sell them."

"To whom?" the stable owner said, his round, steel-rimmed glasses sliding down his nose.

"Maybe to you."

The man snorted. "I don't deal in horse flesh as expensive as these two mares."

"Trade them, then."

"For what?"

"Three good, surefooted mules. You have three?"

"Well, I do, but what kind of trade would that be? You don't look like a fool to me, mister."

"It's just that I need mules right now, not horses."

"Well, I won't ask more. You must have your reasons."

"I'll need to keep our saddles and tack, and for you to throw in a pack for the third mule as part of the bargain."

"No problem there."

Joel walked back across the square to the hotel. There was now first light in the sky, and he felt rather satisfied with himself. He opened the door to the hotel reception room and headed for the stairs in the light of a single small light on the counter that glittered on the keys hanging behind.

"Mr. Devereux?"

He spun around, reaching for a pistol that was not there. The voice had come from the darkened parlor, where he could see nothing but the glowing end of a cigar.

"Do join me."

A tall man stood up, stepped out into the light. It was the Confederate colonel whom he had last seen by moonlight at Dr. Robinson's.

"This is not the first time, I believe, Colonel Alexander," Joel said, in control of himself again, searching for an advantage.

"The third, actually."

The tall colonel put a hand on his shoulder, led him into

the darkened parlor, gestured toward a stuffed chair opposite the one in which he had been sitting.

"A cheroot?"

"I wouldn't mind."

The colonel passed him a cheroot and lit it for him.

"The last time was at Dr. Robinson's, where you eluded me. How, I still haven't quite figured out."

"And the second time?"

"At a watering tank beside a railroad track. It was I who stopped the pickets from shooting you down, you and that telegrapher who had run off with the codes. Codes are easily changed, but I wanted you alive."

"Even before then you were following me. How did you get on my trail?"

"Isn't that obvious? When Marcey, the stationmaster in Savannah, came to me, asking that I countersign the pass allowing you aboard the troop train to Atlanta, vouching for you as a member of President Davis's staff, I was dumbfounded. I was on Davis's staff, and I knew there was no John Dabney attached to it. Being from Virginia, I know all the Dabneys there are. There was a John Dabney, but he was killed at Cold Harbor.

"Marcey being a convicted felon out on parole, it took no more than a hint for him to reveal that your father's cook had requested the pass for you. I was already on the track of the missing gold, and I thought you might lead me to it, but you never did."

"What do you propose now?"

"Your freedom for the location of the gold. It is critical that Richmond lay its hands on it at this moment and in this place. Now or never, so to speak."

"And if I don't know where it is?"

"That's what Judge Stiles says, but he may change his

293

tune. We took him in custody the night we came for you at Nacoochee. I didn't want him playing his own game, offering rewards for your arrest."

"But if you arrested him that night, who are the two assassins that followed us from then on, if not his men?"

"Assassins? I have no idea."

Joel thought that he did. He had shown some gold coins at the barter market, and that had been enough to put two renegades on their trail. It was as simple as that. It was he who had complicated it. As Manuela had warned him, the universe turned, crushing some lives and sparing others, indifferent to what men expected.

"Stiles faces a bleak future unless he talks," Colonel Alexander continued. "He is, however, a stubborn man, and I have no time to waste."

"I could tell you where the gold is, on my word of honor, but on one condition."

"Name it."

"That my wife and I are free to leave Waynesville within the hour."

"Your word of honor. I might accept that in other circumstances. But if you didn't keep it, how could I explain the trust I put in the last of the Devereux, when your father and brothers stole the largest cache of gold remaining in Confederate territory? No, I can't let you go until you lead me to the gold, and even then I would be taking considerable risk with my superiors and compatriots in doing so. Where is the gold?"

"The gold is at Raven's Nest. Do you know where that is?"

"Can't say that I do. Is it close enough for the gold to be transferred here?"

"It is. Do you have good military maps with you?"

"Given my mission, I would be most remiss if I did not."

"I will mark Raven's Nest, a hunting lodge of my father's, on the appropriate map. You will find the gold there at the bottom of a well."

24

For two days they waited, looking out their hotel window for some sign that the men sent out to verify the existence of the Dahlonega gold had ridden into town. When the waiting became unbearable they wandered the few streets of Waynesville until they knew every building in it, every board and shingle of every building, every picket fence, every flower border. Colonel Alexander rode in and out of town on whatever business his mission dictated. Susannah began to suspect that when the gold was found, the two of them would be put under arrest and sent away, all promises declared null and void where they were concerned.

Late in the evening of the second day there was a knock on their room door. The colonel would like to see them in the parlor. Now, finally, they would know their fate—perhaps. The colonel motioned for them to take a seat on a sofa covered in cut velvet. His smile was not particularly reassuring.

"The gold was there, then," Joel said.

The colonel went through the ritual of offering Joel a cheroot and lighting it for him before he replied.

"There was gold there, in the bottom of a well, just as you said." Colonel Alexander—if that was his real name—paused to light himself a cheroot. "There was gold there, but not all of it."

"I don't know what you mean. How would you know how much all is?"

The colonel looked at him thoughtfully.

"Perhaps I had better explain, or we will be talking at cross purposes. Before the war even began, Governor Brown had the head of the Dahlonega mint, who was of course a Southerner, put aside a portion of each month's production of gold coins, reporting to Washington a much less amount than was actually minted. This excess was put into sturdy wooden boxes, each numbered, and stored in a vault in the basement of the mint. When the war came, the gold in these boxes was transferred to your father's bank, after the boxes had been labeled DANGER. LIVE AMMUNITION.

"I don't need to tell you the rest, except to say that almost half of the numbered boxes are missing. Where are they?"

"I have no idea."

"Just what Judge Colcock Stiles says, who has decided to talk on the understanding that he will not hang. My man in Catesville believes he's telling the truth. Well?"

"I could hazard a guess. The rest of the gold is in a bank vault somewhere in Europe—France would be most likely—in the name of Auguste Devereux and may now molder there for many a year."

"I'll accept that since, in any case, there's enough left for my purposes. It's already being loaded onto mules to bring it to a location near Waynesville."

"And your purpose is to prepare for a move of the Confederate capital to these mountains in the last resort."

"Yes."

"Will that work?"

"I don't think the Confederacy has enough time left for that even to be a realistic course of action."

"Which means that the gold that has been the source of so

much scheming, has caused so much trouble, will in the end have served no purpose."

"I won't dispute that."

"Then why are you doing what you are doing?"

"Because that is my job. After I lost a leg at First Manassas, all that I could offer the Cause was my intelligence. Not a bad offering, considering that the war is being run by such numb-skulls as my West Point classmate John Bell Hood . . ."

"Well, if you are going to escape, you had better do so well before first light. You'll have only this one chance."

"Then I had best alert the livery stable that we will be leaving early tomorrow."

"Yes."

Joel turned to Susannah. "I won't be long."

She found herself sitting alone in the parlor with Colonel Alexander. She felt she ought to say something, so why not what was really on her mind.

"Why are you letting us go free?"

"Perhaps because you remind me of my Sally."

"Your wife?" Susannah said to cover her surprise and confusion.

"Yes. She's dead now."

"I'm sorry."

"We thought we were free. We were certainly happy. But then the war came that was supposed to be about freeing the slaves, and it made slaves of us all, slaves to the dark destiny that was sown when that first ship from Africa reached our shores."

Dark destiny was something she understood quite well, but here it was being put in terms not of an immortal soul but of the fate of a nation.

"Please tell me more," she said—immediately regretting having said it.

"I went to West Point—with James McPherson and John Bell Hood, among others—if you know who they are."

She nodded her head. She had been with General McPherson the day before he was killed.

"After graduation I was sent to Paris to study—I was always more comfortable with books about war than with war itself—and I came back to West Point to teach military history. I married a northern girl, my Sally, and we were given a stone cottage on the grounds of the military academy, with a view of the Hudson River valley, and no two people could have been more happy. But then the war came, as any military historian could have told you it would. I felt I owed it to Virginia and the South to resign my commission and join the Confederate army. Sally pleaded with me not to, but my ties of family and sentiment were too strong . . ."

The colonel's voice broke, and tears welled up in his eyes. How she regretted having asked the question that had opened the floodgates.

"And then?"

"And then I had my leg shot off at First Manassas. I was taken to the country seat of some Virginia planter, which had been turned into a field hospital. Two days later I was handed a telegram from West Point, where Sally had been allowed to stay on until our child was born. Mother and child had died in childbirth. I turned my head to the wall. There was a wallpaper design, which I looked at for hours at a time, dark green and dark red, that went around and around, always ending where it began. Well, I thought, that's the way life really is. It just goes around and around, and in the end means nothing. Chances are my amputation will end in sepsis, and I will die, and that will be that . . . But of course I didn't die. It was my fate to live on."

"I'm so very sorry," she said, daring nothing more.

"Best be going," the colonel said, raising himself by the

chair arms. When he was on his feet, he reached alongside his knee, and clicked some device that locked his false leg into a rigid position.

"Thank you," she said to his back as he limped out of the parlor, but he did not reply.

There was only one road north from Waynesville into the Smokies, the Old Cataloochee Road, which led to one of the few coves in the high mountains where there was bottom-land and water enough for settlers to make a living farming. Beyond Cataloochee Cove there was only an Indian trail. Finally there was no trail at all, and to reach the high peaks you had to make your own trail.

The dawn when Susannah and Joel set out for the high mountains, the forest that washed up like a sea to the edge of the town was, as often after a summer storm, Joel said, deep in fog. The trees, even close at hand, were but ghostly shapes, and the regular clip-clop of the mules' hooves was muffled. But the odors were intensified, the perfumes of wildflowers, the incense of pines and firs. This is going to be the greatest adventure of my life, Susannah thought, but she could not have put into words why she thought so.

She soon began to see why mules were necessary. The so-called road was worn down to moss-grown rocks made slick from the underground water that welled up among them. There was water everywhere. A mountain torrent roared down beside them, lacing itself around boulders. Its banks were thick with mountain laurel, of the kind she had nearly died in, but here bearing gorgeous flowers of white and pink and lavender. There were trees with creamy blossoms like magnolias, but their trunks tall and slim. Joel knew them all, the umbrella tree, the cucumber tree, and others.

The morning fog began to lift, and she found herself in an

enchanted place, strange and a bit frightening. The higher they went, the larger grew the trees, until she could not believe that trees of this size existed. On one of them there was a great ragged gash.

"What did that?" she said.

"A bear's been sharpening his claws."

"It must be of monstrous size."

"There're some pretty big bears up here."

"Don't like that very much. Will they attack you?"

"Not unless you happen to get in between a female bear and her cubs. Then the mother will stand up on her hind legs and look around for you, but they can't see real good. So you start backing off, making a lot of noise, singing a song or something, and they'll usually move away."

"Usually."

"Most of the time."

"Now that's reassuring."

"What they will do is come in where you're camping and eat every bit of your provisions. So you have to take all your foodstuffs and put them in a sack, tie a rope to it, and hoist it about thirty feet up into a tree."

"This promises to be an interesting journey."

"I can guarantee it."

"And you love it."

"I do."

She looked at him. Joel was smiling. He was teasing her, but that didn't make anything he had said less true.

"We'll be all right," he said. "We have plenty of food, as much as our pack mule can carry, and I now have the kind of gun to bring in game and a fly rod. There are foot-long trout in these streams."

"How much higher must we go?"

"A lot. Until the clouds are below us at sunrise."

That night they slept under a fly tent, a piece of canvas stretched over a rope tied between two trees, that Joel had bought in Waynesville. He seemed to have thought of everything, including cooking pots and candles, soap and medicines. But then, he said, he had had three summers in the high mountains with Dr. Arnold and knew that if you didn't bring the right equipment with you, it could cost you your life.

The next morning Susannah awoke early, as happy as she had ever been. She went to the stream and bathed in water so cold it took her breath away. The banks of the stream were lined with blackberry bushes, and she filled a pot with the succulent fruit, a gift for her new and wonderful husband, who was further down the stream fishing for trout. As she started to rise from her crouching position, she heard a dry rattling sound like pebbles being shaken in a gourd. She turned her head and looked into the fanged mouth of the largest snake she had ever seen, as long as her leg and as big around as her arm.

The snake's head moved back and forth, as though seeking the best place to strike. *Just not to die this way,* she thought, *after all I've been through.* But then there was an explosion, and the giant snake's head disappeared, leaving the body writhing on the ground.

"About the biggest timber rattler I've ever seen," Joel said, sitting down beside her, holding his smoking pistol.

She began to cry, and then came wrenching sobs. Through all that they had endured she had remained mostly dry-eyed, but this was too much.

"I'm sorry," she said between gasps.

"About time you let go," he said.

"My hero," she said.

"I've done what I thought I had to," he said simply.

"I know."

Joel made a fire, and they ate an unusual breakfast of grilled rainbow trout and wild blackberries. Then they got together their gear and continued on up the mountain, the path ever steeper, the views ever more spectacular. About noon they arrived at a promontory with a view that circled the horizon, where under a giant balsam fir a cabin nestled, a sturdy well-built cabin that had apparently been unmolested in the years since Professor Arnold and his pupils had closed the door for the last time, as war spread across the land.

"Our honeymoon cottage," Joel said.

"Life can be so wonderfully strange," Susannah said, "so unlike what you imagined it would be."

"It can be if you dare, if you don't seek safety in the known, in a circle of people who share the same views, who never venture outside their circle. They are afraid of the unknown, tell themselves it's dangerous, which of course it is. But without risk . . ."

"Joel Devereux, I'm going to make you a good wife. Here on this high mountaintop I'm going to start making a home for us."

The first task of the afternoon was to rid the cabin of the bats and flying squirrels. There was still a broom, leaning against the stone fireplace, and Susannah began sweeping out the cabin. Joel cut wood for the fireplace until she made him stop. He had even thought to bring a mattress cover, which he filled with sweet-smelling twigs from the balsam fir. Then he pushed two bunks together and made them a marriage bed.

By sunset the cabin had become a home. There was a little rock terrace, and they sat there and had a nuptial drink from the bottle of brandy that Joel had bought in Waynesville, while the sun went down in splendor over row after row of mountains below them.

"This is the most beautiful sight I've ever seen," Susannah said.

"We're as far upcountry as you can get here."

"Now I understand. You're home. And this is where I begin making a home for us. We have a little money left, and for a while we can live like the Goodes. I'll learn to make soap from bear fat and ashes, how to weave baskets. I'll start a vegetable garden."

He laughed. "You might even plant some corn, and we could make some money moonshining."

"Don't tease me, Joel. I'm so happy, so full of enthusiasm, so proud to be your wife. I'm glad we're going to have to struggle for a while to survive. When we're old and rich, we'll look back on this time as the happiest of our life. And you're doing what you most want to do. The war will be over soon, and you'll have money regularly. You'll go on to map these entire mountains, with me at your side, and you will become famous and laden with honors. Until then I'll learn how to survive in the wilderness, and we'll make it somehow. And there's the most incredible beauty all around us."

He leaned over and kissed her, held her body tightly against his.

"The happiest time of our life. Yes, that's how we will remember this. We begin our honeymoon."

During the night Susannah had dark and violent dreams, as the demons that might have ruled her were driven step by step out of her life, fleeing before her. As they retreated a light spread around her, finally so intense that she awakened. At first she thought the forest must be on fire, but then she realized it was the dawn, a special kind of dawn. She got up and went out on the terrace. From horizon to horizon she looked down on a vast golden sea, from which dark islands emerged.

"Joel," she called, but he had already come up beside her, put his arms around her.

"What am I seeing?"

"We're above the clouds here. It's like this almost every morning."

"Those dark things?"

He laughed. "The tops of mountains peeking up above the clouds."

"The sea," she said, "the sea. We've made it, haven't we?"

"Yes, we've made it."

"Like survivors of a shipwreck washed up on a faraway shore, to find an empty cottage waiting. I can imagine Jessie and Amos's house in Florida, light coming through dark wooden shutters, and the smell of orange blossoms. And I wonder whether Asa and Elam will reach Halifax, and she will have her house with a garden overlooking the harbor. Colonel Alexander and his wife, Sally, once had a cottage overlooking the Hudson . . ."

"Some are crushed and some are spared," Joel said, half to himself.

"I was spared long ago," Susannah said. "On the day you first noticed me, my way up from the dark places began. We may be two specks in an indifferent universe, but I don't believe that. We may yet have many sorrows, but nothing can ever change what's been forged between us on our way upcountry."

"No, nothing," Joel said.

Barrington King has always had a deep interest in history, the arts and languages. He has a degree in painting from the University of Georgia and was a Woodrow Wilson Fellow at Princeton University, where he did research on the history of the Mediterranean. He has lived in Egypt, Tunisia, Greece and Cyprus. He studied French at the Foreign Service Institute in Paris, and he also speaks Greek. He was Deputy Chief of Mission at our embassy in Islamabad, Pakistan, when it was attacked and burned, and the first American Ambassador to the Sultanate of Brunei, on the island of Borneo.

Barrington King is married with two children. He divides his time between an apartment in Washington D.C., a converted silo in Rappahannock County, Virginia, and a small Spanish fishing village on the Costa Brava.